OBLIVION HAND

BOOKS BY ADRIAN COLE

The Dream Lords

A Plague of Nightmares
Lord of Nightmares
Bane of Nightmares

Madness Emerging
Paths in Darkness
Wargods of Ludorbis
The Lucifer Experiment

Moorstones
The Sleep of Giants

The Omaran Saga

A Place Among the Fallen
Throne of Fools
The King of Light and Shadows
The Gods in Anger

Star Requiem

Mother of Storms
Thief of Dreams
Warlord of Heaven
Labyrinth of Worlds

Blood Red Angel
Storm Over Atlantis

OBLIVION HAND

Adrian Cole

WILDSIDE PRESS

OBLIVION HAND

An original publication of
Wildside Press
P.O. Box 45
Gillette, NJ 07933 USA
www.wildsidepress.com

Copyright © 2001 by Adrian Cole.
Cover illustration © 2001 by James Pitts.
All rights reserved.

"Well Met In Hell" is a fully revised version of *The Coming of the Voidal*, a chapbook published by Spectre Press in February 1977. "The Universe of Islands" is a revised version of the story published in *Airgedlamh* magazine in Autumn 1980. "First Make Them Mad" is a revised version of the story published in *Fantasy Tales*, volume 2, no. 4, in Spring 1979. "The Ocean of Souls" is a revised version of the story published in *Fantasy Crossroads* 15, January 1979. "Astral Stray" first appeared in a slightly different form in *Heroic Fantasy*, DAW Books 1979. "Ever the Hungry Night" is a revised version of "All Things Dark and Evil" which appeared in *Weirdbook* 13 in 1978. "The Lair of the Spydron" was originally scheduled for *Phantasy Digest* (1979), and "Urge And Demiurge" for *Weird Adventures* (1980) but sadly both magazines folded before the tales saw print. They are published here for the first time.

FIRST EDITION

DEDICATION

Originally the components of this saga were written as short stories and in the main they were either published or scheduled for publication in the small presses that flourished around the late 1970's, and I am indebted to the enthusiastic support of the editors and artists who first brought the Voidal to the light of day. This volume is dedicated to them and their own heroic endeavours:

Jim Pitts
Jon Harvey
Wayne Warfield
Dave Sutton and Steve Jones
Jonathan Bacon
Robert Fester
Gerald Page and Hank Reinhardt
Paul Ganley
And to the fond memory of Dave McFerran

EXORDIUM

During the countless millennia of my exile I have been able to ruminate extravagantly, though not without exasperation, upon the more esoteric laws of my fellow Deities. Perhaps, in the spirit of accuracy, I should say my former fellow Deities, as I have no doubt that they would take exception to any presumption of mine to claim equality with them now. As an exile I am not entitled to the status I once enjoyed, though in reality I remain as I was. A god is a god is a god. I simply live apart.

It is an unwritten but embarrassing fact that certain things cannot be destroyed. Certain powers are eternal and remain so, resisting all other powers. I am one such power, but what I have begun here is not my story. No, my personal history would make dull reading and would scandalise no one. I make no secret of the fact that my reputed avarice for knowledge earned me the insular existence that I now endure. The pain of loneliness, like all other pain, atrophies and decays eventually. But no one wants to be ignored. And it has been a long time since anyone did so much as acknowledge my presence, even with a curse.

I feel it is time I caused a stir of embarrassment again. In case I really have been forgotten.

So then how do the gods put an end to the aforementioned eternal powers when they consider it in their best interests to do so? Since we are talking about immortality, death is not an option. Imprisonment? As a temporary measure, but all prison walls crumble as the eons slide by. One could suggest the application of unending pain, but I have already commented on the deterioration of pain. Constant pain dulls and earns the victim's contempt, though I would not wish the theory put to the test in my own case. There is always the bestowing of madness, but madness is relative, and being largely unpredictable, is never easy to control. Besides, madness is something I would only recognise in someone else.

Since my exile so frustrates me, you will understand that few things give me as much pleasure as those which frustrate my tormentors. Thus my history, this partial revelation of secrets, this presentation of indiscretions. I refer to a repressed power: the gods have decreed it a sin even to contemplate this ejaculation of darkness. Ironically I was exiled for less than the injudicious study of this particular entity.

I refer to the enigma known as the Voidal.

Few will know the name, but for those who do, it is synonymous with nightmare and deep unease, which is why it is so beguiling. This dark entity could not be destroyed, though the gods had set their corporate powers to reducing it to nothing, motivated, if you have not already guessed as much, by their fear of it. They took from the Voidal his memory, and with it his understanding of his powers, his soul, his identity, and the greater part of his sanity, as you shall discover in the history that follows. There was little of his own will left to him, but they could no more wrest it from him than they could his life. He could go nowhere unless he was summoned, and yet the gods placed upon him such a mantle of terror that only fools dared call him, as you shall also learn. And they set him adrift in the fathomless deeps of his own nightmares, believing he would be lost forever in their paradoxical inconsistencies and could never rise.

Why? Why did they do this? What did they fear? The question haunts him throughout his bleak quest. As it has me. It is a fragmented history and much of it remains dark and obfuscated, for I have woven it from whispers, myths, hints and rumours. And my work has been hampered by the shadows that ever seek to close in over the grim traveller himself. They may yet be your companions.

—Salecco the Esteemed, of Escaloc, Author of *The Extrapolation of Exactitudes, Towards the Cognizance of Random Creation, Nascent Darkness: Our Responsibilities* and various other Works currently invalidated under the Divine Sedition Acts.

I

WELL MET IN HELL

The demon who gave me the bones of this story was in a state of advancing lunacy on the occasion of its garbled narration. It was told to me long before my exile, but in my enthusiasm for such choice morsels of grotesquerie, I secreted the unexpurgated details among my private collection. It is, I believe, the first reference to the Voidal after his own banishment. In retelling the tale I have found it necessary to remove surgically much of the demon's verbosity, together with a number of references that would serve only to confuse rather than to enlighten the reader. I trust, however, that I have retained something of the mood and flavour of the original, repellent though it is.

For in prefacing my history with this tale, I begin at the very depths, where darkness coils upon darkness.

—Salecco, once Esteemed

There is a world that even the most audacious demons fear, where sane Gods do not tread, whose shifting landscapes ebb and flow like dark tides of the mind, ever restless, ever haunted. Beyond natural laws, at the far reaches of reason, shunned by all but the perverse in spirit. It has many dimensions: they twist and fuse, baffling the mind itself with their deranged patterns, their layer upon layer. A veritable universe, unique to itself, enclosed, locked.

This is Phaedrabile.

It has known many empires, spawned many wars, its demigods rising and falling over the eons, careless of life, of pain, delighting in the dark cloak of entropy that is its only true god.

At the time of the Csarduct Dynasty, many of Phaedrabile's dimensions toppled to the relentless crusades of these self-styled overlords, their vast armies swarming, driving before them a veritable tide of refugees, man and demigod alike, who sought ever darker places in which to secrete themselves from the contagion of conquest. The Csarducts may once have worshipped at the grim altars of the gods of Phaedrabile, but at the height of their greatness they had supplanted them with their own images.

Among those who fled was the sorcerer monarch, Rammazurk, a creature of limitless lust, a slave of extremity, whose hunger for forbidden knowledge exceeded by far the depravities of his contemporaries. Into the very entrails of Phaedrabile he wriggled, creating for himself the nether hell of Sedooc, a labyrinthine kingdom of sorcery. With him he took his repulsive entourage, and they burrowed like maggots in the charnel house of their creation. Far from the eyes of the Csarducts and their own sorcerers they wallowed in new depths of chaos. Rammazurk the Omnipotent, as he called himself, ruled subjects to whom clung only the faintest vestiges of humanity.

Rammazurk trafficked with terrible powers: they bestowed upon him their awesome gifts, and he used these to strengthen his defences against intruders, locking himself and his corrupt empire deeper within itself. He distorted the elements themselves, enslaving monstrous storm elementals and binding them to him, wrapping them about his haven, Windwrack, the stronghold at the heart of his empire. The Screamers raved incessantly about the upper turrets and parapets of the huge castle: no one came near, man nor god. And while the winds of madness fumed outside Windwrack's walls, hell seethed within.

Far down in the echoing halls of Windwrack's labyrinths, a world away from the guardian Screamers, in the Hall of a Thousand Joys, other shrieks and howls reverberated, though this was no storm, unless it were a storm of passion. The obese monarch had decreed that for a month there would be a feast, a brazened orgy that would celebrate his glory and mock not only the Csarducts but also the very gods of Phaedrabile itself. For Rammazurk had lately breached a trove of hitherto undiscovered lore, sorcerous powers previously shunned by even the most adventurous or foolhardy of mages. And he felt himself a step nearer divinity, immortality.

He filled his halls with a veritable flood of sycophants, all of whom were too terrified to deny the monstrous ruler the slightest whim.

And such a feast! There were strange and vile foodstuffs brought forth for stranger quasi-human appetites to consume. Many were the night-spawned denizens that whispered and susurrated at the edges of the festivities, hovering between light and darkness, and they were summoned and cavorted with obscenely under the bleary gaze of the vast monarch. Humanity had lost its shape, its path, in the seething, cacophonous revels.

Rammazurk himself presented a grim spectacle, a bloated maggot atop a mound of sprawling acolytes, his naked folds of flesh dripping with sweat and wine, his bloodshot eyes sunk deep in the immensity of his face. Depravity epitomised, he snarled his derision for all gods but himself.

He was gloating over his new secrets for a particular reason: they gave him power over a principal wife, of which he had many, and whom he had long sought to destroy and toss into the abysses of limbo. He had favoured her years before, for she was only partially human and possessed sorcerous powers that he had yearned to savour at the time. It was said that her mother had mated with several of the slime demons of the Mudwastes (an area notorious for failed expeditions) who themselves were reputed to traffic with the devils of the astral realms.

Thus Issylla was born with her mother's seductive wiles and her father's features and peculiar astral powers. Her relationship with Rammazurk had been a tormented one, but he had profited from it in the doors it unlocked for him. He had added to the grotesque components of his court.

But Issylla had nothing fresh to offer him now. And she was no longer the pliant, obedient creature she had once been. Until only recently she had held his powers at bay: this was soon to end. He had found the means to dispose of her.

Now, with the month-long feast waning about him, his countless courtiers sated, the obese one rose sluggishly to his feet like some beast of the ocean, dragged from its natural element, and gestured at the thralls who yet danced and sported across the hall. Slowly they turned until all watched the towering mountain of flesh, relieved to see the ghastly smile, the hint of new pleasures. The monarch was evidently not yet so full that he could not savour one last act of indulgence.

"Where is Issylla, most beloved of my wives?" Rammazurk belched.

The momentary silence was broken as the queen stepped forward voluptuously, her painted breasts thrust out invitingly at the swaying tower of blubber that was her husband. Her open audacity was clear for all to see.

"Ah," burped the monarch. "My jewel! Unparalleled sorceress of my halls. Most delectable of my treasures."

Issylla revelled in her hold over the monarch. She knew well enough that he had become bored with her long since and that he loathed her, but she knew he was powerless to destroy her. But somehow, in his wicked eyes she saw something new, and within her a sliver of cold fear twisted. She smiled beguilingly as Rammazurk gestured to the inner rooms of the palace.

"Let us momentarily leave our devout followers," he breathed. "We have not indulged ourselves in intimacy for too long, my jewel. There are depths to our needs as yet untrammelled. Let the people feast in our honour while we pleasure ourselves."

Issylla could think of nothing more repugnant to her, but she maintained her seductive pose. She knew the deceit of which her obnoxious spouse was capable. And she knew of his recent delvings into power: she dared not fob him off until she knew what new secrets he had dredged up.

"But first," he said, "let us clean away the filth of the past few weeks." He clapped his podgy hands together and at once six muscular retainers stepped forward, each bearing a huge ewer of beaten gold. Their biceps strained as they raised them.

Issylla's smile evaporated, but it was too late to spin out a curse or weave a protective charm.

"I am sure you will not mind cleansing yourself for your liege!" laughed Rammazurk, with a nod to his men.

Immediately they cast the contents of the ewers over the queen, and as the sparkling liquid cascaded over her, she began to scream, the pitch rising as the steaming concoction bit into her like acid. She stumbled to her knees, beating at herself, her palms slamming into her already molten eyes. The laughter of the king rose above her terrible wails. Her skin was sloughing off like a reptilian coat, dripping to the floor in a thick, viscous stream.

"The slime demons no longer protect you from me, you whore of a thousand beds! They tramp their stinking realm at my whim now! You've lost your protection. Your magical aura is of no avail. Feel the revenge of Rammazurk the Omnipotent. I have only just started!"

Other retainers rushed in upon the unfortunate Issylla, thrusting at her flesh with barbed javelins, ripping and tearing while the onlookers cheered like demons. The stormhounds, chained to the pillars, leaped up, straining at their chains to get at the flesh, anxious to sink their fangs into that rich meat. And Rammazurk tittered uncontrollably as the disgusting scenario unfolded.

Satisfied that the former queen was dead, the king waved the stormhounds forward and they were let loose on the spoiled flesh, snapping and tearing, their wild eyes daring anyone to interfere with their grisly work. When they had finished, dragging away the last of the dismembered bones, they had left only a steaming, pulpy mass. Rammazurk smiled contentedly at the congealing pool of blood.

As the torchlight played upon that dark pool that once had been his queen, other light seemed to shimmer there, strange light that was no reflection, but that seemed to have its source within the reeking pool. Rammazurk's features melted and became a stare shaped from foreboding. Mutters and murmurs rippled through the assembly. Something was coalescing, using the blood as a sickly medium in which to sculpt a bizarre form, drawing upon the very air for its substance.

Rammazurk knew intuitively what amorphous mass it was that suddenly drew itself up like a column of mud and excrement: it was powered by the undead will of Issylla. From a black orifice where a mouth should have been issued a faint, sombre voice. A limp, dripping limb flapped out and gestured at

Rammazurk, who drew back onto his throne in horror, while his houris ran screaming from the foul apparition.

It was a voice that insinuated itself throughout the entirety of the Hall of a Thousand Joys.

"Rammazurk the Omnipotent! Slayer of children, destroyer of the weak, defiler of beasts! Hear me, most accursed of men! You have spat upon the gods for too long. Know that I, Issylla, invoke my last curse upon you, granted to me by the demons that already prepare to suck me into their scalding embrace. The masters of the unknown dark curse you, and grant my invocation! Though I can never reach your realm again, I pass to you my final execration. I send you your bane, Rammazurk.

"I invoke the Voidal!"

No sooner had the grim words been uttered than the shape began to dissolve, slopping down into the pool of blood from which it had so odiously formed. In a moment nothing was left save a dark stain. In all the hall, not a sound was heard. Slowly all eyes swivelled to Rammazurk as he gazed from his silken seat. Even the feeding stormhounds had fallen silent, afraid to offend forces they could not see, but felt all too palpably.

Rammazurk hardly noticed his vassals. He frowned in puzzlement. It was no surprise that his dead wife should curse him. He had expected it, even if it had been a trifle dramatic. But she had disturbed him. She had invoked something alien to his knowledge. The Voidal. Although he searched his memory for a hint of the name, nothing came to light. He was not afraid: Issylla could be no match for his sorcerous defences, and yet he was uneasy at hearing an unfamiliar name.

He drew himself up slowly and waved at the silent watchers. "Why so solemn? Continue the feast! Issylla is no more, her curses hollow. Enjoy the feast!"

He left them and their renewed revels and made his ponderous way to remoter parts of Windwrack. Down through evil-smelling tunnels he went, through slime-walled pens where winged familiars skipped about his feet, crimson eyes gleaming up at him, anxious to serve. The monarch held out his hand and winged things alighted, cloaked in strands of sooty web. Through a maze of spell-hung corridors went the huge figure, careful not to disturb the mantle of conjurations he had woven here. At length he reached a high grotto hollowed out of the obsidian rock, and here he stopped at the shores of an oily expanse of phosphorescent mire.

A cloud of the familiars thickened the air above his head like miniature imps, but his whispered words to the little beings made them subside, settling like a cloud on the rocks and fanged stone of the cavern. Rammazurk made cabalistic passes in the stagnant air, reciting a mournful and rhythmic chant that echoed back softly from the walls. The very stone seemed to throb and pulse to the arcane chant, the vibrations increasing in cadence and the first ripples appeared on the oily surface of the mire.

A vague, saurian form broke from the surface, rivulets of slime cascading back into the lake. Two baleful eyes gleamed like lamps across the expanse of dark mire, and the shape of the awful head began to move sensuously in time to the echoing rhythms of the chant, hypnotised by its suggestive pulse. Rammazurk ceased his cantillation, though the echoing sound prolonged the sounds. He looked across at the awesome, wavering shape.

"Eldereth, traverser of the pits, wallower in the entrails of time and knowledge!"

The huge thing in the mire inclined towards the monarch, recognising the familiar summons, the call of a master to his servant.

"So it is Rammazurk who disturbs my slumbering voyages," came Eldereth's basso profundo. "What secrets do you wish to drag from my storehouse? And more important, Omnipotent One, what will you give me in exchange?"

Rammazurk glowered in the half-light. "You're in no position to bargain with me!" he snapped. "Or would you enjoy the company of the denizens of the Mudwastes?"

A reptilian hiss of anger sounded from the mire, like the escape of steam. Rammazurk was master here.

"The slime demons no longer overawe me. So let's not bandy threats," said the monarch.

"What do you wish?" came the sibilant retort.

"A curse has been placed upon me by my now departed spouse, Issylla. No doubt I can shred this trivial cantrip, but its exact nature is for the moment outside the boundaries of my memory."

"Surely nothing eludes the mind of your omniscience, O divine lord—"

Rammazurk ignored the mocking tone. "What do you know about a creature called the Voidal?"

The monarch studied the gloomy silhouette, confident that the powerful elemental, infamous for its astral delvings, would shortly disgorge the necessary counterspells that would enable him to blast Issylla's curse. But the weaving shape fell silent, brooding a while. This was most unusual.

"Come now! Your answer! Satisfy me in this and you shall be rewarded."

"It is rare knowledge you seek, Omnipotent One. Perhaps the answer lies outside Phaedrabile itself."

Rammazurk looked annoyed, but then an expression of avarice stamped itself on his sweating face. "Outside Phaedrabile? Power from beyond it? How intriguing. But wait! How could a worm such as Issylla traffic with such powers?"

"All beings are mere vessels, Rammazurk, catalysts."

"Don't fob me off with riddles! Speak candidly. What do you know?"

"Certain astral currents are forbidden to me, indeed to all but the Dark Gods. I know only that your late spouse was a bridge between you and your destiny. Some believe that the divinities mould all our destinies. Yet you, Rammazurk grow in power and perhaps will wrest your destiny back from the very Gods."

Rammazurk seemed mollified and nodded pompously.

"As for the Voidal," added Eldereth, "my own knowledge is strangely clouded. I can give you little more than pieces of a picture."

"Yes?"

"He is a complete enigma. From where he comes and on what mission, the Dark Gods alone know. They mask that secret jealously. But I recall a conversation I once had with Juxatl of the Million Ears, who dwells in the heart of Thaumatand, the most potent of the Spellworlds, and he spoke of a being who once offended the Dark Gods, a man who perpetrated so heinous a crime against them that they flung him on a wanderer's course, devoid of soul, identity or fate."

"And this is the Voidal?"

"So it would seem. But he is man you need not fear, for he cannot kill."

Rammazurk looked puzzled. "Cannot kill?"

"So Juxatl had heard. The Voidal cannot kill. The Dark Gods have denied him that power."

"Then why should Issylla have invoked him? What powers does he have?"

"As I recall, he is a Fatecaster. Whatever warped powers the divinities have bestowed upon him lie in his right hand. No other knowledge of him exists, for a cloud of forgetfulness follows him. To recall too much of his passing is forbidden."

Eldereth again fell silent. Rammazurk had to content himself with the dubious morsels of information. As he reflected on them, the shape in the mire drifted closer.

"Even this little I have told you is indiscretion, Omnipotent One."

"So now you want a reward for your outrage? Well, you shall have it. Today I am generous, having cast aside the yoke of that vampiric bride! As to the nature of your reward, I have an army in the field this very moment: it is drawn up outside the walls of Hakyarkuff, citadel of the fleshmen of Vybo, an old adversary of mine. Soon Vybo's minions will be annihilated. I will have their corpses cast into the Lagoon of Grey Movement. I am sure you know of it. Feed well."

"You are indeed a generous master," boomed the voice of the huge elemental as it subsided. Rammazurk grinned and withdrew from the ophidian depths of his fortress.

hortly after his discourse with Eldereth, the monarch was again seated amongst the velvet and silk splendour of his divans, surrounded by the dirge of his subjects, who now sought to divert his attention with even more debased vigour.

Rammazurk indulged them in their excessive outrageousness. But he was thinking of the curse, waiting for news that any stranger had arrived in his domains. He had set his familiars to watch, and they missed nothing, either in the realms of earth or astral.

At last, from high up in the cobwebbed, dust-laden vaults of the roof, came a flutter of thin wings. A gathering of membranous beings dropped down and hovered about the ears of the monarch, delicate as butterflies. The messengers, minute but humanoid, chittered and gibbered like excited children. Two dropped daringly to the shoulders of the monarch and pressed their tiny heads to his ears. Rammazurk listened avidly to their words, nodding, visualising the events they were describing: a strange being had indeed appeared outside the gates of the city, enquiring after the fortress of Windwrack. This must be the promised Voidal.

In spite of his preparations, a clammy kiss of dread touched Rammazurk's skin.

"Tell my storm elementals, the Screamers, to abate. Let Windwrack seem a haven to this intruder. But once he enters, have them seal the skies anew."

Rammazurk's harbingers rose in a tiny cloud and were soon lost to view. The monarch beckoned to one of his revellers. "Go to the Scarlet Tower. Fetch me Dennizor and Nazzim," he snapped and the pale retainer dashed away.

It returned soon after with two tall, gaunt figures, almost identical in their spectral regalia, a cloying air of decay heavy about their shoulders as if they had come fresh from a graveyard. Their devil eyes looked hatefully at Rammazurk, though he sneered at their expressions.

"Ah," smiled the reclining monarch. "The two necrophiles—"

"How much longer will you chain us to your service for sins long forgotten!" spat the first of the skeletal figures.

"You exist only to serve me! One day I may release you, but for the time being I require your metamorphic skills. I am expecting an unusual visitor. See to it that the court is liberally interwoven with the Werespawn, those particular demons that serve you like hounds. Let them sniff out any tricks that this Voidal intends to unleash. Go, perform your arts at once."

The twin sorcerers faced the apprehensive throng and began selecting victims for the possessions.

Outside the odious fortress of Windwrack, the city of Npandil sprawled unevenly across a score of hills, in parts dressed with crumbling, antique temples, in others a bizarre jumble of hovels, raised up in a parody of architecture where the debased and retrogressive servants of empire lived. It was at a remote gate of this festering city that the stranger had appeared. Behind him was an oddly silent sandstorm that obscured the land for many miles, and he recognised in its shifting currents an element of sorcery.

Already the newcomer had begun his enquiries in the city, calling at the first inn. He asked bluntly for Windwrack, saying he had business there, but at mention of the fortress at the heart of the city, the tenants drew into themselves and offered only brief directions.

"What do you seek in the palace of the Omnipotent One?" said one ancient inhabitant.

"There is someone there who will help me."

The oldster spat into the fire, which hissed back at him. "You are a fool. You'll find no friends there. Only pain."

The stranger left the inn, noticing now the tiny darting shapes in the air between the roofs, sensing their fiery eyes upon his every step. Beyond them the skies were shifting uneasily, the air moaning to itself, a huge beast stirring on the edge of wakefulness.

Rammazurk fed excessively, glutting himself. His twin sorcerers had done their work well, drawing forth the Werespawn. These were transmogrified revellers, sub-human, drooling things, barely controlled by the sorcerers: they hopped about like huge fleas, tendrils flicking out like obscene tongues, both caressing and flagellating the ecstatic mass of other revellers. Rammazurk delighted in the array of ghastliness, bound over to him in chains that were virtually unbreakable. Together with this he had ensured that the oldest and most protective of charms and cantrips hung his walls like black drapes. Let this Voidal come to him!

An ominous boom, the deep note sounded by the immense double gongs at the far end of the Hall of a Thousand Joys, reverberated around the walls. Two gigantic doors carved from single blocks of meteoric stone swung ponderously open as the sonorous notes died, and in the light that flooded in from beyond, a single figure was silhouetted, dwarfed by the titanic doors. It paused to gaze with apparent bland indifference upon the now silent hordes of the orgy, then stepped forward, the sound of its boots ringing back from the high vaults.

Rammazurk heaved himself upright, motioning the throng to open a way for the stranger. Down that long avenue of writhing humanity and sub-humanity the monarch and the stranger stared at one another. Rammazurk's fiends hissed and grimaced, claws outstretched, but there was a kind of fear in them all. The Voidal gave them no more than a cursory glance of disgust as he began the steady walk towards the monarch of Sedooc. About him was cloaked an aura of darkness: he wore it like armour.

The stranger was a man of good height, his spare frame draped in a dark shirt of nightweb, his legs clad in black leather, his harness studded with purest silver, the accoutrements of the same glittering material, while from an ebon scabbard protruded the fine-worked haft of a sword, clearly no ordinary weapon, though what its talents were remained as yet, like its owner, a mystery. His face was serene, absolutely smooth, pointed and classic in proportions, while the eyes were a piercing green. The hair was silken, black as the midnight cloak that had been clasped to the shoulders.

As the Voidal drew nearer, he moved with the deadly silence of a spider, his long legs striding purposefully yet gracefully. Yet on the serene face was the unmistakable look of a man of melancholy, the look of a man desperately in search of something he might never find.

He came to the foot of the royal dais, eyes searching Rammazurk's as if for answers.

"I have been expecting you," said the latter, impressed by

the physical presence of his visitor. But he remained outwardly calm. One flick of the wrist would unleash incalculable power upon this dark man.

The Voidal was surprised by the monarch's remark. "Expecting me? Were you told I was coming? Who told you?"

Rammazurk lifted a hand, a demand for silence. "It is I who will ply you with questions. You are here under sufferance. I expect all those who visit Windwrack to show respect. After all, I am lord of all Sedooc. So, who are you, and why are you trespassing in my domain?" He seated himself, resting his enormous chins on his fist.

The Voidal bowed his head sadly. "I am afraid my story is a strange one. I must apologise for any rudeness." He bowed to the monarch, who remained suspicious. The Voidal straightened, his every move watched by a thousand pairs of his eyes.

"I am here in search of knowledge," he said. "No more than that. I seek knowledge about myself, for I have no identity, and my memory is a wretched, broken thing. Of the knowledge that I have accrued, only fragments remain. I neither know who I am or where I am from. The Dark Gods mock me and seem to trifle with me for reasons they do not share. All I know is that here in your palace I will meet with one who will guide me."

"How did you come to Sedooc?"

"I cannot say. I stood on a plain blasted by fogs: your city materialised like a dream. All I know is that I may find knowledge here, and perhaps a friend."

"A friend you say?" The monarch looked sceptical. "What friend?" He was thinking of the grim shade of Issylla.

"Until we meet, I don't know."

"What else do you seek?"

"No more than I have said." He seemed almost apologetic.

Rammazurk looked at the black gloved hands of the man, one eye on the shadowed ranks around him. Among the leering Werespawn, the servants of the monarch readied for the task set them.

"I have among my vassals sorcerers and thaumaturges of no small repute. You may learn your fate here. Perhaps my fortress can accommodate you," Rammazurk smiled, though it veiled a shadow of menace.

The Voidal bowed. "I am indebted to you."

"Ah, yes. Indebted. But you need not be." An almost imperceptible nod of the head accompanied the monarch's words and in swift silence four shapes were at the Voidal's side, pinning his arms in a serpentine grip. Surprisingly he made no attempt to free himself, though he looked askance at Rammazurk.

"If you are to be my guest," said the latter, leaning forward ominously, "then you shall deliver to me a small fee."

"Of course," replied the Voidal impassively.

"Hold out his right hand," Rammazurk said to his retainers, and they did so. Rammazurk then took from the folds of silk beside him a razor-sharp sword, the edge of which glowed with sigils, carved there in some remote demon-hold in which the sword had been forged. Rammazurk rose and stepped down to face the Voidal, eager to destroy the source of the being's power. He unclasped the silver studs of the Voidal's right hand glove, then drew it off. But his grin of triumph dissipated, replaced by a look of shock.

For there was no hand.

The black glove had covered nothing, unless the hand was invisible. The Voidal, still gripped firmly, could not move his outstretched arm, so Rammazurk tentatively felt for the unseen hand with the tip of the sword. But there was nothing. He was puzzled, having been told that the Voidal's strength was in this hand.

"You have no right hand," he said haltingly.

The Voidal's face had clouded, as though a dark power from elsewhere had suddenly taken control of him. His features twisted, his eyes rolled evilly and he spoke in a scathing, reptilian hiss. "Since you have asked for it, you shall have it."

Rammazurk drew back, nonplussed. "Release him!" he snapped, returning to his throne, though he was ready for any attack.

The face of the Voidal changed back and for a moment the strange man looked bemused.

Rammazurk considered him briefly, then waved him aside.

"You are welcome, then. Later you shall converse with my underlings. For now, join the feast. I enjoy a celebration. Let us not mar it. Windwrack embraces you. Take what you need."

The Voidal bowed, picked up the fallen glove and receded into the ranks of the expectant throng. Yet none of them dared touch him, for the stink of fear bathed them all, and even the stormhounds by the pillars drew back, hackles rising as they sensed that about him that spoke of intolerable evils. Rammazurk drew two of his most beautiful concubines close and instructed them to stay beside the Voidal, and to amuse him. They blanched, but they feared Rammazurk's wrath more than the eerie stranger, so obeyed.

Rammazurk continued to drink himself close to the shores of oblivion, for he could not unravel the enigma set him by the words of the elemental Eldereth. Later, mused the wine-sodden monarch, I will find a way to kill this Voidal and toss him to the slime demons. Let them tell the limbo-lost spirit of Issylla that her curse was impotent. The monarch cackled in his drunkenness and waved for a platter of sweetmeats.

Two servants came to him, bearing between them a golden tray upon which were strewn fruits and assortments of edible leaves; amidst the succulent organs and slices of meat nestled a silver dome, under which the subterranean chefs had entombed the very best of their diabolical cuisine. Rammazurk nodded distractedly as the silver dome reflected a beam of light from the overhead firebrands high above, and he casually reached out to lift the gleaming lid. The food that he was already masticating as he raised the lid burst from his mouth as he saw with horror what lay beneath. The lid clattered down the steps of the dais. There on the tray was a hideous object, putrefying and shrivelled.

It was a severed hand.

The forefinger of the foul thing was extended rigidly, directed straight at the royal person of Rammazurk accusingly, as though still imbued with life. With a strangled cry, the huge monarch wobbled to his feet and smashed the heavy tray from the startled grasp of the servitors, sending food spinning and catapulting the gnarled hand out on to the stones of the floor. The cavorting beings drew back in disgust as the loathsome object turned and again pointed at Rammazurk.

"Destroy it! Destroy it!" snarled the monarch and a brand was quickly brought. When the severed hand refused to be burned, it was snatched up by one of the Werespawn and dropped into a brazier of blazing coals. Rammazurk watched the horrible relic smouldering, then turned away and staggered from the feast, his face a sickly pallor. He was so stunned by what he had seen that he momentarily forgot his grim visitor. The Voidal looked upon the incident with perplexity, as though it should have significance, but he could not understand it. His two seductive watchwomen were mildly disturbed by Rammazurk's hurried exit, but soon turned their wiles once more upon the strange but handsome Voidal. They drew him away from the throng, and though he made no attempt to discourage their lascivious attention, he was soon deep in private thought.

"What is it that you dwell upon so moodily?" asked one of the sleek-skinned girls.

The Voidal gazed at her, forced a smile, then looked away into the middle distance of the smoke-hung pillars, ignoring the nearby hoots and bawdy laughs of the resumed orgy.

"I can only tell you that I must have offended the Dark Gods. For that they have set me upon a stormy course for purposes I can only guess at. My presence here is as much a mystery to me as it is to your monarch. Yet I know that I am to meet someone familiar here. As I approached your city, I knew it instinctively. When we meet, he will direct me. In my wanderings I pick up small pieces of the mosaic. When I have them all, I will learn what my crime was. By then I may have atoned for it."

The two concubines listened with dreamy interest.

"And what of your—severed limb?" breathed one of them.

The Voidal's expression soured, but he was not angry. "Perhaps it was my hand that pointed so irreverently at your king. I am minded of the word, Fatecaster. It has a ring to it. But I don't recall having lost my hand—"

"So what will Rammazurk's fate be?" said the other girl, lips beside his ear.

The Voidal drew back stiffly. "Enough questions!"

"You wear a cloak of mystery," the girl laughed.

He nodded. "What I know of myself is not a matter for pride." After that he said nothing.

Rammazurk retired to the depths of his labyrinthine boudoir and deliberated between sleeping or pondering his grimoires in search of further information concerning the Voidal. He had thought merely of destroying the man, but on reflection had decided it may not be that easy, nor a permanent solution. No, this Voidal was a vessel for something greater. Irritably the monarch dragged from their hidden seclusion his dustiest and most damned scrolls and tomes, first securing his doors with spells that were old when Sedooc was but a dream. Then he began a systematic and thorough perusal of the blasphemous rituals and lores concerning curses. For two days and nights he drugged himself awake with heady and potent mixtures, losing himself in the deep and catatonic wilderness of sorcerous study.

But at the end of it all he was no wiser. The Voidal remained a mystery.

Grim-faced and despondent, he flung himself down upon his lavish bed and allowed the caressing fingers of sleep to slide over him. His sleep was like the sleep of the dead, and his snores were loud. The embers of the guardian fires burned low, so that only a dim glow suffused the sacrosanct chamber.

Someone tapped gently on the thick, sigil-woven doors. Several times the inoffensive knocking continued, but the monarch was far out across the ocean of slumber, insensitive to recall. However, the doors suddenly bellied inwards as a horrendous blow was struck upon them from without: the thick wood splintered, the panels bursting like pulp and crashing into the room as though mashed by a giant's fist. Rammazurk stirred fitfully and sat up, rubbing his eyes and gazing vacantly at the open doorway. He cursed vilely as he saw the shattered door, though at first he could see nothing or no one who could have wreaked such havoc.

It was pitch dark throughout the fortress of Windwrack, as though the Dark Gods had clouded the very cosmos. Wan light seeped into the bedchamber from a single taper without, the black candle permeating the air with rich incense. As Rammazurk sat motionlessly, the enormity of this unwarranted intrusion disturbed him, for the spells that he had set in apposition to such sorcery were the most puissant imaginable. He frowned at vague movement. Something had scuttled across the threshold of the room, unclean and verminous.

A single beam of dim light probed the marble floor from somewhere above, and into the beam came the thing that moved, as if taking its cue from the insipid light. Charred, shrivelled, it was a severed hand.

Rammazurk regarded it with utter revulsion, and quickly recited a blasting cantrip. But the hand was immune and continued its revolting scamper towards the huge bed. The monarch called upon elementals and demons from all manner of nether hells, but the host that normally would have rushed to his aid was not forthcoming. The power of the Dark Gods was stronger. Rammazurk leapt up and grasped a rune-coated sword beside the bed, watched as the burnt hand crossed the first of the silken sheets. It stopped, its forefinger pointed directly at his chest. He struck wildly, again shouting some archaic, prehistoric curse, but to no avail. The hand ignored the protests and curses and evaded the sword with ease. Back into a shadowed corner the monarch retreated, his ugly face coated with perspiration as a sheen of terror broke out on those odious features. The hand drew inexorably closer, then pulled with sooty fingers at the hem of his nightshirt.

Rammazurk screamed, calling upon every necromantic guardian he could name. They should have rushed to save him, but they did not. The hand clawed upwards: try as he did, the king could in no way dislodge it or hamper its dreadful progress. He beat at it hopelessly. Paralysed with fear, Rammazurk fell to his knees, gibbering, shrinking into a corner. Those foul, reeking fingers reached up and gripped his fat throat. They tightened. Rammazurk opened wide his mouth to give vent to another bellow. At once the hand moved upwards and the fingers clawed into the mouth itself, so that presently the gurgling monarch was desperately fighting to spit out the hand as it worked its way into his throat. Rammazurk tugged at it, gagging, but it possessed limitless strength.

The screams choked off and the terrible instrument of Rammazurk's torment slithered down deeper into him, passing to his very vitals. Soon he felt it working at him like a rodent, clutching his internal organs. Nothing he did could prevent its abominable workings. The hand began tearing and ripping and clawing as he twisted madly about, hands pressed to his vast gut. His screams and whines grew in volume, shaking the corridors of Windwrack. He rolled about on the floor, eyes bulging from their sockets.

Two vulpine forms appeared at the shattered door of the chamber and gazed with incredulity on the hellish scene. Dennizor and Nazzim, the twin sorcerers, said nothing as they watched. They saw Rammazurk rolling on the floor in his death agonies, and to their horror they saw presiding over the frenetic form a naked woman, her arm buried to the elbow in his mouth, as though she were ripping from within him his very entrails. She turned a brief, ghoulish smile upon them and at sight of her eyes, they fled.

Down a black corridor they rushed, and towards them from out of the darkness came a single, eerie figure. It was the Voidal. He had spent two days in Windwrack, trying to learn something about himself, hoping to meet someone who could help, but had uncovered nothing.

"By all the hells!" snapped the gaunt man. "What is happening?"

"She has returned," blurted Nazzim, his face pale as he made to rush past.

"It is the queen—back from the dead," groaned Dennizor. "She takes an unspeakable revenge upon the king."

And the terrified sorcerers fled. The Voidal, appalled by the awful screams he had heard earlier, went quietly to the now still chamber of the king. A widening pool of sticky blood had run from the darkness of a corner, where something hunched and motionless slumped against the walls. The Voidal could smell the blood, but he felt compelled to examine the corpse. There was something grimly familiar about the scene.

Rammazurk was sprawled in a broken posture, his robes saturated with blood, his face a horrible mask of agony, his mouth gaping. From the shredded orifice hung the pulped end of an organ.

The Voidal turned, a sudden look of revulsion and recognition on his drawn features. Here was the appointed companion—the unseen, the unattainable yet ever near. Death.

A host of disorganised guards with stormhounds was making its raucous way through the passages of the gloomy castle, led by Dennizor and Nazzim, who had regained a modicum of composure. Their terror of the supernatural manifestation responsible for Rammazurk's demise was overshadowed by their dreams of freedom from the tyrant's will. As they led the guards towards the chamber of death, they again met the Voidal, who had evidently seen as much as he wished to.

"Ho!" cried Dennizor, more boldly than he felt, for this enigmatic stranger made him shudder. "Is it over? Did you see Issylla?"

"I saw no one save Rammazurk," said the Voidal coldly. "Though one greater has been within."

Nazzim pointed at the Voidal, his hand trembling.

"Rammazurk's blood is on your hands! It is you who have brought Death here!"

The Voidal looked down. He had not donned his black gloves: he stared in disgust at the two hands, cursing the deceit of the Dark Gods. As the rabble saw the restored appendage, they drew back in alarm, for not only had the missing hand been restored, but it was unburned, unblemished, whole. Yet as they watched, they saw blood well between the fingers and drip steadily to the begrimed floor.

Swords sang out from scabbards and wavered, awaiting the command from the sorcerers to avenge the king's murder. But Dennizor and Nazzim were in awe of this pale man, who seemed to bear upon his shoulders the weight of a greater curse.

"I am cursed," the Voidal whispered, ignoring the wavering steel. "I came here in search of an ally, one who would lead me to a closer understanding of my fate, yet I found only Death. It was another soul it took, for I have none, unless it is hidden among the intersecting dimensions of this vile omniverse!"

Still no one moved against him.

"Rammazurk's followers will call for your corpse, if not your soul," said Dennizor. "If you wish to survive the dawn, you must leave Sedooc at once. You'll be hunted its length and breadth."

"And have you no wish to avenge your king?"

"Not I!" spat Dennizor, and he was echoed by Nazzim. "We had cause enough to loathe him. We owe you a favour for his death."

The Voidal smiled wryly. "If that is so, direct me away from this wretched citadel."

They showed him a way out of Windwrack: a tortuous, secret route that led him through a maze of pits and reeking tunnels bordering on other realms of sorcery and corrupt power. But his mind was fixed on the deceit that had been played upon him, and the way in which the Dark Gods had used him. When he reached the outer walls and penetrated the last bolthole to the desert beyond, he paused, feeling the onset of a familiar, hated lethargy.

The sands began to spin and presently had surged upward in a spiralling column of dust as the winds increased in power. The Screamers, Rammazurk's elemental servants, gathered themselves in anger, eager for vengeance.

As the Voidal stepped out on to the sands, his hand closed around the hilt of his sword. Mechanically he tugged it free of its sheath. It made no sound, and it was as light as air. Without knowing he had said it, he whispered its name. "The Sword of Silence." Another of the Dark Gods' games.

But as the hurricane force of the Screamers began to swirl in the skies overhead, he was glad of the weapon, whatever its powers. And he was soon to learn. The twin sorcerers had been happy to show him the way out of Windwrack, oh yes. They had known the Screamers would be waiting.

They tore downwards like the bolts of an electric storm, but as the Sword of Silence flashed in the wan light of dawn, the demonic winds felt the sorcerous bite of the blade. Not only did it slice into them, disrupting the course of their flow, but it drew out of them their shrieks, shattering them like glass on stone. The sword was like a vent into limbo, a gate through which the Screamers hurtled, unable to prevent the manic speed of their outflowing. And throughout the maniacal din of their passing, the Voidal heard nothing, as though suddenly deaf.

The desert had been whipped up into a maelstrom of dust, blotting out all vision, so that the Voidal covered his face with his cloak. He held the Sword of Silence on high like a beacon. It drained the skies of their movements, the Screamers snared, dragged into the vortex, trapped in the very blade.

At last it was done. The desert subsided and fresh clouds slowly eased their way across the heavens. The Voidal raised his head, studying the Sword of Silence. He thought he heard one last scream of defiance, locked away in the shimmering blade. Then he re-sheathed it. Unwittingly he had served the Dark Gods well.

Tiredness overwhelmed him. Without a backward glance at the black walls of the citadel, he began the trudge into the desert and a fresh rendezvous with oblivion.

II

THE LAIR OF THE SPYDRON

If you were to take a glass ball the size of a small moon and shatter it, I am sure there would be a sliver of glass for every poet that ever rambled the mazes of Phaedrabile's twisted dimensions. I sing the praises of none, being myself immune to their art. Doubtless the fault lies in me: at any rate I am content to consider myself deficient in critical faculties on such matters.

This next tale I had from a poet, Gnompathon, or, as he liked to style himself, Gnompathon the Wiser (there having been, presumably a Gnompathon the Less Wise). It was actually recited to me in couplets, the poet having devised his own rhyme for it. In recording it here, however, I will restrict myself to quoting the opening three lines, after which I will render the entire piece into my own prose, though you must forgive me for the occasional stylistic lapse. Blame that on the poet who is said to be dormant in all of us, striving for release.

Gnompathon began thus:

> *Beyond the walls of Night's abyss, beneath a thousand hells:*
> *Behind the farthest depth of space, where writhing Chaos swells,*
> *Outside the laws of ordered realms, unchained by Reason's spells—*

This from his "Songs of Life and Death."

—Salecco, Author of No Poetry

I have already established that Phaedrabile is a somewhat accursed realm: in its cauldron of erratic confusion there are countless unspeakable marvels, many of which could only have been birthed in this infamous, appalling realm. Myths abound, naturally, for creation, no matter how debased, must needs attempt to supersede its creator. And although most of Phaedrabile's myths are little better than mad dreams or passing whimsical invention, others have a grounding in reality. Of the latter type was the myth of the Spydron.

It is a certain fact that even the Dark Gods scorned and derided this Spydron: they tolerated its malign intrusion into the warp and weft of Phaedrabile's dimensions with open antipathy. However, the Spydron had power of its own, though from what inconceivable well of nightmare it had sucked this remains beyond knowledge.

In its apartness, the Spydron brooded, protecting itself from the full wrath of the Dark Gods so that it enjoyed a solitary existence, for they could not destroy it utterly. Its black lair they twisted so that it wove through the interstices of numerous dimensions, being not wholly in any and only partially in many. Hence the rampant mythology that surrounded the Spydron.

Locked inside its black bubble of night, separated from the remainder of creation by the unique bonds of its prison, the Spydron forgot about time and space: they no longer existed, save within the walls of its inner world. In the confines of its castle, it brooded, all traffic with the outer omniverse decaying into vague memories. Even so, its loneliness was like an infection, insistent and nagging. Its insularity became a sore, running with hate and self-pity.

So the Spydron conceived a creation of its own, populating its Gargantuan castle with debased and ghoulish creatures, things that slithered and scuttled in the dark, unseen and unfit for any other realm. For an age these hideous things amused the Spydron, but again it became bored, the weight of its isolation doubly unbearable. In desperation it sought to flex its power, testing the fetters placed upon it by the Dark Gods. And, turning sluggishly to the dimensions that held it, the Spydron called sibilantly, drawing into itself all those who came too near, incarcerating them in the inner world of its castle, from which there was no exit.

Those wayward beings who found themselves caught up in the endless corridors and spans of the bleak domain soon learned to fear its two extremities. High, high up above them, in leaning vaults and huge lofts and attics there gathered the countless minions of the spiderlings. Most of these creatures were small, scuttling about in silence, secreting themselves in their numerous forms far and wide in the vast castle, forever seeking to link the entire maze into one webbed complex. Among them there were mutations, moulded by the bizarre mind of the

Spydron, crawling things that flopped and hopped above the middle terraces, always hungry for news of the rival lower levels. And in the uppermost places of the dark there dwelt the awesome bulks of the spider overlords: massive, bloated denizens, whom it was whispered cannibalised their own minions when their appetites went unsated. One colossal monster ruled them all, the bristling Arachniderm, feared Spider Mother.

While the lofty vaults of the Spydron castle housed the abominable army of spiders and spiderlings, the lower reaches held no less a terror; for it was far down below, deeper than any ray of false light could pierce, that the ratlings held sway. Here rats pattered to and fro in a perpetual chase, sniffing their way upwards with caution, being a cowardly tribe, devouring any tiny thing that had the misfortune to be edible. They, too, had their mutated masters, for their forms had been created by the Spydron, fabricated from an uneasy nightmare. Far down in the black wells there lurked the swollen ratling underlords, themselves prone to acts of gluttonous cannibalism, governed as they were by the primitive laws of survival, their yoke from the Spydron. Over them ruled the tyrannical Xalganash, he of the Thousand Teeth.

The dreaming mind of the Spydron writhed ceaselessly as it contemplated the ageless struggle of the spiderlings and ratlings, which harried each other about the extremities of their domains in the neutral middle regions. Yet, as always with the introverted Spydron, the products of its own creativity grew insipid and dull. Hence its recourse to the abductions.

The fruits of these practices had made their niches and crannies in the middle terraces and corridors of the castle, cringing away in constant confusion and terror from the perpetual forays of the two warring armies. In time, they, too, succumbed to the rigours of mutation, and became debased and stunted, parodies of the evolutionary process to which they had once belonged. And the name of their lord was Misery.

Trabulic, the thin-faced, silver-haired Songster, woke from a slumber that had plunged him into a stellar gulf so deep that he dreamed space itself had swallowed him. He woke, though the darkness around him taught him nothing about his environment.

The vague memory of splendid drunken revelry in the court of some debased, hedonistic monarch of Phaedrabile stirred sluggishly. Was this, then, the way he had been repaid for the rendering of the lost art, the Songs of Life and Death? Had he been cast into a remote dungeon for those shameless Songs (many of which, admittedly, made crude jest of the gods)? His memory had been all but wiped clean by the escapades of countless years of imbibing at numerous courts. But a piece of dream gleamed for a moment, the vision of a long strand of web, but it vanished. He reached out and clasped the instrument of his art, the many-stringed wooden frame that sang with him. It was enough to comfort him. Darkness and Grabulic were old acquaintances, and on occasion they had been close friends. He shifted in the rank dirt and dust, waiting.

"Art thou, awake, enemy?" grated a voice from so close to his ear that he started.

"Who calls me enemy?" he replied in an octave higher than was usual. "Never call me enemy! Have you not seen my face? Do you not know me? Am I not Grabulic, whose famous Songs are for all the creatures of the omniverse? Grabulic, who calls no man enemy?"

"Awake, then!" came the growl. At this a crackle on the air presaged the brief flicker of a primitive torch. In its green glow, Grabulic saw a hunched, stunted creature bending over him, gazing with eyes that were not eyes. They were two round, white orbs, evidently blind, yet the manling seemed to be studying him.

"Gods of the Abyss, what manner of creature are you?" cried the Songster, with little regard for discretion (a trait for which he was not noted).

A peculiar sound that may have been a laugh escaped the lips of the manling. "You'll know that soon enough. Come! To linger here is to invite the ratlings to feed. And there is nothing that lives they do not call enemy!" This time the creature emitted a gargling sound that was indeed meant as laughter, though Grabulic did not feel encouraged to enjoin his companion.

The Songster was now able to see something of his remarkable surroundings. He had not woken in a dungeon as he had imagined, but saw instead that he sat in some subterranean corridor, which wound its serpentine way through the stone to his left and right, dank and unsavoury as a sewer, sheer-sided and ovoid, like the burrow of some colossal worm. He saw why the manling was so hunched, for the ceiling of this tunnel was but a few feet high. As the Songster got to his feet, the manling hobbled ahead on stocky legs, holding aloft his sputtering torch.

"Say! Where is this miserable domain?" said Grabulic, sensing that the gargoyle was for the moment an ally.

Its white orbs turned back to him. "You trespass in the castle of the Spydron, unfortunate traveller. You are the first to do so for a long, long time," it croaked.

Grabulic's expression at once altered to match the colour of his silver hair. "Gods of Chaos and Madness! The Spydron? But it's a myth, its castle a place of pure legend!"

"Nay, 'tis the rest of creation that has become myth for you," the manling cackled. "Touch the stone. It is real enough, eh?"

Grabulic was about to utter an obscene retort, when the little figure ahead abruptly stood upright, its squat nose sniffing the air in the manner of a questing beast, more rodent than man.

"They come! Their stench is unmistakable. Hurry, traveller, or you'll dream no more of anything." The manling turned and rushed on ahead, and as he did so the torch guttered, almost out. Grabulic followed, crouched low, clutching his beloved instrument. Behind him now he could hear a strange pattering that grew rapidly in volume, and the cold sweat of dread began to break out on his brow. It was the running of the ratlings, hastening to the feast. Grabulic looked back down the tunnel, and in the dim light saw the first of the horrors come squealing into view, teeth gleaming. Whiskered noses high, the horde rushed on like a wave, tails white and bleached, thrust up in the hunt. But the eyes were the most fearful aspect of the ratlings, for they were round and seemingly sightless, like the manlings, but they were the bright crimson of blood.

Grabulic took but a single glance before the light went out. He bumped into the dwarf, who was scuttling up a crude series of holes in the stonework.

"Climb for your life! Quickly!" cried the manling, and the Songster needed no second bidding. Already he imagined he could feel the sharp nips of a hundred teeth in his scrawny legs. The manling had climbed above the tunnel and through an invisible hole, while the squealing below had assumed frightful proportions. Grabulic thrust himself up and through the hole and at once something clanged down, shutting off the ghastly sounds of pursuit. Another ball of green light ignited, a new torch in the manling's fist.

"It will hold them until one of their underlords comes to force it open. With luck and the Spydron willing, we'll be safe by then. Come!"

Grabulic immediately followed the figure, having no wish to be left to the vicissitudes of this dreadful place, particularly if it truly was the castle of the heretofore mythical Spydron. What manner of nightmare had he been pitched into?

Turning through corridors and wriggling up tiny stairwells of black stone that wormed up into the heart of the castle, the two figures hurried on fearfully. From time to time the manling stopped, sniffing for a hint of pursuit or to learn if any other revolting denizens of this place had been awakened by the rapid flight. At last, high on the middle terrace, he drew Grabulic on all fours through yet another of the burrows and they came out into an open area, though it was neither high-roofed nor bright. No sun ever shed light within this nocturnal realm. The walls and floor were heavy with table-like fungi, grey and daunting, the air trembling with spores. Other life stirred in this alien plantation, for in the shuddering torch-glow Grabulic could discern a score of diminutive manlings, each as stooped and bent as his erstwhile protector.

They were atavistic and beast-like, their apparently blind eyes questing, their gnarled limbs like wood, grained with vessels and corded muscle. Their skins looked mildewed, their hides toughened by this inhospitable environment. Thick, tousled hair tumbled in ringlets down their broad shoulders, and black beards spilled out on to shaggy chests. They spoke in grunts, brief, guttural and rude. Beyond them Grabulic could see a few women with children clutched to them, hiding behind the trunks of the thick fungi. The Songster sensed that he was not welcome.

"What has Mnam-Mnam brought from the lower reaches? A ratling spy is it? Some new monster cunningly wrought so that it may breach our defences?" growled a stocky, muscular dwarf, thrusting its hideous face close to that of the Songster.

"I think not, brother Kulkurakk. 'Tis but another traveller, caught up in the cruel web of the Spydron, tugged here by the same foul sorcery that sucked in our own ancestors," vouched Grabulic's companion.

The huge white orbs of Kulkurakk came close to those of the Songster. "It has been long since any such came! What proof have you of this? Show it at once, lest we commit you to the embrace of the catacombs."

Grabulic shuddered. "Noble sir!" he cried, swallowing, but the burly Kulkurakk snorted in derision.

"Hah! 'Noble' he calls me! Your eyes may look intact, but their sight is not! 'Noble'! What is there in all this vile world of the castle that is noble?"

"Your pardon, I did not mean to mock you," blurted Grabulic.

"Nay, I see that. Oh yes, I see! We all see, in both light and dark, though the manner of our doing so is by no method known to you, I'll wager, if you are truly an outsider. Our kind has festered here in the castle for many an age. Necessity has bred us a strange sight of our own, as it has with the other monsters of this lair of madness."

"I am no offspring of this castle," insisted Grabulic. "Let me show you my own peculiar gift. There is no other Songster who can give you such diverse joy as I, and no other instrument that can speak to you with the silver tongue of Layola. Here, within this musical device, is said to be imprisoned the Lady Layola, one time Songstress of the lost world of Gnardril, held now within by an eternal spell." He lifted his stringed frame, and the dwarf people all stared at it, fearing for a moment that it might be a grim talisman, forged through sorcery by an enemy within the castle.

Kulkurakk looked most suspiciously at the instrument and the others drew back.

"A trick!" someone cried, and there was muttered agreement.

"Sorcery," breathed Kulkurakk. "You are on a demon's mission."

"Brother Kulkurakk," said a voice. A wizened oldster had come forward, bent even more than his fellows, his own burden that of time. His hair was pure white, a white beard trailing in the dust at his feet. He used fungoid sticks to wriggle to Kulkurakk's side. "I have seen the like of this before," he said hoarsely.

"You recognise it?" said Grabulic eagerly, holding it under the old one's very nose.

"Indeed! But I have not heard its melodies for a lifetime: perhaps it was even in a former life, for this one has been as endless as the vaults of the stars that none of us shall see again. Play for us, stranger, that we can recall the existence outside this prison in which the Spydron has encased us."

Grabulic looked to Kulkurakk for instruction and the dwarf nodded sourly. So the Songster began to play, and the mellow notes of his instrument chimed and rippled through those sombre shadow-vaults of the middle terrace. His voice was sweet, painfully sweet, evocative of a universe and a time that had no relationship to the nightmare and despair of the castle. He sang of things of beauty, of light and of love, and the stone hearts of the dwarves were melted. He sang of the fishers of the fire seas of far Mnurgh and of the sea-waifs from the sulphur pools of Gennarus and of the sleek willow-folk of Wendlewarren, and of their tragic loves. And as he sang, the notes of the Lady Layola soared in perfect harmony with him, as if the instrument embodied the very lost love of which he sang, his own forlorn passion, locked away, so close yet so unreachable.

Even grim Kulkurakk felt a current of emotion stirring and flowing through him like magic, so that as the Songster ended his last song, the dwarf clasped his arm fervently. "You are no spawn of the castle! By all the old gods, you are indeed from some other place! A place we knew must exist, but which we can only reach in our dreams!"

Grabulic looked at them as they shuffled closer, eager to look upon his instrument, his beautiful Layola. "So you are prisoners in this place?" he said.

Kulkurakk grunted. "Hah! Not prisoners, no, for we have the freedom of the castle, though there are places we dare not venture. The castle is our world, its dimensions our entire universe, for there is no way through its walls. It is all we have known. In dreams we touch the places of which you sing. So we are both free and enslaved at the same moment."

Grabulic set down his instrument and considered the dwarf's words gravely. The others were nodding sadly: through the echoing cavern passed a wave of deep melancholy.

"Have you no means of escape?" he asked them, for it had come to him that their predicament mirrored his own, and that he, too, was therefore incarcerated.

"None," affirmed Kulkurakk.

"But—is there no god you can pray to?"

"Gods! Pah, they deserted us long, long ago! There are no gods here, unless you call the Spydron a god. What god would come to this misbegotten realm?"

"You have no demons, no elementals, no Werespawn you can call on for supernatural aid?" said Grabulic, his concern for his own plight mounting.

But Kulkurakk shook his head at each. "None."

"No sorcerers, no masters of arcane lore? No one who can wield cantrips or conjurations or hurl spells? No adepts?" Grabulic's voice had become a wail.

Again the reply to his questions was a solemn negative. Gloomy silence hung over them all. Grabulic looked dejected beyond words.

Presently the old manling with the long beard came forward again, sniffing at the Songster like a hound. "Our memories are bereft of such things as you mention, traveller," he croaked. "But what of yours? Perhaps you have some deity to which you can appeal for succour? Can you not urge it to find an aperture in the walls of the castle?"

Grabulic scratched at his silver locks. "I fear that I have been so wayward in my journeyings and so erratic in my obeisance to the gods, that none of them would turn a whisker in my direction."

"Yet there must be gods with which you are familiar?" growled Kulkurakk.

"Well," blustered Grabulic, "that is so. But they are gods of another dimension than this. The walls of this castle must be inordinately thick. Surely no god would hear my invocations! I am no wizard, no priest."

"Nevertheless," said Kulkurakk, "you must try! We shall bring you food and drink and give you such luxuries as there are in this sinkhole. And then you will begin. You must call upon every god you can remember until you solicit a response."

Grabulic paled. "But—but—surely none will hear me!"

Kulkurakk stood close to him, features grim. "They must! Play to them! Your songs and your music would charm stone! Your gods will hear you."

This brought an optimistic if ragged cheer from the gathered ranks of the manlings.

"And if I do not?" gulped Grabulic.

Kulkurakk deliberated silently, but then an expression of satisfaction moulded itself out of his bellicose features. "If you fail us, Songster, then we will feed you to the Many Mouths in the black orifice of the Wall-that-Hungers."

A cry went up at this, for the manlings were loath to lose someone as gifted as Grabulic, and one who could so touch their heartstrings with every movement of his fingers along his instrument. But Kulkurakk growled and thrust out his chin in defiance of their complaints.

"Hear me, you fools! This traveller weaves magic in his songs, yes! He sings of wonders and of lost places that we all long for. Yet we cannot reach them! To be reminded of them will be like having a flaming brand searing our hides! If this Songster cannot take us to the places of which he sings, then let us have none of him and his impossible promises! For, consider this: he may well be a trick of the Spydron, sent here to torment us!"

Grabulic anxiously awaited another outcry of defiance from the manlings, but they began to nod soberly, then mutter, then call out that Kulkurakk was wise, was far seeing, and was right. The latter turned to Grabulic, orbs wide.

"So be it! Find a god to aid us, or you feed the Many Mouths!"

Thereafter Grabulic, who could not protest his case as he was outnumbered vastly by the gathered manlings (and who was blessed with not one iota of courage or fighting skill when it came to matters of conflict) was led by the eerie torchlight along low tunnels to a small chamber, lined with old hides and scarcely tall enough to accommodate him, and was then brought water and slices of thin meat. He would have preferred the sting of wine to dent his fears, but the manlings knew of no such commodity; as for the meat, it was tough and salty, yet he made no attempt to ascertain from what creature it had been hacked. After he had been allowed to rest and to gather what he could of his palpitating wits, he was again visited by Kulkurakk.

"Do you need anything to aid you?" he said.

"Without powders, alembics, pestles, skillets, grimoires and all the paraphernalia of even the humblest wizard, I am more or less impotent—"

"Enough! You have your instrument, your voice. Begin! And do not cease until you have called upon every god and every other manner of power you spoke of." So saying, the gruff dwarf disappeared, closing the thick door, while from outside Grabulic's cell could be heard the shufflings of many manling guards.

Grabulic had but a tiny green brand to see by. He scowled at it, deep in thought. This was a dreadful pass he had come to. He reflected upon the many gods that he could name: Aabun, Aacrol the Lurid, Aberboomeroth—to list them alone would take an infinity. But his past and his sins had sealed a particular fate to him, unbeknown to the manlings (and indeed to all but Grabulic) namely that by his jesting at the expense of the gods in his Songs, and also by his errant tenets and faith in many of them (whom he alternately praised and rejected to suit himself) they had combined to deny him a single favour, so that it was his lot to be a man without a god. However, he felt that if he had explained this to the impetuous Kulkurakk, his journey to the ominous-sounding Many Mouths would have been significantly accelerated.

At this moment, three sets of white orbs peered in at him from a grille set in the black door, to see, doubtless, why he had not begun his rituals. At once he started an incoherent incantation, calling out loud the names of Fnobollion, Regurjaj, Ctelpotl the Slitherer, Numm of the Hundred Wills, Hoi-Hoi the Soul Gatherer and many more, not a few of which were entirely his own invention. The white orbs withdrew in amazement and no less in trepidation. Thereafter Grabulic was not disturbed; occasionally, though, he called out the name of some nether world divinity. As had been promised to him, none of the gods saw fit to acknowledge his appeals for aid. If the Spydron heard him, it remained immobile and insensate as stone.

Grabulic felt the onset of despair, knowing that a prolonged recital of unspeakable names would not delay his unwanted confrontation with the Many Mouths indefinitely. He slumped against the cold wall, cursing and profaning, vilifying the gods he was supposed to be invoking. But in time, as his wasted rage spent itself, the seed of a faint plan evolved in a dark corner of his mind. A single name slipped elusively through the halls of his memory, and he tried in vain to corner the name and grasp it, bringing it out into the light of recollection. The words of an old rhyme came to him:

> *"Ye who seek the Hand of Fate*
> *That points the way to Future's gate:*
> *In deed your will is best employed—*
> *Invoke the shadow from the Void."*

Now the Songster recalled the slippery name.
The Voidal.

It meant *from the Void*. This Voidal was the enigmatic fragment of an old myth or legend from a history or nation unremembered. But of the smattering of lore that surrounded the perplexing figure there was an element of sorcery as old as the omniverse itself, or so Grabulic believed. No god would help him shatter the walls of the Spydron's hold, but this Voidal, this ancient curse—who could tell what powers his incantation might unleash? This comer from the Void knew no allegiance to gods and obeyed no laws that they made.

Grabulic straightened as best he could, gazing deeper at the green light. Of all the gods he had tried, only this Voidal might answer him. And yet—surely there would be a reckoning, a dire emolument. The Songster frowned at that, but quickly his cunning mind compromised with the dilemma. There was a way. So, committed to his course, he drew in his breath and spoke.

"Hear me, timeless vault of the omniverse! I invoke the Voidal! In the name of the creatures of this castle and by their will, I invoke the Voidal!"

Out into the ether went the words, absorbed at once by the indifferent stone. Grabulic could think of nothing else to add weight to his words, for very little was known of the thing he had summoned. He had no idea what effect his invocation would have, nor was his confidence surging. Yet he struggled to the door of his cell and called upon his captors.

"Ho! It is done. I have summoned the one who will aid you." At this, word was quickly sent to Kulkurakk and shortly afterwards he appeared, glancing about him suspiciously, as though expecting to see some terrible and grisly deity.

"I see no god! Have you caused an invisible spirit to enter the castle?" he boomed. His manlings surrounded him, each holding a crude fungi club, ready to be used.

"The one I have summoned is not yet here. But he will come in time. You will know him when he comes. In the meantime if you would release me, I will—"

"You may enjoy the hospitality of your room until such time as your god does come," laughed Kulkurakk, and calling to his followers, strode back into the black tunnels.

Grabulic returned in despair to his hides. He would be glad of any aid this Voidal might bring. He tried to recall other fragments of the legend, for if the being did arrive, it were best to be prepared.

long a remote tunnel in the lower regions of the castle, a host of ratlings was gathered together about a carcass. Some unfortunate creature had strayed into the ratling domain, a mutated hybrid from an unspecified part of the hold. There were many such strange ones, spawned at some point in the castle's timelessness by sires and dams the nature of which had become totally obscure in its weird evolution. Whenever a lone creature found itself far from the safety of its hole, it was sure to fall foul of a thirsting horde. And now it was the ratlings who had struck. They were stripping every last vestige of flesh and organ from their victim. But then, as if at a given command, they all ceased their gnawing and began sniffing the air in unity, their blood-red orbs gleaming in the faint effulgence of light diffused by the mould on the walls, their noses high, twitching.

Something approached. Something *alien* to the castle.

From around a bend in the narrow confines of the tunnel appeared a solitary figure. Though it had the appearance of a man, it moved almost like a spider, its long, black-leather encased limbs striding forward in silence. It saw at once the lately feeding ratlings and from the ebon scabbard that depended from its belt slid a sword, without a sound. The ratlings amassed for a singular charge: their crimson eyes beheld the brazen stance of the newcomer. It was a tall man, thin and dressed in funereal clothes studded with a brief silver harness. The hair was sleek and black, and the cloak was of a midnight hue. The face was sharp, the eyes a piercing green, enhanced by the aura of silence and darkness in which the figure was swathed. The Voidal had come to the castle of the Spydron.

Their sense of smell told the ratlings that this spider-like being was not possessed of fear: the very fact introduced the same emotion into each of their own tiny brains. Was this an enemy from the upper vaults, spawn of the hated spiderlings? Instinct told them to rush forward and destroy it, but their fear quickly mounted to terror, for in the right hand of the Voidal was that awful sword, its sinister purpose a mystery they would rather not unveil. The ratlings began to squeal in indecision, then ran about in a fervour. Soon they were scurrying ever backward. The Voidal strode nervelessly toward them. It was enough. They fled.

rabulic, exhausted by his lengthy incantations and lulled by his introspective ponderings, had fallen into a light sleep. From outside came muted voices; eyes looked in at the somnolent figure as it cried out in its sleep or gave voice to hoarse whispers. The manlings assumed that the Songster was merely continuing his chants and supplications to the promised divinities, whereas the recumbent body was dreaming a sequence of ghastly nightmares in which some invisible being was tearing the bones from within it.

Kulkurakk, meanwhile, pacing up and down the corridors of his immediate domain, followed by a murmuring band of his people, was first to come upon the stranger. This dark figure had come out of the shadows, a sinister, wispish light following it like a familiar. In the figure's pale, green-eyed face and angular tallness, Kulkurakk recognised another being alien to the castle. At its side swung an ebon scabbard, from which the pommel of a sword stood up brightly, scattering beams of light, shimmering as if holding within it powers that writhed, eager to be free of its grip.

The Voidal stopped as he saw the manlings. Kulkurakk sniffed, but from this foreign creature came no noticeable aroma. The weapons of the dwarves wavered. Could this be the promised god, or his servant?

Kulkurakk stepped forward haughtily, chin out-thrust. "You lookin' for the Songster?"

The Voidal mouthed the word, mulling it over. "I come in search of a companion," he said after a pause.

"And his name?"

"I don't have it. But he is here in this intolerable region."

Kulkurakk grunted. "Very well. Come with us."

As there seemed no immediate hostility from this stranger, the manlings were content to allow him unhindered passage to the cell of Grabulic. Keys rattled in the low door, and as it swung open, Kulkurakk motioned the stranger inside. The Voidal bent and entered, looking down at the snoring Songster. A nudge with his boot brought the latter into sleepy wakefulness, muttering his innocence in the affair of the deflowering of the daughter of a certain King Nyordias. The Songster stared at the green light, gasping and drawing back from the night-hung stranger. The manlings had again retired, though they had not locked the door. A god could shatter such things with his breath.

"Who are you?" burbled Grabulic, clutching his instrument.

The man in black looked puzzled. "Who am I? I wish I could answer that to my own satisfaction. I am a wanderer, set adrift by the Dark Gods, whom I appear to have offended. My memory of such matters is a fragmented thing. But I seem to sense that I am to meet a friend here, someone who can help me."

"I summoned the Voidal," said Grabulic tremulously. "Though I did it in the name of the manlings. It was their wish, not mine!" he added, still mindful of the potential price of the calling.

The Voidal considered the name. "It seems familiar to me. I may be him. But you say you summoned me? How? From where?"

"I—I—merely invoked your name."

"Why?"

"To aid me—I mean—the manlings of this castle. They have no gods, being neglected by them, as indeed, am I, and as I had heard of you, they forced me to invoke you, in their name, to aid them—"

"To what end?"

"To free them from their plight. This is the world of the Spydron. Do you know the myths? Well, they are not myths here, but lunatic reality!"

The door opened and Kulkurakk entered slowly, hand grasping his fungi club. "Is this the one you promised us?" he asked Grabulic bluntly.

"Indeed!" said the latter, getting to his feet. "It is."

"Will you save us?" Kulkurakk asked the Voidal.

The Voidal considered. "If it is in my power to help you, very well. But if I am to be of service, there is something I would have you give me."

Grabulic visibly paled, his fingers twitching.

"Name it," said Kulkurakk.

"Knowledge. All that you know. And you—" he pointed to Grabulic. "All that you know also."

Kulkurakk looked relieved. "Well, that one is a Songster. He has already sung to of us of many wonders outside this place. What we manlings know we will soon impart to you. But he is the one with true knowledge."

The Voidal's green eyes focused on the Songster. "A Songster! That would seem a stroke of fortune."

"All that I know is yours," Grabulic assured him with a lavish bow, and the dark man seemed satisfied.

"Let us to a more comfortable place," said Kulkurakk, "though there are no luxuries in the castle of the Spydron."

Far below the middle terraces where the manlings and the outsiders conversed, the squealing ratlings had scurried ever downwards in search of their masters and the repugnant monster that had set itself up as their supreme monarch, Xalganash, he of the Thousand Teeth. Now word was being carried to the hybrid that sprawled in wasted, gelatinous bulges of blubber in the lowest catacombs of the castle, far from the eyes of other creatures, where only the ratlings ever set foot and where only the Spydron could otherwise peer. Into the vast and bulbous presence of this grotesquely mutated ratling came a quartet of great rats, each black-skinned and huge, bellies never empty, often filled with their own kind. They stopped well short of the foul-smelling nest of their ruler, telegraphing to Xalganash in their own peculiar way the facts concerning the arrival of the strange being in the upper tunnels of their domain. They told also of the fear this grim harbinger had instilled in the minds of the ratlings. Whatever Xalganash felt about this uncalled for intrusion, the degenerate monarch made no reply, dismissing his four underlords curtly. They were glad to remove from the presence of the Thousand Teeth, their duty done.

When they had gone, the monarch continued to masticate the bones of the carcasses that had been brought to him, leaving nothing. As his many teeth worked with the efficiency of knives, he considered the news he had been brought. As he did so, an oblique configuration appeared upon the far wall of his huge, stifling chamber, where the stone had been smoothed near flat by the beating of a million ratling tails over the ages. There, upon the wall, was a shadow, coalescing out of nothing, deepening in umbra, forming into a shape. Xalganash spat out bones in anger. Who dared work sorcery here in his very lair? But he was cautious: it may be the Spydron, whose power alone he respected.

Upon the wall the shadow was complete. It was a creature with legs. At first it seemed to be an image of the Arachniderm, the loathely monster that ruled the rival spiderlings who thronged the highest reaches of the castle. But it had five legs, not eight. What creature had five legs? As the shadow moved, it formed into a huge human hand, its forefinger directed straight at Xalganash. However, after no more than a few moments, the hand shimmered and dissolved. The rat monarch roared out his scorn and went back to crunching his bones, the incident soon forgotten.

Kulkurakk and his manlings had gathered around the fire in the Chamber of Bone, the tall part of their middle terrace which was sacred to their ancestors, the worship of whom was the only kind of worship in which they indulged. Guards had been placed at the entrances to see that no spies or advance parties of ratlings or spiderlings harried those within. Kulkurakk and his elders had then recited to the Voidal all they knew of the castle of the Spydron, its geography, its history and its inhabitants. To this small store Grabulic was able to add only a smattering of the myths and legends he had gleaned from his wanderings. The Voidal sat in silence, a graven image, but at the end nodded, masking his emotions.

When Kulkurakk had done, Grabulic turned to him. "Now, I beseech you, leave the Voidal alone with me for a while. Such other knowledge as I have for him is secret and for no other ears." In spite of evident misgivings, Kulkurakk agreed to this request, leaving the two outsiders beside the sputtering fire, surrounded by the stained bones of the manling ancestors that festooned the walls, a forest of trophies.

"Their trust in my ability to help them escape may not be

well founded," said the Voidal. "The Spydron appears to have erected an impregnable barrier between this inner world and the external omniverse. If I am to breach it, the method of my doing so has not made itself apparent to me. Can you help, Songster? What can you tell me? You summoned me. Why did you invoke the Voidal?"

"Since I called you, I have managed to scour my memory and come up with certain songs and fragmentary pieces of legend that may shed some light upon you," said Grabulic. "For example, it was in the court of King Bendool the Braggart that certain mages, seeing their master's pleasure at my rendering of the Songs of Life and Death, gave me access to some ancient rhymes and odes that had long been secreted in their private library. Of these, the majority was only of interest to a scholar of orthometry or a Songster such as myself, but others—well, you shall hear. One spoke of a being, seemingly a man, that would 'come from the void' at the behest of the summoner. This being was apparently bound by the invocation of its name to perform some deed useful to the invoker. Usually this deed itself was a 'rendering of future events' (to quote Julius Julian the Minor) or a prophecy, rather than an actual physical act (such as any common demon would perform). The collected rhymes of which I speak referred to the being as 'Fatecaster.'"

The Voidal's eyes flared with jade light. The mantle of melancholy that had draped him seemed temporarily pierced by the Songster's words. "Fatecaster! Yes, I recall that name. Then I am a prophet?"

"It could be that you shape the future with your words, or indeed, your very presence."

"Perhaps. Go on."

"In the Forbidden Odes of Oyboldornix, a scribe of the Csarducts, whose Empire sprawls across all but the extremities of Phaedrabile, there are to be found certain lines concerning a 'walker in the void.' These I can quote, as far as my faltering memory will permit. They read:

"You who walk the void of night,
Whom immortality are shown

By Gods unseen and recondite:
The death you seek may be your own,
Yet you may be destroyed by none.

"This suggests that you are immortal, unless the dark Gods will it otherwise," added Grabulic uncertainly.

"Your words have the shimmer of familiarity, as though I lived an old dream in which the fabric of your words was more substantial. An immortal prophet! And the gewgaw of these Dark Gods, whom I have sometime enraged. Yes, they have cast me out into a void of ignorance, and they have taken something from me, my soul, perhaps. Without it, how could I die?"

"One thing more I recall," went on Grabulic, masking his personal feelings of relief. "The venerable scribe says:

"Not by thy will shalt thou kill."

"By whose, then? That of the Dark Gods? They who forge my every step, for I seem to have no will of my own. If the manlings are to escape this place, it will not be through my will."

Grabulic tossed more fuel on to the fire, while the dark man brooded. "What mischief have you worked upon these Dark Gods?"

"I have no memory," said the Voidal.

"Could their fate for you be to make you atone for your sins by using you to dispense fate to others who have offended them? Whose fate have you lately cast? Where were you last?"

The Voidal looked up at him, face sullen. "Each time I move from one realm to another, my past slips back, a spectre that dogs me but which will not show its face! Perhaps I do bring doom, catastrophe, love or fortune, but I cannot say. But—your words have the ring of wisdom. You have solved me one riddle. I must do the work of the Dark Gods, work which they will not do openly—"

"And work which you would not do willingly, perhaps."

"Yes," agreed the Voidal with a dry laugh. "I believe you have it, Songster. You are a friend indeed for teaching me this. I know that I was to meet a friend here. That much was planted in my mind. I knew as much when I found myself walking the tunnels."

Grabulic returned his smile, relieved to be considered the friend of such a redoubtable ally.

The Voidal clenched his right fist in its glove, shaking it at the stone walls as though in abjuration of the Dark Gods. "I shall wrest back my fate!" he avowed. "Though it takes an eternity!"

Grabulic looked at the leather-sheathed fist uneasily, recalling yet another line of forbidden poetry. He spoke it aloud:

"The curse of might lies in thy right. Your hand, Voidal. Your right hand. It is the key to your power."

The Voidal did study the gloved hand, unclenching it, though he did not unclasp the glove. For a long moment he was wrapped in thought. "You wake strange emotions within me, Songster. It was you who summoned me here, but who, I wonder, was it that sent me?"

Grabulic swallowed, preferring no to answer. He had already earned the scorn of too many gods himself. Though the Voidal had pronounced him friend, and did not have the power to kill him, the Songster knew only too well the deceit of the words of gods.

"For now," said the Voidal, "let me hear you sing and play. Let us put aside the despair of this wretched place and of our purloined destinies. Call back the unfortunate manlings. Bring them all to us and let us drink the forgetfulness your art can give us."

Grabulic was much pleased by this, hastening to gather his audience. Now that Kulkurakk and his people had been assured that the Voidal was here to intercede with the Spydron for their deliverance (as Grabulic swore by all the other gods that he was) they were charmed to hear more of the incomparable Songs of Life and Death.

In the castle of the Spydron there was no light and day, only the eternal gloom and chill of the convoluted tunnels that wound in manic spirals ever across each other from one far reach to another, like the inside of a monstrous fruit, eaten away.

The ratlings had no light save the dim glow of phosphorescence radiated by the moss and mould of the lower pits, while in the remote and lofty vaults, the spiderlings neither had nor needed light. Only the manlings in the middle terraces used torches, old bones soaked in oil that burned slowly. For their artificial night they were content to find an unlit tunnel or hole wherein they snatched what sleep they required.

Grabulic and the Voidal both found a guarded place and sat. Kulkurakk was always near, constantly seeking proof that the two outsiders meant to help his tribe. Since their private talk, he insisted on being present at all times. To appease their impatience, he feigned sleep, but one white orb was only half closed. The Voidal was glad of rest, for his dreams often prompted knowledge.

When darkness had all but blotted everything out, Kulkurakk was alarmed by a slight movement and sound. His ears had long been attuned to the most minor of shufflings and scurryings, for they could easily betoken the prying passage of an enemy, always eager to drag the manlings away to a grisly death. Kulkurakk opened both eyes and watched his two charges with deep trepidation. But they were both silent and unmoving. From the shadow of the Voidal, however, a smaller shadow detached itself, quickly melding in with the pitch of the tunnels.

Kulkurakk leapt up with a hoarse cry, casting his weapon after the retreating thing. Light was struck up at once and guards rushed in, spreading the green glow. In its radiance both the Voidal and the Songster were awake, staring at the cursing Kulkurakk.

"What is wrong?" snapped the Voidal.

"Spiderling! Sneaking through the dark, crawling over you to see what manner of intruder you are!" He searched in vain for the corpse of the tiny spy, for of it there was no sign.

The Voidal nodded as he rose. "I have met the ratlings. Now both your enemies know I am here." As he spoke, he slipped his right arm inside his nightweb shirt. As he did so, Grabulic turned away to conceal his great surprise, for he had seen that the right hand of the dark man was absent.

ust as the ratlings had their silent methods of communication, adapted over the ages in the insalubrious castle, and just as the manlings had developed vision through eyes that seemed blind, so did the spiderlings have their own ways of communicating, through telepathic impulses. Each tiny spiderling transmitted to the larger overlords, while these sent an endless stream of impulses to the brain of the huge Arachniderm, the Spider Mother, whose web sprawled through each and every tunnel of her kingdom, each strand a road to her terrible door.

In deep gloom the great Arachniderm curled up in a trelliswork of threads, thick, sticky cables that suspended her over the abyss of her kingdom. Around her the spiderling overlords moved gently, anxious for news of all that transpired outside the web, but mindful not to interfere with the dreams of the Spider Mother. They were beginning now to receive messages from the countless tiny spiderlings that made up the minions of the community.

From far below came the word: something harmful approached, some remorseless enemy bent on death. Already the tiny spiderlings told how they were amassing at the lower reaches of their domain, trying to stay the advance of this enemy. It was a spider, yet not a spider. When it became evident that even a great host of tiny spiderlings could not halt the nameless invader, the strongest of the Arachniderm's guards, he that was known to his kind as Zithadrl, scuttled on his eight thick legs down to meet the challenge.

In a black corridor he came upon the terrible struggle. Here there were countless thousands of spiderlings, a solid wall of them, a veritable sea of crawling, undulating creation; yet they could not halt the steady advance of the enemy. Zithadrl saw it was a single entity, no bigger than the hand of a manling, and as the fat spiderling overlord studied this thing, he saw that it had but five legs, though it moved like a spiderling. Covered in a black leather skin, it clawed and strangled its way through the hundreds of bodies that tried to smother it: behind it stretched a hideous trail of carnage where numerous broken and twitching spiderlings had been smashed aside.

Zithadrl, realising the futility of his minions' efforts against so irresistible a foe, bade them desist. Then he alone squared up to the intruder, spreading his eight legs across the tunnel. Without halting for a moment, the disembodied hand came on. Zithadrl attacked, but the thing moved with such speed that it could not be checked. Zithadrl felt one of his limbs wrenched and snapped, then another and another. Soon he was upon his back, with this diabolical creature tearing at his vitals, ripping and clawing.

The spiderlings scurried forward en masse, trying again to smother the enemy with sheer numbers, but to no avail. In a few minutes, Zithadrl had been destroyed, his limbs broken and folded in, his carcass leaking fluid from a score of wounds. The frightful Nemesis brushed away the spiderlings easily and advanced, weaving ever upward.

Quickly the word of Zithadrl's slaughter had reached the mind of the Spider Mother and at once she stirred herself on the swaying fronds of her web. Her other principal guardians had come rushing in to surround her, but she chose to confront this vile intruder herself. In a dream she had seen the eight and the five. Long had it been since she had experienced a real battle and her killing instinct gushed through her veins in anticipation. There in her huge web she waited, fuelled by a rare lust.

The coming of the enemy was heralded by an inrush of spiderlings, for they fled from it now in their multitudes. A boiling tide of the tiny creatures spilled over into the great chamber beneath the web of the Spider Mother, filling it with living matter. She waited patiently, throbbing with ungodly lust. Soon the enemy entered the choked vault.

The Spider Mother tried to analyse the thing. It was a hand, a manling hand, small and puny. How could this ridiculous thing have engendered such mass terror? The hand turned, and a long forefinger pointed upward, directly at the Arachniderm. At once, outraged by such blasphemy, the bloated overlords raced down the cables of web to crush the hand in a single assault, but before they reached it, they pulled up, bristles quivering in indecision.

For as they watched, the hand began to grow, taking on grim proportions.

Terrible, demonic sorcery must be at work, for the wriggling member had reached the size of the Spider Mother herself, dwarfing the overlords. The latter decided that it must be a scion of the Spydron itself, for nowhere else in the castle were there such powers. Thus they held back, for no one defied the Spydron.

Slowly the huge hand reached out for the cables and began to pull itself up towards the Arachniderm. The Spider Mother was still, knowing that this would be no normal contest of power. If this hand was, as her minions believed, a servant of the Spydron, then the outcome was in the hands of the Spydron. But if it were merely an intruder—

Moving quickly to maintain her advantage, the Arachniderm rushed down upon the hand. She had immense legs, bristling with wire-like hair, and her mottled underbelly was thick with fat, creased with sickly folds of skin. She hissed as she scuttled downward, and below the spiderlings rolled back, afraid of the grim confrontation.

The huge hand rose up and plunged into the attack, both creatures grappling, locking. They rolled to and fro on the cobweb, shaking each other violently in a blur of movement. The whole framework shook to the colossal struggle, and in places the moorings in the stone walls began to tear loose. Into the palm of the hand the Arachniderm thrust her fatal sting, discharging gallons of poison that would have killed a human army, but the hand evinced no sign of injury.

An automaton, it fought on, indestructible, indefatigable and unstoppable. More cables ripped from the shuddering walls as the two titanic forms writhed and hurled to and fro. A rending sound split the cavern and suddenly the whole of the great web burst to cast the two locked antagonists down upon the cold embrace of stone. Four of the Spider Mother's legs smashed to pulp beneath her. Before she could recover, the hand encircled her grotesquely misshapen body. And squeezed.

The spiderlings and overlords realised the outcome: they could do nothing. The giant hand was crushing the life from the hissing Arachniderm. The awful pressure increased, the power of a blood-crazed god, and the insides of the huge spider queen burst out through her ruptured skin and between the iron fingers. It was soon over, the Spider Mother mangled beyond repair, hideously crushed. The murderous hand drew back from its frightful triumph, beginning at once to shrivel back to its original size.

In the middle terraces, a lone figure stood at the gaping corridor that sloped upwards in the fashion of a hungry maw. The Voidal, cloak wrapped about him, studied the incline. Behind him there was movement: he swung round, ready to meet a challenge. But it was the Songster who materialised from the gloom.

"Not asleep?" he called. Behind him were Kulkurakk and a dozen others. Evidently they had prodded Grabulic here, for Kulkurakk's club was close to the Songster's back.

The Voidal shook his head. "I've slept enough."

"They made me come," spluttered Grabulic. "They won't wait any longer. You must act soon."

The Voidal nodded. As he did so, something scurried out of the dark tunnel. Kulkurakk took a step forward and made ready to bludgeon the spiderling that ran for the legs of the Voidal, but the dark man bent down, obscuring his aim. Only Grabulic caught sight of the brief motion as the Voidal snatched up the thing that had come to him.

The Voidal turned, holding out his right arm. Grabulic gasped and stood back, for in the gloved hand were a mass of pulped spiderlings. The hand was again one with the arm.

"The horror above you is no more," the Voidal told Kulkurakk and his followers. "The spiderlings no longer have a queen. Their Arachniderm is dead."

Kulkurakk looked at the bloodied hand. "How do you know this?"

"The Spider Mother's blood is on this hand."

"He does not lie," said Grabulic.

But neither Kulkurakk nor his people looked convinced.

"Go to your Chamber of Bone," the Voidal told them. "Secure your doors and wait for me there. I have other hellish work yet. My dreams were full of terrible things. I understand what I must do. You, Songster, you go with them."

"The ratlings?" said Grabulic. "But you cannot mean to go alone?"

"I will not be alone. The spiderlings have a new master."

No sooner had he spoken than there came a whispering from the slope up into darkness. The first of the myriad spiders appeared. At once Kulkurakk, Grabulic and the manlings turned and fled, leaving the Voidal in the swelling flood of the spiderlings. The dark man raised his right hand and pointed to another tunnel, leading downwards.

He led the descent to the realms of the ratlings, his obedient army following.

X alganash of the Thousand Teeth roared and smote one of his underlings bitterly so that the huge black rat span and crashed into a wall of the lower caverns. The bulk of the master quivered with rage. Where was the promised food from the last raid upon the middle terraces? Where were the succulent corpses of the manlings? Where were the libations of blood? Xalganash's underlords cowered before his stentorian outcries. They had tried to explain that the ratling host was afraid of something: the grim intruder they had seen, the one who walked without fear. Xalganash had shown his many teeth in a grimace of pathological fury. Very well, since he had fathered a brood of querulous cowards, he would lead them himself. They would rise up from the depths like bile and quaff their hunger upon the manlings, eradicating every last one of them.

Word that Xalganash himself was stirring from his nest to lead them quickly spread to the entire ratling horde, and in excitement and resurrected courage they prepared themselves, their ranks thick, choking the lower tunnels. Xalganash squeezed his huge carcass along the corridors, around him the air filled with squealing and squeaking as the host flowed, red eyes alight like those of devils from a forgotten hell. Up and up ran the living river of rat-flesh, Xalganash roaring, flexing his huge claws, eager to rend and rip.

Barely had this awful army come to the lower end of the middle terrace, when extraordinary sounds reached the alert ears of the front runners. Soon the coming of the amassed spiderlings was apparent. Xalganash received the news without fear: it was time the ratlings and spiderlings confronted each other and contested sovereignty of the castle. When he had killed the Spider Mother, long would he feed on the monstrous carcass!

Rounding a tunnel into a broad, flat-roofed chamber, the ratlings came upon the advancing spiderlings. Without a pause, the two forces rushed together like opposing thunderheads in a storm. They clashed with much noise, ratling teeth snapping, claws slashing, and spiderling poison jetting. A milling carpet of writhing life, feet deep, blocked the chamber. Frightful scramblings and gnawings churned the place into a maelstrom, creatures whirling in a lake of flesh around and around, hundreds smeared up against the black walls. Xalganash was set upon by a trio of stumbling spiderling overlords, all eager to fill him with venom. Yet his many teeth sliced them to strips of ragged flesh before they could do their worst.

As the walls of the chamber rang to the conflict, the incoming hordes raised the level of creatures, the dead and dying squashed under the blind and berserk fury of the battle. A number of tunnels ran from this broad chamber, some up, some down, others to unvisited extremes of the castle where few things stirred. In the mouth of one of these disused corridors stood the Voidal, watching the fantastical heavings of the swell of battle. As Xalganash eviscerated the last of the spiderling overlords, his huge red orbs alighted on the human figure. Instinctively he recognised his true enemy, as though the Spydron had whispered it in his ear. He forced his mighty bulk through the writhing mounds of the interlocked armies.

Seeing the rat monarch coming for him, the Voidal backed into the tunnel. He did not do so out of fear, for he was not without a strategy. Xalganash saw the hated man disappear into the dark chute and quickly reached the edge of the battle. Thousands of tiny spiderlings clung to him, but he ignored them, rushing after the Voidal, knowing the black figure had everything to do with recent events in the castle. A cold vault of night swallowed him. His huge claws scrabbled against stone, his ears picking up the sounds of retreating footfalls. On he plunged, certain of success.

At length he had to pause, coming as he did to the lip of an unfathomable canyon. It may only be yards deep, or plunge to the very bottom of the castle. Of the Voidal there was no sign. The great rat sniffed, but still could not detect the man. Yet there was something here. Strange distant sounds, issuing perhaps from the drop before him. Sucking, gurgling sounds. Water? A lost drain? Xalganash listened for a while, thinking the man must have plunged to his doom. Then he turned, deciding to go back to the battle, the waiting victory.

But behind him rose a black shape, an immense shadow, equal to his own bulk.

Five-legged, a mutated spiderling, it clenched into a fist and pounded at him like a ram, its rock-hard knuckles smashing into the rat's bloated chest, caving in a dozen ribs and bones, rupturing organs. With a squeal of horror, Xalganash twisted backwards, claws raking the lip of the abyss. Then, with a final howl, the great beast plummeted into the eager darkness.

The Voidal abandoned the niche where he had secreted himself and stood above the yawning pit. He could see nothing, but he could hear clearly the smacking, drooling sounds of the Many Mouths as the invisible denizen of this Western Wall feasted on the obese form of the rat monarch. Something scuttled to the Voidal's feet: he bent as though to retrieve a fallen glove. Then he made his silent, thoughtful way back to the middle terraces of the castle, by-passing the death throes of the two armies.

Kulkurakk opened the doors to the Chamber of Bone and admitted the Voidal. "What has happened?" said the manling, unable to conceal his agitation. Behind him the other manlings rushed forward like children.

"The ground trembled!" said another.

"What of the spiderling tide?" said Kulkurakk.

"They fight the ratlings to a standstill," said the Voidal. "Neither army has a monarch. The Spider Mother and Xalganash are no more. The armies will soon cease their orgy of destruction and the remnants will scatter to all parts of the castle. I found the one I sought, and his name is Death."

"What of us?" said Kulkurakk.

The Voidal's expression was one of sadness. "I have considered your plight. There is a way out, shown to me in a dream." He pulled his sword from its scabbard, and there came a faint sound, as of distant winds. "This is the Sword of Silence. I used it once to trap the elemental slaves of an evil monarch, so my dream told me. If you listen, you will hear the frustrated cries of the Screamers."

But Kulkurakk and the others drew back, afraid. Only Grabulic stepped forward, clutching his beloved Layola.

"With this I can free you all," said the Voidal. "But there will be a price, a reckoning."

"Name it," said Kulkurakk. "Already we owe you everything for your part in the scattering of our enemies." The manlings shouted their agreement.

"The reckoning is not one of my choosing, alas," sighed the Voidal. "It is what the Dark Gods demand. I am simply their vessel."

Grabulic's face became grave. "Then what is the price?"

The Voidal tapped the gleaming sword. "The walls of this castle will split open before the power of the released Screamers. But the sound will deafen you. For always. You also, Songster, you who play so beautifully. Those who hear the fury of the Screamers will hear no more thereafter."

Grabulic looked mortified. "Not hear—but, I cannot pay such a price!"

"Then you must remain here."

Kulkurakk drew in a great breath and threw out his chest. "I will pay for my freedom with my hearing if I must! I have had my fill of this place. Take me with you!"

At this the manlings voiced their uniform agreement, and soon there was only Grabulic who had not acceded. Tears had welled in his eyes as he looked down at his instrument.

The Voidal came close to him. "The castle is safe now. You can remain and be in no danger. The choice is yours: your music or unimaginable loneliness."

Grabulic gasped. "How can the gods so abuse me! They would take from me my only pleasure. If I sacrifice my hearing,

I will lose so much more. Why can they not be content with what they have already done to me?"

"What do you mean?"

Grabulic slumped. "There was once a beautiful girl, and she sang sweetly. One of the gods, infatuated by her, bestowed upon her the gift of even greater sweetness of voice, so there was no other comparable to her. In exchange he made her promise never to love anyone but him. But she met a young musician, whose music married to her voice was the envy of the world. And they fell in love. Her name was Layola."

The manlings gaped, all of them as silent as if the sword of the Voidal had touched them.

"The god was so incensed that he imprisoned Layola within the instrument, saying to me, for I was the young musician, that now I would be together with my love. We are together, yet apart. But if I am to be made deaf, then I will be truly alone. Those who mock the gods are punished, beyond enduring."

"I called you friend for your guidance," said the Voidal. "It seems the Dark Gods marked my words and thus punish you. I, too, have been cursed by them. I am to go my way alone, for those who pity me are made to pay. Yet still I call you friend, Grabulic. And I say, pay this toll! When we next meet, I will seek true justice for you, for know this, we shall meet again! I will swear it on the blackest powers of every hell if I must! Do your penance, but it will not be forever."

Grabulic clutched his Layola lovingly and nodded glumly.

The Voidal then led them all through the winding tunnels to the remote boundary of the castle. Here he drew out the Sword of Silence in readiness for the blow that would free the Screamers and open the way. But the company asked Grabulic for a last song, one they would keep in their minds, and he obliged them.

Thereafter were the walls of the Spydron's lair shattered and the cruel powers of that tyrant were maimed, leaving the Spydron confined within itself, never to meddle in the affairs of outside again. The last sound that Grabulic heard before silence clamped down on him was the whispered voice of the Voidal.

"We shall meet again."

III

THE UNIVERSE OF ISLANDS

You will learn what became of Grabulic in due course, provided I have whetted your appetite sufficiently enough for you to pursue this dark history.

But I must complete other pieces of the elaborate Voidal mosaic first.

Not all of the realms through which the Voidal toiled were as steeped in nightmare and torment as the hellish empires of Sedooc and the Spydron's lair, though even the brighter regions he was cast into had their shadows. Let me speak now of one such realm, one for which I confess a particular fondness, for I have visited it myself in the past and have luxuriated in its creative excesses.

On one such self-indulgent sabbatical I met one of its more loquacious denizens and I had from it this tale of the dark man and what befell him in the Universe of Islands.

—Salecco the Irrepressible

hroughout all the strange, interwoven dimensions of what I have called the omniverse, there is no realm so unique as the Universe of Islands. Dreamed, perhaps, by some sleep-tossed, delirious god, born of his meandering whim, the Universe of Islands lies in a far flung region of the omniverse, its character, its indigenes, its laws all peculiar to itself, its single link with other dimensions the forgotten god who formed it. In other places, such as Nyctath the All-Night, the Wendlewarren and maniacal Phaedrabile, the black and airless vault of space cements the numerous worlds, but it is not so in the Universe of Islands.

For here the tissue that unites all is the Ether, which is neither air nor sea, but which combines some of the favourable properties of both most propitious to life. In this Ether, this boundless, misty ocean of salubrious matter, life spawns ever anew, for here there is warmth and light, inherent in the very essence of the Ether: it is like some macroscopic womb-fluid, nurturing its insular offspring. No suns blaze in the Universe of Islands, and no spinning globes of dead moon-rock whirl about endlessly: there are no worlds, no stars, no comets such as there are in other realms. There are only the Islands.

These are innumerable. Their variety is unlimited and as myriad as the particles of dust in any other universe. Greatest of all the Islands is the Continent at the Heart of All Things, a titanic, immeasurable mass of floating organic matter that exists principally in the myths and legends of the beings of the Universe. Many are the speculative fables and superstitions passed among lesser Islands concerning the fabulous Continent. And like a gargantuan magnet, the Continent is said to be pulling to it slowly all the numberless particles of Island throughout its Universe, like a parent drawing in its spawn.

There is such a variety of Islands that no individual knows how far they extend: I suspect even the gods are vague. There are Gaperoots, omnivorous Islands that hunt in packs, drifting together for their mutual forays, snapping up and digesting smaller, less mobile Islands—often these Gaperoots turn upon themselves, slaughtering, rending themselves uselessly to fragments; there are Viscerals, huge stomach islands that move sluggishly through the Ether, scenting out hosts of small Islands that gather communally—the Viscerals, who then begin their dread revolutions that establish an irresistible gravity, drawing into their rapacious stomachs their unfortunate prey; there are also the Poisoners, execrable Islands that move about freely, having the external appearances of places of paradise, but whose exotic surfaces trap and destroy everything that touches them; there are so many other Islands, many of which are more conducive to life than those I have named above. But other dark shapes also slip through the Ether, always avid for sustenance.

Each Island, vast or minute, is a single, living organism, mobile, sensitive and sentient. Most have millions of roots that act as propellers, guiding the Islands through the sluggish drift of the Ether. Others have huge clusters of leaves that are as versatile as sails, sweeping their Islands on at speed, catching the enigmatic aerial tides of the Ether; still others have many orifices which draw in the Ether and expel it behind, thus insufflating and exhaling at an exaggerated rate, for all things breathe the Ether. While many of the smaller Islands exist solely on the microbiotic harvest of the Ether, the larger ones feed principally on one another: some are purely cannibalistic, others produce food for parasitic Islands, some dwell in symbiotic harmony, while others support degrees of animal life which is the common prey of many. The inhabitants of the Islands (the genetic variations of which are as boundless as the Islands themselves) remain for the most part insular, confined to the world that is their Island, but there are species who bridge the Islands in a constant search for richer knowledge about the Universe.

Not all life is confined to or dependent upon the Islands: flying constantly between them in the Ether are the Snapwings, colossal, ornithic saurians that are never still, nor ever sleep. Their diet varies, though few of these winged monsters are carnivorous; they are cartilaginous and light, yet their size often allows the lesser creatures of this Universe to dwell upon their backs, as though they, too, were temporary Islands. Thus the Snapwings have come to play a vital role in the colonising of the Universe and the spreading of the smaller species. Because of this unique mode of travel, the commonest of all genera in the Universe of Islands is Man.

"I'm thirsty!" the child said petulantly, squeezing its mother's hand hard to emphasise its words, which were a demand, not a statement. The child was plump, green-eyed, succulent with bright health. Its mother shook it irritably, looking around at the group of people who were sitting quietly and patiently, hiding their anxieties. The flora here was sparse, bent low as if in conference as to whether these people should be allowed to wait without molestation.

"Quiet, Urgollo. What little water we have, we need for the remainder of the crossing. And we have little else to give to the Tallyman for our fare. Be silent!"

A few heads turned in the girl's direction, but nothing was said. Each of them, Pilgrims they called themselves, had his or her own reasons for being here, crossing from Island to Island, their fates temporarily in the hands of the Tallyman, he who knew the whims and impulses of the Snapwing they rode, as though his mind were mysteriously linked with that of the huge aerial creature. He was their guide, their pilot, and for the duration of the crossing, their lives were his. For a moment he had left them, tending to his self-chosen, obscure duties; his absence left a void that the minds of the Pilgrims filled with colourful speculation and soaring wings of fantasy, for the men who spent their lives as pilots of the Snapwings were a breed as secretive and unknowable as the Gods.

Shebundra, the dark-skinned, olive-eyed girl who tended the excitable child Urgollo, seemed far too young to be more than its sister, or so thought some of the Pilgrims, though they did not say this.

Why are they here? mused Abal the Farmer. I am here to seek new pastures, new Islands to seed with crops for my enterprises, and of the Pilgrims here that I know (through but a brief encounter it is true) each has his reason for travel. Zoig there seeks men to pioneer a voyage to the fabled Island of Silver, Glimmerdale, while scurrilous Krasdo flees the barbed justice of the Lomixians (may they catch the oaf). Isc of Ydril is to join those of his clan who have made a new and promising home on the peaceful Island of Waterwillow and the sallow-faced triptych there, garbed so splendidly in bright green robes, they are Hysterics, members of that odious but remarkable cult who forever seek the Heart of All Things, their ineluctable god. But the girl—she is a rare beauty! Where, I wonder, is she bound? Fleeing her spouse for a lover, perhaps? O, fortunate man if he indeed awaits her at her destination; though if I were a companion to him I would warn him of the child's boorishness. A firm hand is required there. Still, there may yet be an opportunity to open converse with her. Only the Tallyman knows when we shall reach the next Island.

And so the Pilgrims mused on their individual thoughts. The only sound was the gentle soughing of the hair-trees; above them the endless vault of misty green seemed motionless, though they knew the Snapwing never ceased its movement and thus must always feed (and glad they were that it found vegetable fare ample). One of the Pilgrims kept himself apart from the rest: it was true that each had his own course to pursue and that friendships forged on such crossings were rarely lasting, but it was not uncommon for Pilgrims to gather together and share the mutual strength of unity. This Pilgrim, however, had shown no inclination to bind himself to them in any way, no matter how superficial. He preferred to sit alone and brood deeply, for his eyes centred on a tuft of hair-grass before him as though in study of its vibrating cilia.

Abal the Farmer turned to look him over. He saw before him a man garbed outlandishly for this realm of light and warmth, for the stranger wore only black garments. His legs were clad in dark leather, his shirt woven of an unknown material, black as pitch and conceivably the webbing of an arachnid, while his hands were always hidden from the light by gloves of equally dark material. Beside him he had temporarily discarded a cloak, and by its lightless colour it suggested a cold embrace. Abal considered himself a jolly man, for all the hardships of his roving existence, and it would not have been out of character for him to have made subtle jest of the strange man's morbid habiliment. Yet there was that about him, a force as dark and suggestive of the unnatural as his clothing that prompted no such taunt. Abal left the stranger to his thoughts, which seemed as dark, and turned his own once more to the delectable girl with the child. He winked at it.

Presently there came through the monadelphous hair-tree a short, stocky man whose arms and legs suggested that he had been seeded and grown more in the nature of a tree himself than a normal man. He was the Tallyman, whose entire life had been spent here on the undulating tracts of the Snapwing's back. He screwed up his already wrinkled, comical face, spreading yet more lines like latticed bark and stood in the midst of the Pilgrims.

"Your journey will soon be at an end, for a group of Islands is barely visible on our forward horizon. If you will prepare your fares, I will receive them now." Earlier, at embarkation, the Pilgrims had agreed their fares: water was the most precious commodity to the Tallyman, for though the Snapwing occasionally passed through the vapour clouds that drifted like the Islands through the Universe, their dew lingered only briefly on the growths here. The Tallyman was, however, able to procure enough sustenance from his unusual surroundings. As he gathered up the water pods and various trinkets and valuables that the Pilgrims paid over to him, he was thinking what a poor lot they were—and so few of them.

Abal the Farmer was again looking to the jet-clad stranger, who had not moved and who watched serenely. He had arrived here late, keeping aloof. The Tallyman had temporarily placed his fares in a small heap and now came before the silent figure. "I do not recall your embarking," he growled.

The stranger looked up at his gnarled face, his own expression vaguely bemused. "No. Nothing of this place is familiar to me."

"The Islands draw near. How will you pay me?"

The dark man sighed. "I have very little. What would you have?"

But the Tallyman had already cast a covetous glance at the jewelled ebon scabbard and the protruding sword haft that rested alongside the stranger's thigh. The latter saw the greedy look and a subtle smile flickered for the briefest of instants on his gaunt features.

"Perhaps you desire this?" he said, unstrapping the weapon and then holding it out in its sinister black sheath. The eyes of the Tallyman gleamed and his trembling fingers stretched out tentatively. Every one of the Pilgrims watched in silence. Then one of the green-robed Hysterics leapt forward.

"Touch it not! Infamous, blasphemous thing! Leave it be, Tallyman, or your soul will bear its stigma until the very day the Heart claims you."

At this shrieked outburst the Tallyman's fingers curled back like scorched paper, as though the sword were a bar of red hot iron. Its darkness rippled, ominous.

"No need to fear," said the stranger.

"Keep your sword," grunted the Tallyman, reaching a brief decision.

The stranger nodded sardonically and strapped it back against his thigh. "What else will you have of me?"

Abal the farmer, intrigued by this most unusual of exchanges, had inadvertently shuffled closer. His burning curiosity prompted him to interject. "Pardon me, but I have heard it said of the Tallymen that they enjoy a good tale and that from a travelling Bard they crave no more than a finely rendered ballad for his passage. Perhaps you should ask of this wanderer a tale, a portion of his history, for he is certainly no ordinary man." He made a bow to the dark man.

The Tallyman considered this with a grunt and a nod; he scowled at the stranger. "How do you answer that?"

"It is a small fee. Ask what you will, though you may be disappointed."

"It is unwise to traffic with this lightless creature!" hissed the spokesman for the Hysterics, drawing back to his companions. But the Tallyman snorted, for they were indeed a hysterical sect, bowed under the weight of their dogma. He nodded to the man before him.

"Very well. Who are you, where are you from, and for what Island are you bound?" he asked.

Abal the Farmer remained close at hand, for he had no intention of forgoing the opportunity of hearing what must certainly be a bizarre story. Zoig, too, the adventurous fortune-seeker, kept well within earshot. Here, he thought, may be a man to join my cause. Others were not too anxious to know secrets that may be harmful. Krasdo quietly comforted himself with a sac of mead.

Now the man in black began his tale. "There is little to relate. You ask who I am: I have no name, no identity. You ask where I am from: I am from many places yet can recall them only vaguely. You ask where I go: I cannot tell you. Both my destiny and my soul have been stolen from me."

At once the Hysterics, who had been slyly listening, began wailing and moaning in a most despondent manner, like feral treerunners, those wild cat-beings of the tropical Isles of Bubuji. The Tallyman shuddered, himself as nervous as a treerunner, while both Abal and Zoig exchanged glances of unease.

"Once," continued the stranger, "I visited some grave mischief upon the Dark Gods, the shadows behind the walls of this bright Universe. My lot is to wander and sail the tides of their whim. I have eyes to see, but I stumble in darkness."

The Hysterics had subsided, now drawn away into a secret conclave, muttering orisons and incantations to their supreme deity, the Continent at the Heart of All Things.

Abal the Farmer was greatly fascinated by the sorrowful words of the stranger. He leaned forward, speaking for the Tallyman, who nodded furiously to mask his puzzlement.

"You say you do not know where you have come from?" said Abal.

"I was dreaming. Tortured visions in which I saw many things, many places. Worlds and dimensions beyond this Universe. Perhaps some of them exist only in my mind. I have clung to shards of the dreams, for they are part of my past. When I awoke, I found myself here, among you good people."

"Dreams?" murmured a voice behind Abal the Farmer. It was the comely girl, Shebundra, who had also been listening, and who was now deep in thought. "He speaks of dreams," she whispered so that Abal barely caught the words. "I have known dreams. Evil dreams."

Abal would have questioned her discreetly on this, but the Tallyman was speaking.

"What will you now? Journey at random through the Islands?"

The stranger shrugged. "I have no control over my fate, though I seek it. But I will be guided."

"You are not without purpose, then?" said Zoig, with a cough.

The Pilgrims found themselves looking into an expression of deep sorrow. "I am not my own man."

Zoig thought for a moment, then his own fierce features broke out in a smile. "Well, then, why not be my man! For a time, at least! I am Zoig, of no Island and yet of all Islands. Treasure is my quest—riches beyond dreams. I seek the fabled Glimmerdale where 'tis said there are mounds of silver for the taking! I gather a band of worthies about me to make good my search. Come, cast your lot with us. Should we succeed, you will have riches enough to set yourself up as a monarch and forge a new destiny for yourself!"

Abal the Farmer chuckled. "Ho! Your band of plunderers must be singularly remarkable men, for they are invisible!"

Zoig frowned gruesomely and the man in black chuckled warmly at the subsequent banter. "My thanks, Zoig. I will consider your generous offer. I do not easily earn the friendship of men."

The Tallyman gathered up his fares, twining together and pocketing the smaller gew-gaws. "Ready yourselves, Pilgrims. The archipelago of Vinewalk floats ever nearer. Soon the Bladdermen will arrive to take you down, unless any of you wish to travel further. Here, we are within the outer tropics, but our journey on the Ether current takes us inward to less temperate zones. Decide quickly, for my Snapwing will not linger."

It was agreed by all but the three Hysterics that they would vacate the Snapwing and go down to the Islands of Vinewalk, which promised to be an auspicious place. The archipelago was now visible relatively near as drifting green banks of tightly compacted vegetation, each several scores of miles long. They floated like huge green clouds, and from those closest to the Snapwing could be seen countless waving roots and rootlets, wriggling like worms, while those Islands closest to each other were attached by long, trailing vine-like growths, festooned with lichens and tufts of dense green foliage. The archipelago seemed to be webbed by the thick cables of vegetation.

The stranger stood with the other Pilgrims on a knoll of the living landscape and watched the archipelago in fascination. Presently he saw from the closest of the Islands a cloud spray out, as though a gigantic plant had abruptly issued a shower of spores: these quickly conformed into a regular unit, however, and commenced a distinct arrowing for the incoming Snapwing. As they came on across the Ether, the man saw that they were indeed plants of some kind, long, transparent bladders, trailing tendrils at their rear and with lateral membranes. Upon each of these slender shapes there sat a man, guiding the bladder with his knees, his hands gripping further tendrils at the front of the re-markable aeronautical mounts.

With a whooshing of air from the rear of the bladders, the first of the riders eventually came gliding down towards the group of Pilgrims. The Tallyman was first to greet them. Overhead the main body of Bladdermen hovered like a cloud of humming insects, waiting. None of the Pilgrims could hear the conversation between the Tallyman and the principal riders, but there appeared to be a heated discussion ensuing. After a while the Tallyman and two of the riders came across to the Pilgrims, their expressions taut.

"What's the news?" said Zoig bluntly, sensing the great fear of these men.

"It's bad," growled the Tallyman. "Ofestron here says his Bladdermen cannot take you down to Vinewalk."

"Cannot?" said Abal. "They have a veritable fleet of bladders, which seems a little extravagant for a welcoming party, as there are but a handful of us—"

"It is not that," said Ofestron. He wore a brief tunic, and the dark man noticed a thick belt encircling his waist with several weapons thrust into it. "We have to evacuate the entire archipelago. No one can remain here."

"Evacuate?" echoed Abal, somewhat stunned. "But these Islands seem so serene, so fruitful. The vegetation is lush, young. What ails the Islands? Is there some subtle disease at work we cannot see?" He paled as he spoke. "Gods, don't say they have the grey mould—I have seen it only once, and it pervades all things instantaneously—"

Ofestron shook his head. "Vinewalk is perfect in all respects. The danger does not come from within, but from without." He pointed into the limitless Ether. There was not one among the original Pilgrims who did not blanch at the words, for they all knew well enough the many perils that drifted through the Universe of Islands. Only the dark man seemed unmoved, for clearly he did not understand.

Ofestron explained. "Coming towards us is a rogue Island. We have had word of it from a cloud of fleeing refugees from Softwood. Its proportions are vast, incalculable. There is nothing to be done to avert the horror. Our Islands move but slowly. They have been drifting with all possible speed for a great length of time, since we first learned of the rogue, but still it comes on. It has set its own course implacably. This is no chance meeting. Vinewalk is its target."

"What will happen?" said the stranger. Eyes turned to him at once.

"I have said this intruder has gone rogue," snapped Ofestron. "Do you not understand? Are you not aware what this means?"

"He's a traveller from great distances," said Abal the Farmer, placating the scowling Bladderman.

"Oh? Well, traveller, a rogue Island is one that has lost its reason. We never know why this happens. Perhaps a clash somewhere in the deeps of the Ether with another Island, or perhaps serious damage to its membranes in a skirmish with a pack of Gaperoots. Or a partial succumbing to a Vampire Isle. Whatever the cause, the rogue Island has become a berserker, crushing everything in its path, destroying or devouring all things that are too small to resist."

"Yet," said the stranger, "this rogue has selected Vinewalk as its target?"

"Rogues are unpredictable. But this one is set on Vinewalk. It adjusts its own course to cause a meeting."

"Why?"

Ofestron furrowed his brow, sighing in exasperation. "Nothing changes the insane purpose of the rogue. Vinewalk is doomed. Who knows why? But we must all ride on the back of the Snapwing. The exodus prepares."

The Tallyman nodded, for the Snapwing was immeasurable and could easily accommodate the refugees from the Islands.

One of the Hysterics suddenly rushed before Ofestron, pointing wildly at the man in black. His voice rose in a high scream of indictment. "See, Bladdermen! The omen of doom is already here! Why should the rogue seek you out to destroy you, he asks! Why, indeed! From emptiness has this blasphemous wanderer come, cast out by the Dark Gods, weavers of infinite evil. His very presence is an abomination! He will bring death to all that traffic with him. It is he who has brought the rogue Island upon us!"

Another of the Hysterics babbled, "Fatecaster!"

And the third, "He is the comer from the void!"

Ofestron scowled in anger and confusion at the three howling Hysterics. He had no time for the intricate ravings of their religious doctrines. Yet they had clouded his mind against the strange man, who was indeed most unusual to look upon.

"How do you answer these charges?" he asked, noticing for the first time the weapon of the stranger. Swords were not common, their metal being such a rare commodity.

"I have neither willingly nor knowingly brought any fate upon you. By what power could I hope to control an Island? Least of all an Island that will not respond to reason, by your very words?"

Ofestron did not have the wit or the patience to respond to this logic. He snorted and turned upon the Tallyman. "There is no time to waste squabbling. The exodus will not be easy nor as swift as we would hope. I will begin at once, before your Snapwing flies on past us. See that the traveller from afar is kept under surveillance. I neither like the manner nor the bearing of the man. And keep those infernal Hysterics away from my people: they evoke nothing but fear and apprehension with their perpetual ranting. I wish their great god would swallow them all!" So saying, he strode off with his companion, remounting and drifting skyward.

Many Bladdermen had come drifting down, their strange mounts attaching themselves to the surface of the Snapwing, their tendrils burrowing parasitically, though to the gigantic creature they were less than fleas. Several of the riders had been discreetly commissioned by Ofestron to watch over the dark man, though the latter did not object, accepting their ill-concealed vigilance lightly. He had found a quiet place to observe the now hectic activity of the Bladdermen communities, and had soon fallen into a deep slumber. There is no night in the Universe of Islands, for the Ether knows no suns, only perpetual glowing mists of warmth; its creatures sleep briefly whenever their bodies need it.

The Pilgrims were uncertain how to react to the exodus,

for there seemed a great many bladder creatures rising from the many Islands of Vinewalk. Yet the oncoming rogue Island brought real anxiety into their hearts, and their eyes never left the horizons of the deep green Ether, expecting at any time to see the enormous mass of the oncoming monster.

Shebundra controlled the child Urgollo with difficulty, for he sensed the tense aura of anticipation that had clouded all of them, and though he was afraid, he was more excited, for the crossing had so far been, in his youthful opinion, quite boring. The girl was watching the stranger, who had fallen asleep. It concerned her, for she had sensed in him a terrible power from the moment he had appeared. He had spoken of dreams: did he, like her, glimpse things that must come to pass, grim, shadowed visions of possible futures? But she knew, in spite of self-recrimination, that her fate and his were somehow bound together, though she would have had it otherwise.

As the exodus continued, with streams of the Bladdermen darting to and fro in endless spore-like processions between the Islands, the stranger woke from another turmoil of dreams. He watched the movement of the distant creatures along the vines as though they were gnats, so small were they made by distance. His dreams had not been cheering, but they never were. Near him sat Abal the Farmer, Zoig, the girl and her child, and a few of the other Pilgrims. Thankfully the Hysterics had moved elsewhere upon the strange terrain. There were a number of the silent Bladdermen about, but their watch was only casual: there was nowhere for their ward to flee, so their concentration focused on the exodus.

"Zoig," called the man in black, and the adventurer turned to him quizzically. "Tell me, Zoig, this advancing rogue Island—has it a name?"

Zoig screwed up his face in uncertainty, shaking his head. "Possibly. Ho, riders! This Island that comes to engulf us, has it a name?"

One of them looked across and nodded. "Aye, Pilgrim. We call it Dreamwarp. It has an evil reputation, for many have travelled to it in the past, seeking one thing or another, as men are ever wont to do on new Islands. Little is said about those who have returned from Dreamwarp. They have never come back as they went. The things they dreamed there stole their sanity. Evil place! It is no wonder the madness infested the entire Island and no wonder it has gone rogue."

"Dreamwarp," breathed the dark man softly, as though the word had touched a live nerve of understanding.

"What does it mean to you?" said a gentle voice. It was the beautiful young girl.

"The name," he mused, shaking his head.

"I also know the name," said Shebundra, and there was fear in her voice. Abal the Farmer leaned closer to her, fascinated as much by her words as her beauty.

"Tell me of it," the stranger said to her.

"I have been to Dreamwarp," she replied and there were gasps from the listeners. "It was—I know not how long ago. Now the memory has become just like another dream. But I was there. There were many of us at first. We were adventurous, a small clan from an Island called Reedwater, and we were lured by the excitement of Dreamwarp, thinking it would be a wonderful place to colonise and spread ourselves, for our numbers on tiny Reedwater were growing quickly. On Dreamwarp we found a world of contrasts, for it was beautiful, a wellspring of wonders, rich in fruit and harvest and in pure, sweet streams, though our dreams were plagued by grim visions. I will not speak of them. They—changed us. A kind of madness came over us. We fought. We killed one another. In the end a few of us escaped, by pure chance, for the Island of Dreamwarp is a cruel master, avidly possessive of its slaves. Those of us that escaped were fortunate that a Snapwing passed, else we had succumbed to madness and perished on Dreamwarp. I may speak prematurely, for none of the other runaways that I know of is yet sane."

A hush had fallen over the listeners, for the words of the girl were like a tapestry of magic that had drawn them all in.

"Dreamwarp," said the stranger again, picturing her description.

"We must quit this part of the Ether in all haste!" cried Abal the Farmer. "The rogue Island seems a frightful place, best put to the torch." Normally such words would have met with bitter resentment, for nothing was more fearful to an Island-dweller than fire, but none of them could find words to defend the unsavoury image of Dreamwarp.

The stranger spoke again, as though saying aloud thoughts that were not meant for any other ears. "Yet I must come to you, Dreamwarp. My restless dreams have said as much."

"What!" ejaculated Abal. "You must go to Dreamwarp! Have you already lost your reason?"

"Alas, my destiny is no longer as shapeless as I thought. Yes, I must go to Dreamwarp. Whatever purpose I have, it lies there."

Shebundra was nodding. "I, too, must return to Dreamwarp."

Abal looked mortified. "You—but, but—you?" he blustered.

"Urgollo and I will go. We must."

"Lady, on what mad enterprise?" asked Zoig, also mystified.

"You would toss your life away so carelessly?" said Abal.

"I cannot explain. I have to go. I have always known it would be so," she said simply. Urgollo, beside her, listened, but for once was very still, patient.

"Will you journey there with me?" the stranger asked Shebundra.

She smiled. "Very well."

Abal the Farmer controlled his palpitating nerves with great difficulty. Emotions welled in him over which he seemed to have little control. "Would it be impertinent of me to—request—that I come also?" he blurted.

Zoig emitted a sudden guffaw. "Hah! This Dreamwarp exercises its influence from afar! Already its madness spreads before it. What, are you also set on doom, Farmer?"

Abal looked sheepishly at Shebundra. "Such a radiant flower must not be allowed to wither," he said. "I am a Farmer, a tender of crops, of herbs, of beautiful growing things. My calling was ever thus. How could I betray such a bloom as this?"

"Well said," grinned the dark man. "Though I fear you may yet rue such fine words."

"Nay, I'll come."

Shebundra blushed prettily, but said no more.

"Who else?" called the stranger, but the Bladdermen drew well away as though he was already plagued.

Zoig was puzzling it over. "I seek Glimmerdale, Island of Silver. What treasure would I find on Dreamwarp? What tales of fabulous wealth can you tell me of this place that could whet my appetite? None, I'll warrant!"

The stranger nodded. "You are right, Zoig. There is nothing on Dreamwarp for you, save perhaps an early grave."

"Indeed! I'll none of the place. You are welcome to savour its crazed embrace without me!"

Four figures stood on a knoll, set apart from the main gathering of refugees from the archipelago of Vinewalk. They looked ever outward into the Ether, watching and waiting for the vast shape of Dreamwarp to hove into view. The Ether here was thick with its own mists, so that distance soon became lost in a haze of green. Below the watchers, in a shallow valley, the last of the refugees had landed, and now the Islands were uninhabited, save for a few resolute souls who would not leave their ancestral home and who were prepared to die with it. The Tallyman approached the four; at his side was Ofestron, and both their faces were grave.

"The Snapwing senses the coming of the rogue. I cannot restrain it, nor do I wish to," said the Tallyman. "If you still wish to destroy yourselves, you must leave at once!"

"Take the bladders and supplies we have given you," said Ofestron, pointing to the nearby bladder creatures that still fed lazily. "I may yet regret letting you loose, though I cannot see how a sojourn on this monster will benefit you." But I am well rid of you, he thought.

"We have chosen our course," replied the stranger. "Go your way."

"See!" cried Abal the Farmer. "It comes! Gods of the undergrowth! What a size!" He automatically put his arms around the child Urgollo to comfort him and the youth, who had been quick to show affection to the big man, pressed close to his chest, awed. The Tallyman and Ofestron gaped, then ran back to their fellows in horror.

Towering over them, spreading out on either side, dropping below their horizon of vision, came the rogue Island of Dreamwarp, like some enormous creature through the eddying green mist, suddenly and abruptly there, jarring the mind with its fantastic proportions, a giant, living world. Urgollo shrieked and hid his face; Abal staggered back; Shebundra looked frightened, though it was her memory that chilled her; the dark man watched without visible emotion. Onward came the awesome bulk, like the greatest ship ever conceived.

"We must mount," he said, leading them to the bladder creatures.

"Gods of the Ether, we will be engulfed!" stammered Abal, but the dark man shook his head.

"No. We will rise over its rim and float down slowly. We are far too small to be hurt by any collision. Follow!" He seated himself, drew on the tendril-reins, and rose upward. The others followed, Shebundra astride a bladder creature, Abal and Urgollo on a third. She did not mind that the good Farmer tended her son, for he gave the boy more strength than she could.

Out into the Ether and up away from the colossal, though now dwarfed Snapwing, they drifted, straight toward the incalculable mass of the rogue Island. Some of its features had now sharpened as the green haze of distance faded. Innumerable thick roots and curling tubes of vegetation twisted and convoluted in a massive wall on the underside of Dreamwarp, an incredibly entangled labyrinth of rampant vegetation, slick with moisture. Huge patches of greenery and trailing vinery spread across the middle tiers as they rose ever upward. The top of the Island was still lost high above like a thundercloud. Up and up the bladders whirled, made giddy by the oncoming shape. Slowly they soared way up to a point in the Ether where they could at last see over the crest of the huge Island; below them now stretched a wildly exotic jungle landscape, rich in verdure, clustered with titanic trees and dazzling with vivid colours.

Abal looked back once, and far away he saw the great Snapwing winging out into the fathomless green Ether, now no bigger to his eyes than a small bird. Urgollo was pointing down at the luscious tropical terrain, his sense of wonder washing away the terrors of earlier. It was indeed a sight to make the heart flutter, thought Abal. Already the magic begins. The dark man led them down, and it seemed that their slow, spiralling descent took an infinity to encompass, for they had been so high above Dreamwarp. Its terrain spread away on all sides, and the first of the colossal trees reached up like avid fingers to claim them. Yet the bladder creatures were perfect mounts, for they wriggled obediently, unerringly between these vast arboreal columns. Down, ever down they drifted, into the silent canyons of the forest, seeking out a safe place to land, if there were such a place on this notorious Island.

They found at last a small clearing, in the centre of which there was an inviting pool, its surface profuse with huge lilies and radiant yellow blooms. On the knotted grass beside this water the four people alighted: at once the bladder creatures attached themselves to the terrain, feeding.

"The vegetation has run riot over the whole Island!" exclaimed Abal, looking around in astonishment at the fantastically entwined plants, trees and leaves that crowded in almost eagerly around the clearing. "Even the rampant jungle Isles exercise more control than this. This Island will choke itself!"

"It is strange," said Shebundra. "The silence. Nothing stirs. No birds, insects, creatures in the underbrush. It is not as it was."

"Well," said Abal, "the Island is rogue. All life flees a rogue."

"Either that, or it is dead," she replied.

"No," said the dark man. "There is life here."

"Aye, the Island lives," began Abal, but Urgollo let out a piercing shriek and pointed to the bladder creatures. Their insides had swollen with what they had ingested and now they burned a livid crimson colour. Presently they were so bloated that each of them ruptured, bursting horribly and emitting a dreadful, charnel stench. The four travellers drew back from the miasma as one.

"Poisoner!" gasped Abal. "The Island is a Poisoner!"

"No," said the dark man, shaking his head emphatically. "It is far more evil."

Abal now felt decidedly rash in having come here, and for the moment even a glance at the beautiful Shebundra could not alleviate his mounting uneasiness.

"Come," said the dark man, leading them on through a maze of paths that looked more random than deliberate. Old animal tracks, thought Abal, leading down to the pool. Through the grimly silent grave they went.

"Where are you leading us?" Abal asked the dark man.

"To the heart of the Island. There we will learn the truth about it."

Abal would have objected, but Shebundra placed her arm on his with a smile. "We must," she said. Abal returned her smile, though his mouth was set and he held Urgollo's hand tightly.

Their walk seemed interminable, but at length they came to another clearing, though this appeared to be unnatural, as though originally cut back by men. Abal could see wooden columns and strange carvings. "So there were men here," he exclaimed. "This must be the remnant of a village or temple."

"Yes," nodded Shebundra. "This is where my clan built their village. The wooden images, the strange engravings—they were all set here to ward off the evil dreams that haunted us. Do not look too closely into the undergrowth, for you will find many bones. Unless Dreamwarp has already drawn them into itself. How did you know they were here?" she asked the dark man, but he was silent.

Abal scowled at the thick tangles of brush and gnarled wood, whose secrets he would rather not know. "Why have you come back?" he whispered, but it was the girl's turn to be silent.

"I'm hungry," said Urgollo.

"Make sure he only eats what we have brought," said the dark man to Abal, and the Farmer unslung the food sack he had diligently packed on the Snapwing, for the Bladdermen had been able to afford generosity in spite of their misgivings.

They ate quietly, watching the brooding, motionless jungle.

"You seem to understand all this," Abal told the dark man. "Now that we are here, what are we to do? Do you expect the Island to speak?"

"It has brought me here for a reason," was the blunt reply,

and the Farmer could see he would learn no more for the moment. Instead he began talking quietly to the girl and her son, trying to cheer them in spite of the dreary foreboding that had drifted over them. It was more silent than the Island of Graves.

Time passed lazily, and it was inevitable that they should all drift into a sea of sleep, for the Island would not be thwarted in its purpose now.

He was accustomed to the wells of dizzy darkness that whirled within him, an inner universe of night, spangled with dreams that substituted for stars. The Dark Gods who had set him upon his erratic path often taunted him with such dreams, hinting at his fate, teasing him with keys to doors on enlightenment, knowledge of his past, his crime. But now, asleep on the Island, he guessed that the dreams here were from Dreamwarp itself, its gift or its curse.

He saw himself again in the huge hall of Windwrack, surrounded by the vile minions of Rammazurk, heard again their gibbering and shrieking, and on the floor at his feet, a spider-like creature scuttled out of the shadows, a hand, his hand. It pointed at the repugnant monarch, who cried out like a mortally wounded beast.

In another vision he saw again the tunnels of the Spydron's lair, watching a contest between two huge monsters, two spiders of immense proportions. One spider had only five legs, but it triumphed, tearing its opponent apart. Looking down, he saw again that he had no right hand.

Lastly he saw himself before seven sorcerers attired in grey, their faces round, featureless, without character. He was pleading with them for something, but each one shook his head and laughed. Looking down, he saw that his right hand was gone, stolen by the seven.

Laughter chased away his visions like a howling wind

Voidal, came a voice over the sound, *you cannot die, nor can you kill.*

His dreams reminded him that he had only one true companion, and its name was Death.

She slept in peace for a time, no pit of dark night to immerse her, only a golden glow, deep and limitless as the Ether. It soothed, warm, radiant. The Island was kind to her, as it had been once before.

She dreamed of that last visit, when she had stretched out on the then soft sward of the glade, watching the brilliant plumage of the birds overhead, hearing their trilling and warbling. The smell of floral perfume. Peace—Dreamwarp was a paradise and the clan would prosper and flourish.

She dreamed again of the golden man who had come like a wraith to sit with her in past dreams, stroking her hair, whispering enticements and irresistible murmurings, promises of love, devotion, ecstasy. In those heady dreams, which were like perfect wine, she had lain with the beautiful golden man and he had made gentle, soothing love to her, a cooling stream of tenderness.

She dreamed now of his face, his memory, but he did not come to her again. I am closer than you know, a voice whispered in her dreams, and she was happy.

Abal the Farmer and Urgollo had nodded into sleep close to one another and the child was now sleeping with his head on the Farmer's gently heaving chest. Both faces were serene in sleep, for they were without dreams. Dreamwarp had permitted them rest.

A cry awoke Abal and he turned to see Shebundra sitting upright, her eyes wide as though something had startled her.

"Are you well?" he asked her anxiously.

"I—seem to be. Why, yes. I was dreaming," she breathed.

"Dreamwarp may not be so hostile as we imagined, for you are intact, and my own sleep was refreshing, untroubled. And, see, the youth is more at peace than he has been since first I saw him."

Urgollo opened a mischievous eye and with a laugh, Abal tousled his hair.

"But where is the stranger?" said Shebundra, looking around uncomfortably. The dark man was not to be seen, but presently some tall growths strained apart and he stepped into the clearing.

"Did you sleep well?" said Abal. "We are better for rest, in spite of our earlier fears."

The other looked sad, even bemused. He glanced briefly at his gloved right hand, quickly lowering it. "The Island knows me. It presented me with evil memories that had been better left in darkness. But I sense it understands me more than I do myself. I may learn something from it."

"Ah—the Island is not without reason then? Not so mad?"

"I don't think so. But what did you dream of?"

Both Urgollo and Abal confirmed that they had had no dreams, and Shebundra said she had dreamed of her past on the Island, though she said nothing of her golden dream-lover.

The dark man nodded. "You are part of this."

She looked afraid. "What must I do?"

"You must all wait. I have been searching. I have found a place that leads down into the vitals of the Island."

Abal was horrified. "Down? You consider going underground? Do you not fear the pitch darkness? I know of few men who leave the glow of the Ether willingly."

"If I am to learn our fate, I must go below."

"Then I am glad you are willing to go alone," said Abal.

"I will return."

"And if not—"

"I will return," he repeated, turning away to the jungle.

Abal would have hailed him again, but Urgollo was tugging at his sleeve.

"I'm hungry," he said.

The Voidal thrust his way through the overgrown paths and the encroaching limbs of wood and foliage, making for the place he had found earlier. In another small clearing he had discovered a large hole, a vent in the earth, a dark well that led down into the dank, loamy darkness. The trees here towered, almost blotting out the gentle greens of the Ether, and though the thick leaves and verdure were resplendent with gorgeous colours, it was cold. But the Voidal moved on, pausing briefly at the hole where lichen and green mould hung over its lip in a frozen cascade.

Around him there gathered the first signs of life other than plants he had discovered on Dreamwarp—they were lightworms, tiny creatures that floated like phosphorescent insects on the air; they formed a tiny cloud around his head, leading him into the hole, lighting faintly the way as though sent by the Island. The hole inclined steeply, exuding a rank stench, but the Voidal ignored it, resolute in his purpose. Below him, in the subterranean bowels of the Island, his fate awaited him—there would be no avoiding it.

He took little stock of the thick roots and interwoven tendrils that bound together the walls of the hole, and though there was a suggestive retraction of the roots from the aura of light, he paid no heed: he knew the Island had not brought him to its depths simply to kill him. Not here.

Far, far down, the hole widened, its incline flattened out to become a fathomless gulf, so dark that even the glow of the lightworms made no impression upon its immensity. The Voidal walked slowly inward. He had not gone far when he came to the lip of a vertical shaft or pit that dropped vertiginously away to infinity, possibly into another dimension. The lightworms hovered clear, obedient to some force, and by their faint glow the Voidal saw the edges of this vast pit disappearing in curves on both sides of him. The shaft was like an artery to the heart of Dreamwarp, which must be enormous indeed to house such an abyss.

"You have come!" said a voice, as though the invisible walls of the huge cavern echoed back the words of an unseen mouth. "Look down into the pit, Voidal, for it is I who have summoned you, I who have invoked your name."

The dark man edged to the very lip and looked directly down—into madness! For there below him, fifty feet down, was a gigantic face, its extreme proportions twisted and screwed malignly as if enduring terrible agonies. Darkness bathed it and it was like a floating, disembodied vision, a huge bubble. Its eyes blazed with unearthly fire, focusing upon the minute figure that looked down upon its inestimable pain.

"Are you yet another vision conjured up by the Island? Another dream?" shouted the Voidal.

But the huge mouth gaped, answering as though real. "Look upon my face! Study it! Do you not know me?"

The Voidal had been confused by the staggering proportions, but now he saw the face more clearly. "Yes—I know you," he nodded, dazed. "Yet I cannot recall you."

"It is part of the curse that is laid upon you," agreed the voice.

"You know of my burden?"

"Yes, for I am Dreamwarp. It was I who sent the dreams to you as you slept."

"You are Dreamwarp?"

"Yes. Though when last our paths crossed I was another and not in this guise. Once, if you could but recall it, I served faithfully the same Dark Gods that so torment you. In my infinite folly I sought to become one with them. For my impudence and my vanity they cast me out into this remote Universe, making me a prisoner of myself, for Dreamwarp is my body now, its shape, its terrain, its life all bound to the laws of this accursed dimension. I languish here, only my thoughts capable of drifting outward in the form of dreams that I fashion. My old powers are sterile! For a while it has pleased me to send mad those who have chanced upon me and in my fury and frustration I have wrought much havoc in this Universe. But I weary of it and dream always of freedom."

The Voidal nodded again. "I know your face, but not your name. I cannot remember—"

"It is not given to you to recall much. Perhaps I can refresh your memory. I know certain things about you."

"I know that much from the nightmares you sent."

"The Dark Gods are punishing you. They make you do their work, work that is too unsavoury for them."

The Voidal leaned as close to the chasm as he dared. "Tell me of my sins. What was their nature?"

But the huge head shook. "I cannot reveal that. Already I have angered the Dark Gods anew. But if you will aid me, I will tell you of yourself and give you the power to recall all that you learn."

"Restore my memory?" gasped the Voidal.

"Partially, Voidal. I can only give you a fragment of what you seek to know."

"And your price? How can I help you?"

"It is a small thing."

"Name it! I will decide upon its weight."

Again the face contorted in ill-disguised pain. "Then hear me. There once came to my shores a clan, which sought to colonise and settle in peace. I chastised them with madness, but while they lingered I dreamed a plan, a slender, cautious plan that might somehow free me from this hated bondage. Among the clan was a girl, a young, beautiful creature that any young man with good red blood in his veins would have desired. I chose her to be the mother of my offspring."

Confusion shaped the Voidal's face, but he waited.

"She left Dreamwarp with the last of the survivors, and she did so bearing in her womb my elemental seed. She dreamed of a golden man who loved her and seeded her, and the dream was pleasing to her."

"And now she has returned," said the Voidal. "With the child."

"Yes! He has grown. Not yet a man, but I cannot wait any longer. They are above us now."

The Voidal saw a look of longing cross the tortured face.

"I want the child," breathed the huge being.

"Is that all you wish of me?" said the Voidal suspiciously.

"Oh no, man of darkness! Not all. First bring me the child. Already it possesses a part of me, a raw elemental force that slumbers within it. Bring it to me and I will pour myself into it and possess it utterly! I will quit this monstrous Island body and secrete myself, my essence, within the body of my child. The mother can tend to me, knowing nothing of my true self. And the man will be her new husband, for already I have sewn both their minds with a dream of communion. When this is done, I charge you with taking us, father, mother and child, out of this Universe of Islands, for you alone have the power to traverse the many dimensions."

The mouth closed and a deep silence fell. The Voidal dwelt long upon the words. "Your demands seem strange, yet not unkind. Will the child or its parents be harmed? What will you do once I have led you elsewhere?"

"I will quit the child and flee before the Dark Gods are aware of what has occurred. I have no desire to be their victim again! I will cause no harm to the three. Their lives will be their own. They will know happiness together."

"In another dimension? It will disturb them."

"Man is an adaptable creature! They will survive. Think on my offer! I can give you knowledge that you could not obtain elsewhere! Think hard, Voidal."

For another long moment the man in black stood like a carved image of stone, thinking long on what he had been told. At length he broke his reverie and spoke. "So be it. I will bring you the child. You have my bond."

"Your bond? I am satisfied, for you cannot lie. I will speak of your fate. What do you know of yourself?"

"Only what you have shown me in dreams."

"That you cannot die, cannot kill? Trickery, for you are no immortal! But that is a riddle I will not solve for you. Cannot kill? Another riddle, for did you not see yourself killing?"

The Voidal looked in disgust at his right hand. "This hand does the work. It crawls from me, as if a separate entity. I would cut it from me, but it would crawl black, fuse itself anew to my flesh."

"It is not your hand. It belongs to another, an even more terrible power than you."

For the first time since descending to this hidden place, the Voidal felt the great cold seeping into him, though it was the coldness of fear. His eyes remained fixed in horror at the gloved hand.

"It is the Oblivion Hand, the hand of one of the thirteen Dark Gods. Through it, you do their will, for it destroys their enemies. Separate entity! Yes, indeed. You cannot control it, nor could you sever it and escape it. Always it will return. It will never leave you, unless one day you appease the Dark Gods. Perhaps then you will retrieve your own hand. By the Oblivion Hand are you known as Fatecaster, and the finger of the hand marks those who will die by it."

The Voidal shuddered, putting the hand from his sight.

"There is more," went on the deep voice. "You ever seek a friend, one to guide you, the image never focused. Another trick of your tormentors! This is Death you seek, and only after meeting with him can you move on. Death is the key that unlocks all doors for you."

The Voidal scowled at the massive face. "If you speak the truth, then I am to bring death here, to this Universe. Yet you told me no harm—"

"It is the body of this Island that will die, not those above."

"I see. What else can you tell me?"

There was a pause, followed by an odd laugh, which seemed incongruous coming from the anguished face. "One thing more. Your sword."

The Voidal touched his left fingers to the ebon hilt. "The Sword of Silence?"

"Yes. I know its power. For their own reasons, pity perhaps, the Dark Gods have given it to you. It has remarkable qualities, but I have already taken precautions against it, in case you attempt to use it on me. You will have noticed that Dreamwarp is clothed in silence. Strike with the sword and you will accomplish nothing."

"You expected an attack?"

"I trust nothing! You are an agent of the Dark Gods, their pawn! Only your blind service can ever earn you a degree of freedom."

The Voidal laughed sardonically, a mirthless sound. "I have agreed to help you. I will not strike."

"No. But they may yet chastise me," came the rumble from below.

"You have kept your part of the bond. If you've said all, I'll do my part."

"I have, Voidal. Your dreams will ever be fitful, but among them you will recall all the things I have said. My ailing powers can achieve that much for you. Now, hence! Fetch me the child!"

y the depths of the Ether, Shebundra, I swear the child has a greater capacity for food than I!" said Abal the Farmer as Urgollo finished the succulent fruit he had been eating.

The girl laughed. "I fear he will eat us out of provisions."

Urgollo giggled, tossing away the core. "Look," he said, pointing. "Here comes the strange man."

The Voidal stood before them, his face set grimly.

"What did you learn?" Shebundra asked him anxiously.

"We are not in danger. Neither, it seems, is the archipelago. But from this moment on, you must put your trust in me. What I must do may seem unpalatable to you, but it will be for the best, for the good of us all."

Abal looked dubious. "Explain yourself," he said gruffly.

The Voidal turned to Shebundra. "You were here once before. You dreamed of a golden man."

She bit her hand, her eyes alive. "How did—?"

"The Island has told me. It is not hostile, least of all to you and your child. I am to take the child. No harm will befall him. When we return, in a short while, he will be enriched beyond your imagining."

Shebundra looked uncertain.

"No!" protested Abal. "I don't like this!"

The Voidal looked at him directly. "When this is done, we will quit this place and go our own ways. Neither Dreamwarp nor I will enter your lives again. This I promise you."

Abal remained uneasy, for his protectiveness towards mother and son had trebled since their arrival on the Island.

The Voidal spoke softly to Shebundra. "The Island wishes to see the child."

Her eyes suddenly widened, as though a new understanding had burgeoned within her. The Island—the child. She nodded, and the Voidal took Urgollo by the hand and led him away.

"Do not be afraid," called Abal, but the child had a strange, fascinated look in his eyes.

"All is well," he called back.

But Urgollo's sense of wonder became a sense of stealing dread as the Voidal led him down the murky depths of the black tunnel. However, up from the abyss came gentle waves of dreaminess to soothe him as the Island calmed him. Fresh clouds of lightworms drifted about the two descending figures, casting long shadows up the tunnel so that Urgollo began to respond once more to the magic of his bizarre surroundings. Down they went, ever down, the Voidal as silent as stone, and at last they reached the huge chamber and stood near its central chasm.

"What lies beyond?" asked the child, afraid to look.

"The one I have brought you to meet. He who will speak to you," said the Voidal. "Wait here." He strode the brink and again stared down into the huge face. "I have brought the child."

The eyes closed as if in a prayer of thanksgiving. "Then your bond is kept, Voidal. Bring him to me. Show him his sire!"

The Voidal offered his hand to Urgollo and the child came hesitantly, for the vast well before him suggested unimaginable terrors. He clutched at the fingers of the Voidal and stood close to his side. As he looked down into that enormous visage, a scream escaped his lips, but the Voidal held him tightly so that he could not flee.

"Peace, peace, Urgollo. This is not an enemy. It is the one who sired you."

Urgollo continued to struggle, his eyes looking down. The face looked up at him avidly.

"My—father?" gasped the child, stilling himself, watching in amazement. His fears were soothing away, responding to the part of him that was elemental.

"Yes, Urgollo,'" thundered the voice. "I am your father, who once was almost a god!"

"He is bound," said the Voidal. "Only you can release him."

Urgollo nodded. "How?"

The Voidal looked down. "How is the child to serve you?"

An unholy smile played upon the lips of the great face. "I will be free at last! The child and I will be united, forged as one. And we will break away from the curse of the foul Dark Gods!"

The huge mouth gaped open, a crimson well. "Cast the child within!"

Urgollo flinched at the gaping maw, its frightful stench. The Voidal's face creased in sudden doubt. "Cast him within? You said nothing of this. You were to enter him—"

"Cast him within!" repeated the voice angrily, bellowing with impatience. "He will be reborn. Do it now, damn you!"

As the Voidal looked down into that slick maw, he saw for the first time the shapes and writhing horrors that crawled and coiled within it, the spawn of a deep evil, and he drew back, appalled. The child, too, sensed the insane shapes. "NO!" he wailed, all sense of wonder shattered, replaced by wave upon wave of revulsion. Both he and the Voidal pulled away, for there was no hint of succour in that malefic hole.

"I will not make this black sacrifice," said the Voidal, holding Urgollo well clear, shielding him.

"Again I say, cast him in, or I shall destroy you all!" roared the voice, shaking the invisible walls of the cavern with the intensity of its rage.

But the Voidal drew the child further away. "There is some other foul purpose in this. You deceive us! Evil is your purpose. Stand with me, Urgollo. I'll not cast you to your doom." With this, he drew from its scabbard the Sword of Silence, but a great bellow of laughter gushed over him.

"Do your worst! Your weapon is impotent against me! You cannot silence your minds—they will hear me yet! You cannot silence that which is already silent."

The irony of the riddle was not lost on the Voidal, who had retreated well back from the pit. Urgollo was trembling, too frightened to move away from him. The dark man held up his right arm, but the hand within the black glove was lifeless.

"See!" roared the voice. "I have already had my punishment! The Dark Gods have done enough. You cannot cast my fate. The Oblivion Hand does not obey you!" And there was more frightful laughter.

Its booming shook the cavern walls like an earthquake, building in intensity, bringing black loam down from above. The Voidal and the child were rooted, held by a tangible force, staring in shock at the rippling blackness that was engulfing them. Now this darkness pulsed and swelled like a living thing. The child fell to the floor, hands closing over its head in an effort to blot out the growing menace. But the frightful din seemed to have sped outward, awakening something else that was far older and far more sinister.

Far in the distance that could have been lost in remote space there were deep, sonorous sounds, thunders that were muted, but growing, like reversed echoes. They approached, slowly but implacably. The voice from the pit and the stentorian laughter cut off abruptly. But the Voidal and the thing in the well listened intently. The sounds were not of their making. Somewhere out in the limitless ocean of darkness, a force coalesced, drawing ever inward, like a coiled serpent of unthinkable magnitude, a core of evil more terrible than any mad dream the Island could ever dredge up.

A whisper came from the pit, couched not in mockery but in extreme dread. "What have you done? What have you unleashed?"

The Voidal was motionless, listening to the pulsing of growing sound. "Not me. Your own laughter woke this. You scorned the silence, mocked the Sword. It is not me you laughed at." In the darkness he could see movement, ebbing closer like a black tide, huge, malignant, nebulous and yet as palpable as stone. In the cavern's darkness, around the limits of vision, shapes were materialising, blacker than space, blacker than hate. Black as Death.

Upward they soared, looming inward, heads lost in dizzy heights, unseeable but awesomely present.

"Who comes?" breathed the voice in the pit.

Thirteen colossal shadows ringed the cavern. The Voidal put his left hand upon the shoulder of the shivering child, drawing it to its feet. His insides had run cold as freezing ice, his every bone, artery and fibre had become chilled to the essence. For these he recognised out of nightmare, the promised memories: they were the Thirteen seneschals of the ineffable Dark Gods, shadows of the ultimate doom. Silence fell upon the cavern, and it was absolute.

The Voidal felt movement. His right hand stirred like an animal rousing from hibernation, clutching tighter the Sword of Silence. In the faint glow of the lightworms, the hand rose up with the Sword, holding it in salutation to the grim watchers without eyes. The Voidal looked into the darkness that clad them and saw that each of them held a sword: each of them save one, who had no weapon, and no right hand to hold one. From the terrible darkness that was its incomplete arm, a tendril of thick shadow curled towards the Sword of Silence as it rose, blotting it from sight.

From the pit came a gibbering, the first hysterical whimperings of a being in utter terror. The face looked up around the rim of its prison and saw the Thirteen shadows. It saw in their clouded hands the swords of power, each one possessed of an individual strength, each with devastating potency. One of the Thirteen leaned forward and the face in the pit screamed.

The Voidal saw the shifting of shadows, powerless to move himself. His right hand, lost in shadow, came back from the great cold before him. It now clutched another sword, no longer the Sword of Silence, which had been recovered by its original keeper. This sword had another name, and the Voidal knew it, though no words were spoken.

The screams from the pit increased, but the Thirteen remained stoically silent and cold. Their own swords winked out like lost stars: now only the one remained, in the right hand of the Voidal, their slave. Aloof, they did not deign to speak to him, though he knew their desires. Like dimming illusions they slowly drew back into the embrace of the Night that had sent them, the screams of Dreamwarp a requiem to their passing.

Soon the great cavern was empty again, save for the thing in the pit, the Voidal and his whimpering charge. Turning to the child, who cringed in fright, the Voidal directed him to the way back.

"Go there, Urgollo. Go back up to your mother and the good Farmer. Go quickly, for nothing will molest you. The lightworms will guide you."

Urgollo stared around at the dark, expecting to see the grim titans looming above. But they were gone as if they had never been. With a last cry of fear, the child scuttled away up the incline, soon lost to view, racing for the light of the Ether. The Voidal walked slowly to the edge of the pit. He looked down for the last time, fearlessly now, into the face, which had become a writhing mask of lunacy, all semblance of sanity shredded away by the appearance of the fatidical seneschals.

"Your treachery has once again sealed your fate," said the Voidal without compassion. He pointed the sword downward at the slack-jawed mouth from which the last of the vile things wriggled and died. It was the Sword of Dispersal.

A single, endless scream was ripped from the black mouth. The Voidal felt the ground heave, then tumbled outwards in an arc, falling with the Sword pointing before him into the huge orifice. The sound became a rumble, a boom of thunder, then an explosion of tremendous force.

Darkness snuffed out the Universe as if it were a candle.

Dreams.

Floating in that familiar well, faint stars scattered like dim jewels, the Voidal dreamed. He saw a huge Island, drifting, drifting.

Suddenly it began to heave and shudder like a great beast in mortal agony. It throbbed, then burst, sending its countless fragments outwards in every direction, spewing forth a hundred thousand new Islands and tufts of debris across the far reaches of the green Ether, spreading ever outwards so that what had once been a single Island was now strewn throughout all the Universe in a billion particles. Dreamwarp was no more.

One spinning piece of detritus from the explosion whirled past the eyes of the dreaming Voidal, a dream within a dream. There was life on the tiny Islet, for clinging to it were three beings. A stout man, a beautiful young girl and a bewildered child. This youth looked radiant, for a darkness within him had dissipated.

As they sped out of his dreams, the Voidal saw them embrace. For them the nightmares had ended.

But not for him.

IV

FIRST MAKE THEM MAD

At this juncture it is necessary for me to introduce one of the most vital components of the entire Voidal canon, although in some ways I am tempted to play down the involvement of the particular character to which I refer. Had I merely set down his escapades verbatim, for he himself is a notorious spinner of yarns, the Voidal would have been relegated to the background, while the creature to which I refer would have assumed monstrously heroic proportions. And nothing could be further from the truth.

This tale has many variations, being a favourite among the familiars and imps of sorcerers and mages throughout the omniverse. However, I have exercised considerable editorial license in my recording of it.

It notes, significantly, the downfall of an extremely powerful empire, but ironically earns its place here because it introduces the reader to the abovementioned character, a familiar by the name of Elfloq.

—Salecco the Long Suffering

I have spoken already of the immense empire of the Csarduct Dynasty, and of how it held sway over almost the whole of Phaedrabile. Like all tyrants before them, these quasi-human conquerors were greedy for expansion, avid for the secrets of the many dimensions. Phaedrabile was never enough.

Their dreadful mages and sorcerers schemed and plotted, calling upon demiurges and demons long plunged into the depths of antiquity (and for good reason). No powers were too terrible for the Csarduct sorcerers to tap. They plumbed the very depths of their arts, seeking to reincarnate old and forgotten gods and hideous powers that would obey them and sweep aside all forces. There was no god, spirit or demon feared by the sorcerers of the Csarducts, and no power to which they bent the knee, save their overlords, the invincible Csarducts themselves.

They established a bridgehead on the world of Moonwater, a foothold to other realms, first step to new tides of bloody carnage and conquest. Moonwater, entirely coated in a phosphorescent ocean of living matter, harboured the great citadel of Quellermondel, which had been artificially grown from the green mooncoral of the planet's ocean over a period of countless millennia. Seven aquamarine moons dominated the Dryunic skies and looked ever down on Moonwater, where the bright ocean reflected in iridescent splendour the emerald glow of the heavens.

Up from the curling, glittering glory of the mooncoral city the ragged towers of the sorcerers thrust like jagged spears seeking the moons: for each heavenly titan there was a tower, seven in all, and from the names of the seven moons the Seven Sorcerers of the Csarducts took their names—Quar Mordo, Mage of Pain; Endellys, Mage of Dreams; Jundamar, Mage of Prophecy; Lucedrix, Mage of Knowledge; Quarramagus, Mage of Spells; Zomakh, Mage of Necromancy; Tephlemytho, Mage of Immortality.

Moonwater hid them all from the curious, prying eyes of the Empire. High in their fantastical towers the sorcerers practised their outrageous mysteries, always seeking paths of discovery, new powers. The seven towers glowed and reverberated to strange energies as the Seven pursued their endless missions. Quellermondel had once been no more than a huge outcrop of mooncoral, but over the centuries, coaxed by unnatural magics, it had thrust upwards towards the bright moons, defying laws of sanity, piling itself layer upon layer upon twisted layer, shelf upon leaning shelf, so that now its planes were countless, its walks twisting and turning through tunnels, over arches, across dizzy abysses, high, high upward, ever upward. The bizarre pile ludicrously mocked geometry and architecture.

As the mooncoral rose higher above the level of the phosphorescent sea, transmogrifying into a harder, more resilient rock form, the life within the city also changed, migrating upwards and mutating. Dwelling in the uppermost Tiers were the great Houses of the Csarducts and their principal acolytes, familiars and Conquistadors. Below them in the Secondary Tiers dwelt the mass of the city's inhabitants, servants of the rulers; below in the Tertiary Tiers were the low-born, those that still interbred with the lesser dwellers of the sea, who were undermen and who did the menial labours of the higher Tiers. In the underwater Weedcoves dwelt the strangest of the city's inhabitants: these were the amphibious Orgae, ocean dwellers who had once been masters of Moonwater, until the scions of the Csarducts had imposed upon them their cruel slavery. Now these Orgae served as sea-harvesters and as helpless, jaded servants to the whims of all the Tiers of Quellermondel. Many were the indignities heaped upon them.

While Quellermondel rose in majestic blasphemy towards the seven aquamarine moons, symbol of the rise of Csarduct glory, its submarine catacombs thronged with a race whose destiny seemed to end in ruin and extinction. High above them the rulers laughed: from far across their engorged Empire they had come to Moonwater, preparing for the new crusade that would spread worlds at their feet.

Two figures, both small and squat, peculiarly batrachian in facial characteristics, dropped soundlessly upon an isolated arm of mooncoral, high up above the sleeping city of Quellermondel. Shadows crossed the seven moons, shadows that had been drawn by sorcerous fingers like veils, for there was undoubted evil abroad. In the twinkling glow of the distant ocean the two figures were limned like gargoyles, their scaly skin a deep green. Bulbous eyes reflected phosphorescent light from far below as the thick heads turned to study the shadows. They were alone. Satisfied, they drew together, fused in their conspiracy.

"Not at your Master's side this night, Owlworm?" croaked the first, a hint of amusement in his tone.

"No, nor thee, Elfloq? There's sinister work afoot," replied the other, pointing. His thin arm waved upward like a twisted stem of bone, singling out a dome set high above them in the shade of the rearing sorcerers' towers. From the few slit windows of the dome came faint, unnatural light; it had not shone from that cold place for many a long year. Too many black ghosts walked its echoing galleries for comfort.

"Strange work indeed when there's not a place for we familiars," said Elfloq, scowling at the dome. "Quarramagus sent me from him long since with strict words that I shun him until summoned back. Most strange."

"Aye, and Zomakh likewise sent me hence," nodded Owlworm, tugging at his lip thoughtfully.

"The Seven have dredged up many a filthy relic of lore before now. Yet I don't recall having been cast out, dispensed with. Not before this night. Are there deities we know nothing of, Owlworm?"

The other familiar looked out over the sea. "You know as much as I do. Who knows the extent of the Gods? Who can guess the far reaches of their power?"

Elfloq grunted. He prided himself on his knowledge of the labyrinthine mysteries his master trod, and to be shut out from a new enterprise irked him. "So you are no wiser than I am?"

Owlworm hawked and spat. "Even less, I suspect, knowing your keenness of eye and ear for—detail."

"Oh, I know nothing," muttered Elfloq. So, he mused, Owlworm would be no help to him and his sounding out of the other five familiars had also been fruitless.

"There is one thing I did notice," said Owlworm casually, picking at his nose with studied indifference.

Elfloq tried not to appear piqued. "Yes?" He was always burning to hear the least breath of gossip, as his fellows well knew.

"Well," went on Owlworm. "The information is hardly priceless, but at the same time it is not completely without value—"

Elfloq puckered his features sourly. "Tell me what you know and I will hang a price on it. Not before, my wily friend."

Owlworm snorted. "A small spell from your master's trove will suffice—"

"First the titbit," growled Elfloq.

"Very well. We are agreed that some new and dire conjuration is in progress," said Owlworm, again aiming a noisy hawk in the direction of the dome.

"I'll not dispute that. The Seven have been preparing strong cantrips and spells these last nine cloudpasses. Binding spells of surpassing power, too. But this much we all know, having aided in the preparations."

"Hmm," went on Owlworm, enjoying his brief moment of power over his fellow, who so rarely needed enlightening on matters of news in the city. "I have sensed several ripples on the astral realm." He fell silent, allowing his words to hover as though weighted with awe.

Elfloq grimaced, unimpressed. "Ripples? But the astral is a cauldron of movement, perpetually. What ripples?"

"Most odd. They began not here, but distantly."

Elfloq nodded, biding his time patiently.

"Something," said Owlworm, with feigned momentousness, "moves beyond. Beyond all the regions we know, beyond all the planes, real or astral. Something outside all experience."

"Yet there are other dimensions—" put in Elfloq.

"Whatever disturbs the astral sea with these ripples is not fettered by any dimensional barrier. There may be Old Gods awake. They watch."

Elfloq sniffed, knowing that the supposed revelation was over. Yet it had served him to a degree. "You should be the Prophet's familiar and not the Necromancer's," he muttered.

"Is my news of value?" said Owlworm.

Elfloq chuckled. "Arguably." He leaned over to his companion and spoke softly into the tufted ear, reciting a simple spell for him.

"My thanks," said Owlworm. "So—I'll not linger. Will you accompany me elsewhere?"

"Not yet," said Elfloq with a shifty glance at the dome.

Owlworm nodded, spitting, then spread his delicate, membranous wings and slipped away into the air and out of view. Elfloq remained on the arm of mooncoral, mulling over what he had heard. He was deeply disturbed, for the omens were decidedly unhealthy. Earlier he had conversed briefly with Dagwort, familiar of Jundamar, Mage of Prophecy, trying to sound him out as to the potential of this conclave of sorcerers, but the tiny familiar had been tight-lipped and evidently far more distraught than he habitually was. No good would come of any of it, Elfloq deduced.

But I would know more. I will see what I may. Then, like a wisp of air eddying up into the darkness, he flitted toward the great dome and to one of its slitted windows.

ach of the Seven guarded his knowledge and powers jealously, sharing what various secrets he had hoarded in the name of the Csarduct Dynasty as infrequently as possible. They rarely met outside the hallowed halls of their overlords, the Csarduct families, who came and went on Moonwater and their Empire as they pleased. Yet now the Seven had come together, and after many long discussions and muted whisperings had agreed to unite to perform one particular conjuration, more ambitious than any other previous working. It was to be the result of an age of scheming and surreptitious plotting, for the arm of their lords was long and there were few places where the shadow of the Csarducts did not fall. Furthermore, the conjuration that they planned required the combined sorcery of them all, for the dangers inherent in its performance were colossal.

Yet if it were to succeed—and it must!—the Seven would usurp the Csarduct thrones and rule in their stead, all Phaedrabile would bow to them, and no god would stay their hand.

Jundamar, Mage of Prophecy, had hinted at the possibilities first, for he claimed to have foreseen the debacle of the Csarduct Dynasty: his tremulous, discreet revelation soon reached the ears of all the others and the meetings began. Lucedrix, Mage of Knowledge was consulted, and thereafter spent many wearying periods in his tower, searching for clues as to how the Seven could accelerate the downfall of their masters.

The Csarducts had decided to come to Moonwater in force, seeking oracles, guidance for the new crusades. Lucedrix had then found a weapon, but fear made him caution his colleagues against its use. However, Quarramagus, Mage of Spells, avowed that he could set up a barrier to bind the terrible weapon, if the others would lend him their strength. And so they had gone beyond idle speculation.

Now, inside the ancient dome, where once the arcane priests of the Orgae had practised their unsavoury arts before being ousted, the Seven had gathered to begin their own unholy rituals. Cloaked in grey, their faces smooth and devoid of features, blanked thus by certain of their magics, the Seven had described for each of themselves a charmed circle; they sat within them, surrounded by invisible guardians, focusing their wills and concentration upon the large pentacle that was the central point of the gleaming floor. Around this pentacle the sorcerers had erected their strongest spells and incantations so that the air hung blackly like a wall of power, unbreakable. Thick magics hung like incense, and terrible sigils flickered like beads of light, spangling the smooth walls. While the Seven remained seated in their potent formation of circles, nothing could form and tear free from the central pentacle. All the combined sorcery they had gathered about them had never before been so co-ordinated. Silence cloaked them as they concentrated. Nothing moved within the pentacle. Even the air there was still.

"Let the summoning begin," came the sonorous voice of Quarramagus, breaking the silence. "I have compounded the strength of our barrier. That which we invoke cannot break free."

"I have sown the air with the Incantations of Pain as set down by the Highmost Nehacc. They will be the scourge of anything moving outside the charmed areas," said Quar Mordo, Mage of Pain.

"I have made ready the dreams that will hold he who comes," said Endellys, Mage of Dreams.

"I have found the myths relating to he who comes and I am ready to question him," said Lucedrix, Mage of Knowledge.

"I have spoken to the dead, who will take him when we are done," breathed Zomakh, Mage of Necromancy.

"I shall rip from him the secrets of immortality to enhance my own lore and render us all beyond death," said Tephlemytho, Mage of Immortality.

"And I," said Jundamar, Mage of Prophecy, "have been shown many paths, all obscured by shadows."

This had an unsettling effect. Quarramagus directed an angry retort at Jundamar. "The time of the invocation is at hand! Do you falter in our purpose? We must be strong!"

Jundamar was silent, but then he whispered, "Forgive me. I am ready. Let it begin."

Quarramagus nodded: he began a cantillation, slowly, rhythmically and low in an alien tongue. It was taken up by others until all of the Seven chanted in unison. The air pulsed with the evil sounds. Within the pentacle a gentle diffusion of light began, its source unknown.

Quarramagus spoke. "Hear us, ye who dwell in the timeless void between the dimensions. We invoke you. Come to us. Come, Voidal. We invoke thee."

A careful scrutiny of the obscure records of Lucedrix had shown that to invoke the mythical dweller in the void it was but necessary to call upon his name. Now the inner light grew in intensity. For brief seconds the vision of the Seven shimmered disjointedly. They closed their eyes, focusing again, then saw a man standing in the centre of the pentacle. He was garbed in black raiment, with high leather boots, a shirt of nightweb, and with a jet cloak draped behind him like a storm cloud. At his side was an ebon scabbard and within it a glimmering blade. All these things the Seven had anticipated and all that they knew of the Voidal they had been careful to counteract with the awesome barrier of thaumaturgy that surrounded the pentacle. Yet the most difficult part of their scheme was yet to follow.

The eyes of the Voidal flickered open as though he had been in a trance, or perhaps a listless dream. He stood serenely, unable to see beyond the rim of the pentacle, where black mist seemed to rise. He smelled sorcery and was wary.

"Voidal," came a croak from the wall of night.

"I am he," said the man in black, recalling his name.

"The Dark Gods have chained you, forcing you to perform their petty deeds."

"I am he."

"You are the immortal one, who can neither die, nor kill."

A sardonic smile crossed the face of the Voidal. "These are riddles, voice from the shadows, and I'll answer you with more. I am he and yet I am not he."

"You are without name, without destiny, without soul."

"You have named me Voidal, which is no name, but a curse. Those Dark Gods you spoke of—they hold my destiny, and my soul."

His words were answered by silence. But beyond the ring of night, one of the Seven growled quietly to his fellows. "I sense a snare. Be wary. None of these answers is satisfactory. Part of his curse is that he has no memory. And yet he knows something of himself."

Silence fell again. The Voidal was patient. Then a voice drifted out of the darkness. "Do you recall your past?"

"A little. In dreams, perhaps."

"Speak of it!" hissed the voice.

"Is my fate to tell of it? You have invoked me, yet I do not come of my own accord. My past is not clear to me. It rests about me like a torn mantle, yet it is mine and mine alone. Why should I divulge it when I have striven so hard to wrest it from the Dark Gods?"

The voice grew impatient. "You have been invoked! You must obey us!"

"You are not my masters. It is they who must have sent me. They move me like a pawn and I am powerless to resist. We are all their vessels."

These words brought a distinct murmur of unease from the ring of darkness, but the cold, imperative voice of Quar Mordo speared the air like an icy javelin. "We are vessels of none! We bow to no gods! We have brought you here for our own purposes. You no longer serve these Dark Gods. Our combined powers mock them, wherever they skulk. Aye, skulk! We shall wrest your power from them with ease. You will see."

"Your destiny sits in our hands now, Voidal," added the mocking voice of Endellys.

But the sharp features of the Voidal revealed no emotion. No smile, no contempt, no fear. "If I am in your hands, I am indeed your pawn."

"He laughs behind his face," whispered Jundamar, but was ignored.

"We do not seek to manipulate you," said Quarramagus. "We seek the source of your power. We shall steal that from you, Voidal. After that we will do you a kindness, for you may wander where your own will takes you." The sorcerer laughed.

A slight frown of puzzlement crossed the Voidal's face at this, but he remained very still.

"Hold high your right fist that you keep from sight within your cloak," Quarramagus told him. "Hold up the Oblivion Hand."

Slowly the Voidal drew out the hand, looking down at it with a grimace of loathing. Holding it from him, he raised it, fist clenched.

"The hand of the Fatecaster," said his tormentors as one. "The key to your power. We have studied all that is known of its vague secrets. If it has been a curse to you, then our deeds here will be a blessing."

The black-gloved hand was oddly lifeless. "A blessing?"

"You have no need of confusion, nor of fear," said Endellys, now more soothing. "See, I will bring you dreams that calm any torments of the Dark Gods." As he spoke, a soft wave ebbed out from the darkness like cool air and in its blanket the Voidal felt the stirrings of images that writhed, worming into his mind, drawing out from him all his concern, his doubts and his fears. Slowly the visions—bright these, not the tortured, enigmatic sendings of the Dark Gods—burrowed deeper into his psyche. He quickly began to succumb and a strange, lethargic peace settled over him.

The Seven observed. Endellys gloated over what he had done. In the pentacle the man in black had dropped silently to the floor.

"Now," said Quarramagus. "Our real test begins. Whatever powers work through this creature will put our mettle to the test. All of you, remember your parts in this."

Once more the Seven became a softly chanting unit, the flow of energy from their potent cantillations drifting into the pentacle, unlocking with occult keys their ultimate designs. The right hand of the dreaming Voidal, which had been so lifeless, now stretched its fingers as though coming awake. It was the only part of the slumped figure that moved. Inside the pentacle a deep blue aura formed, coating the hand, sheathing it like silken mist. The mist pulsed; inside the hand its veins throbbed like wires, livid with force. As the voices of the sorcerers rose, so did the strange hand detach itself from the fallen body, and like a drugged arachnid, it began a lurching crawl across the pentacle. The blue aura moved with it, surrounding it completely. Gradually it neared the edge of the pentacle, well away from the body, then stopped.

A sigh broke from the combined ranks of the Seven as they saw that they had achieved their prime design. Their mumblings ceased and they looked upon the glowing hand in awe. Lucedrix spoke in triumph. "See! The very hand of the Fatecaster! The Oblivion Hand. By this grim member are the dooms sealed of those whom the Dark Gods have marked. It shall do their work no more, for we shall never return it to their minion, this Voidal."

"The hand will do our bidding now," agreed Quarramagus. Around him the other sorcerers breathed more easily, for the great spells they had worked had been taxing.

"What of the Voidal?" said Quar Mordo.

Quarramagus stared coldly at the inert figure. "If he is immortal, as the writings say, he cannot be destroyed. He must be sealed away. Endellys has conceived a plan."

"Indeed I have. I will create an endless maze of dreams in which he shall wander in contentment for the rest of eternity."

"Very well," nodded Quarramagus. "The hand is secure. Break the pentacle."

Jundamar mouthed his doubts once more.

"The hand is sealed!" snapped Quarramagus. "And the Voidal is as one dead. Cease your tremblings. You have seen only doom for the Csarducts, not us. You jeopardise us all with your lack of faith."

"Forgive me," breathed Jundamar. "My dreams are not as untroubled as yours."

"Break the pentacle. Take the hand to the Moonglobe we

have prepared. There it will repose until we are ready to put it to our use."

"And the fall of the Csarducts will begin," said Zomakh.

"Endellys," said Quarramagus. "Attend to the removal of the Voidal. You know what to do with him."

"Oh yes, I do indeed."

Shadows clung to the Seven as they began the final stages of their devious work. High above them, peering down through the slitted window in the curved dome, the squashed features of Elfloq looked on in wonder, marvelling at the things he had seen. Now the full ambitions of the Seven were made known to him, for his sensitive ears had caught it all.

"Bring down the Csarducts, eh? Flaunt the servant of the Dark Gods in their very faces, eh? But what are these Dark Gods? Those whom Owlworm spoke of? And those whom Dagwort fears? I note that his Master, Mage of Prophecy, is also tremulous. What has he glimpsed down future's tunnel, eh? I'll know more of this before I cast my fate with my own Master. 'Tis well Quarramagus is the spokesman in all these schemes, for I'll learn his will ere long." After a last glance within, the figure evaporated into the shadowed city.

The dreams were kind.

There was light and warmth, and the sombre cloud that always hung about him, a cloak of foreboding, was gone, lifted by gentle hands. Here in this vale of soft repose, he was able to put aside all that he had detested. No longer was he tortured by the enigmas of his exile.

He glimpsed himself in a pool. He was complete. A new hand had replaced—what? But he had already forgotten. He was in Paradise, the journey done.

Peace was an ocean: he swam it alone.

East of the city, overhanging an extraordinarily bulbous mass of mooncoral, the tower of Lucedrix, Mage of Knowledge, rose majestically from the layers of the city. It was to this isolated pinnacle of mooncoral that Elfloq now sped, knowing that the Seven would yet be attending to the last of their affairs with the one they had invoked. Elfloq anticipated that here in the tower he would find Lucedrix's familiar, Surefly, who still owed him a few favours. Here would be an opportunity to find out more about the Voidal.

Elfloq brazenly popped into being in the centre of Lucedrix's massive library of cluttered arcane lore, in which could be found a multitude of tomes and grimoires, most of which were duplicated nowhere else. To his surprise, and then delight, Elfloq found Surefly already here, himself buried deeply within a dusty relic of elder works. Silently Elfloq padded through the dust and looked over the tiny shoulders of the familiar at the crimson runes spread out on the page.

"You find that interesting?" said Elfloq with a chuckle.

Surefly sucked in his breath with a start, slamming the book shut, covering himself and the delighted Elfloq with swirling motes. His head bobbed, seemingly larger than his body. "I was just—uh—Elfloq! How dare you materialise in here! You flaunt familiars' privileges—"

"Fortunate for you I am not your Master. I am sure he would be most annoyed if he saw you pillaging his treasures."

Surefly's face screwed up like a wrinkled fruit. "What do you want?"

Elfloq's smile widened. "Oh, nothing much, friend. A little information, that's all."

"The price being your silence—"

Elfloq waved this aside magnanimously. "Perhaps, but we must be swift. I am not here to tease you, which I can't deny is common enough with me."

Surefly noted the tone. "Oh? There is something amiss?"

"Even so. It began, as you recall, when we familiars were ordered to keep clear of our Masters. Most contrary to procedure."

"Indeed," sighed Surefly. "Though in my Master's absence I have been able to—ah, indulge myself a trifle."

"Have you learned anything?"

"Have you?" replied Surefly suspiciously.

"There is an atmosphere overhanging the city. Can you not smell doom in the very air?"

"I sense the unease. It is more widespread than I thought. The Seven are embarked on some dire exercise."

Elfloq nodded. "They are indeed. Already the old dome reeks with magics most unfamiliar to me. Unhealthy magics."

Surefly tapped the tome he had closed. "I will confide in you, Elfloq, though it is only the uniqueness of the situation that—"

"Come, come, there is nothing in this for me. We are both familiars. Is that not enough?"

"Usually, no. But in view of the air of darkness that clouds Quellermondel, I will speak."

"Yes?" pressed Elfloq, containing his eagerness badly.

"There is a great fomenting of apprehension in the lower Tiers and more specifically in the Weedcoves. The Orgae are inordinately agitated."

Elfloq showed his surprise: this was not the direction from which he expected enlightenment to come. "The—Orgae?"

"Yes. Whatever our Masters are doing in the dome, it is causing unique alarm to the Orgae."

"But why? How can they possibly be affected?"

Surefly held up a gnarled finger for silence. "That is what I have been trying to ascertain, at some pains. This tome deals with the deities and demons and such like of the ancient Orgae, most of which are virtually forgotten, having withered away long ago when the Csarducts usurped power on Moonwater."

"Gods? The Orgae have gods?" sneered Elfloq, but secretly he was piecing together more of the puzzle.

"Of course! Slumbering, perhaps, but they exist."

"And this enterprise of the Seven—it invokes the old gods?"

"I rather think, my friend, that it antagonises them. Have you spoken to Owlworm? Well, he keeps blabbering about ripples. Something moving in the deeps. Astral deeps, he says, but I have been reading this, and I rather fear that he may be mistaken. The deeps of Moonwater, which are unplumbed, may be a more accurate epicentre for these supposed ripples."

"Ah," said Elfloq. So he was not the only one to be investigating the chain of abnormalities. "And what exactly do you foresee?"

Surefly grunted. "I would usually recommend you to a conference with Dagwort, but the Prophet's familiar is unseemingly tight-lipped with regard to prophecies. Cloudy, he mumbles. Typical incompetence. In view, however, of this clime of unease—"

"You envisage something unpleasant?"

"If only our Masters had confided in us! Their own familiars! We must assume they are in control, but—"

"They are ambitious beyond their normal dreams," mused Elfloq.

"Their appetite for power is insatiable."

Elfloq nodded thoughtfully. "Yes. But, come. Tell me more of these old gods, my friend." And together they perused the ancient book.

In a secluded chamber of the tower of Quarramagus, the Seven stood in a half moon, looking towards the dais upon which the shimmering Moonglobe rested. Inside the translucent globe the deep blue mist swirled ceaselessly, like a living cloud; at its heart invisible chains had gripped the hand of the Voidal. It had now been rendered immobile by the tremendous strength of the spells of the sorcerers. Quarramagus boldly crossed the mosaic floor and stood close to the lambent hues of the Moonglobe. He smiled in self-satisfaction, turning.

"We have tamed the Oblivion Hand. Now it will dispense fate at our whim! Its finger will single out those whom we choose. Whatever doom comes, comes at our command."

Zomakh came forward, still looking at the quiescent hand with apprehension. "When do we begin?"

"The Csarducts are on Moonwater in force, preparing for new conquests. I will summon the first of them to this tower, promising him all that he seeks for his murderous brethren. I will summon the feared Dan Zar Enzo himself."

"And the Oblivion Hand?" said Quar Mordo.

"It will lay his doom upon him, as is our will. For now, let us disperse. When I have prepared the ground for our evil seeds, I will send my familiar with word to your own. They know nothing of our coup. Later, perhaps."

With a few muffled comments and last brief glances at the hand in the Moonglobe, the sorcerers left, satisfied at last that their grim work neared completion. Last of them to go was Endellys. As he reached the door, Quarramagus put an arm on his, gently.

"What of the Voidal, Endellys? Have you seen to him?"

"I have. He will dream for as long as we desire it. He is secreted in a remote place, where no one of Quellermondel will find him. My familiar tends him and will do so until I call him off."

Quarramagus nodded, permitting himself a chuckle. "Good. All goes well."

Endellys bowed courteously and left.

Quarramagus turned once more to the Moonglobe. "Yes, all goes very well. Yet I have one more magic to work before it is done. One more—" From his gown he drew a slender, sharp blade.

Elfloq had left the library in Lucedrix's tower where Surefly was now hastily tidying up the various books on Orgaen civilisation they had been perusing. Time now to investigate first hand, Elfloq decided. He took himself deep down into the city, past the levels of the Tiers, dropping through into the perpetual shadow to the very level of the phosphorescent ocean where it slopped over the uppermost of the Weedcoves. There was an old den down here where lowborn sailors gathered, and there was always news.

Elfloq was fast moving, quick as the breeze, and able to meld with shadows so that most of the inhabitants of Quellermondel were no more aware of him than they were of the air he breathed. Now, at the base of the Tertiary Tiers, he paused, for his extraordinary senses told him that another of his fellow familiars was nearer at hand than would have been expected.

"Well," he muttered to himself, scowling behind a damp slab of mooncoral that had barely raised itself from the whispering sea. "Has Surefly dipped down here to experience the Orgae first hand, too? Though he said he had no mind for it. These are indeed grim times when even familiars do not trust each other.

But—no, not Surefly." He placed his tufted ear close to the slick mooncoral, ignoring its saline reek, and listened in to the subtle vibrations. Patiently he waited, calculating distances in silence. After a while he nodded to himself.

"Nighteye, or I'm a lump of stone!" he hissed. "But what is Endellys's familiar doing so far below the heights?" Cautiously he began to weave about the alleys and slideways of the Tertiary Tiers, evading the hunched figures that slumped along expressionlessly, cold and lifeless like men raised from the dead. It was a dreary, chilling domain without a soul. Moving away from the packed squalor of mooncoral slums, Elfloq crept out on to a spur that poked like a disused jetty into the deep green sea, its end lost in seeping mist. No one had observed him, so he scuttled over the broken chunks of mooncoral and approached the end of the finger. A rift led blackly down, seemingly to the Weedcoves. Elfloq disappeared like a fish, expecting to drop into the swirl of cool water, but the cave was of air and he realised that to remain in it he would have to skip into the astral. A few simple spells had been set to guard it, together with some rather unpleasant visions, but Elfloq grinned at them—child's play to him, familiar to the Mage of Spells. But why here, in a remote pocket of the astral?

Darkness presented no problems to Elfloq, for he had other senses capable of penetrating it. Deep in the crevasse he found a little chamber, as remote as anywhere in Quellermondel, he thought. Secreting himself with care, he looked and saw a crystal slab, gleaming and shot through with waving light. Lying prone upon it was the one who had materialised in the dome of the sorcerers, the Voidal. He was asleep.

Elfloq knew that Nighteye was here somewhere, but being unable to see him for the moment, he quickly slipped across the chamber and stood before the sleeping figure. The pale face was expressionless, but Elfloq knew that the Voidal was dreaming. Both hands were upon his chest, hidden by the black cloak. With a sly glance around him, Elfloq gently lifted the hem of the cloak and nodded. The right hand was missing.

Something cold stabbed at Elfloq's back and he stood rooted in terror.

"Why are you here, interferer?" hissed a low voice, recognisable as Nighteye's.

"Nighteye, my friend," said Elfloq, not daring to move. The knife remained touching him.

"Interferer first, friend second. Why are you here? Who sent you?"

Elfloq swallowed with difficulty. "Oh, come, come, Nighteye. You know me and my curiosity well enough—"

"Only too well. But whose errand are you on?"

"My own. My Master appears to have temporarily disposed of my services—"

Nighteye was briefly silent, but the knife withdrew. Elfloq risked turning. The sleepy-eyed familiar of the Dream Mage was studying him.

"There are things afoot that baffle me," said Nighteye with a yawn. "First my Master sent me off on some fool's errand, and I gather the other familiars were all likewise discharged for a time. Then I was told to guard this creature you see before you. I know nothing of what transpires, as usual. I have only released you, wily Elfloq, because it is evident from your presence that you know something, which is also no uncommon thing. So, allow me to ask again, less belligerently, why are you here?"

Elfloq nodded at the sleeping Voidal. "I came to see if I could learn anything from the sleeper. The Seven invoked him and then stole from him his right hand, the vessel of his powers. The Seven will use the powers of the hand to their own ends—"

"More powers? Have they not enough? Must they seek to bring every last god of darkness under their sway? They will go too far."

"Just as I fear," nodded Elfloq. "I am my Master's familiar above all else, but should he choose to rebel against the Gods—and lose—well, I fancy that my own fate would be seriously jeopardised."

"What are you suggesting?" said Nighteye sceptically.

"Nothing, my friend. Only that I value my existence. I would rather not have it tossed to the winds of chance and have to pray blindly for their favours."

"You feel our Masters overreach themselves?"

"I would be more inclined to faith if they had confided in us."

Nighteye nodded. "Your tongue frames my very thoughts."

"Then?" urged Elfloq gently.

"Then——? What do you suggest?"

"Merely that we learn more of what is afoot. I know something already, as you anticipated. Well, I shall impart it to you, my friend, and at once."

Nighteye looked even more sceptical. "And——what would be the price of this information, dear friend?"

"Simply a few words with the dreamer."

"Yes, I thought that might be your price."

"Well?"

"I can unlock his sleep for but a short time. My Master's magic is of the most puissant nature."

"Good enough," grinned Elfloq. "First I will tell you what I have learned." He then did so, though careful to edit the details so that it would be more than a little difficult for Nighteye to shape the entire puzzle. The latter listened with mounting interest, nodding and grunting. At the finish he decided that, for once, Elfloq had played him fair, and agreed to wake the sleeper for a short time. Thus he stood beside the figure, leaning over its ear, and began reciting something soft that Elfloq, to his annoyance, could not hear. Presently the figure stirred and then came out of its deep sleep slowly, like a creature of the sea surfacing very slowly.

"He wakes," said Nighteye.

"Is he secured?"

"Aye. The lethargy remains. He has no strength to move. Speak when you see his eyes open."

Soon the man was awake and his lids fluttered. Elfloq leaned over him. "Voidal," he said softly. "Do you hear me?"

It was like another dream to the dark man, seeing the puckered face, the thick lips and peculiar features. He nodded to the odd creature hovering so close to him.

"Good. I am Elfloq, a familiar of the sorcerers who brought you here. Do you understand?"

The face was calm, but it began to change, a mask of doubt. "Dreamwarp is no more. But the child is spared, and the others. Are the ill dreams to begin anew?"

"You dream no longer. You are awake. Do you not recall where you are?"

There was a long pause, but then the figure nodded. "Sorcerers—"

"Do you know why they brought you?"

"Invoked me—"

"Yes. To do what?"

"My fate—is not mine to command."

"And your power?"

"Power?"

"How do you discharge your power? By your hand is it not, Fatecaster?"

The Voidal was alert now. Nighteye looked nervous, but the persistent Elfloq pressed closer, eager.

"My right hand," said the Voidal. "I remember."

"Show me," said Elfloq.

But a look of terrible anguish crossed the man's face. "You don't know what you ask! It is a foul instrument. I dare not show it."

Even so, Elfloq abruptly reached under the cloak and pulled out the Voidal's wrist, showing him the severed stump, neatly bound in black cloth. "See! You have no right hand."

Stupefaction replaced fear on the Voidal's countenance, quickly dissolving to horror. "No hand? Yet in the dreams I again had two. And they were clean. My own, restored at last."

"Well, your hand is with the Seven now. They command it. Why? Why have they stolen it?" demanded Elfloq.

The Voidal shuddered. "Stolen it? Yes, I recall. Dreamwarp's gift grows strong within me. But how foolish to think the curse had been raised! Your sorcerers are insane. They have no true conception of what they have done. They have no further use for me, hence this phantom paradise in which they have set me. But the hand will seek their destruction. They cannot control its monstrous energies."

"They have easily controlled you," interrupted Nighteye.

114

"So is it not easier for them to control your mere hand?"

A cold, cynical laugh burst from the Voidal's lips and both familiars shrunk back at the wild sound. "My hand! It was never my hand. The Dark Gods purloined my true hand: the hand of which you speak is theirs. It forces me to do their work, though I would shirk the task if I could. If your Masters have truly stolen it, I am well rid of it. But they are mad to think they can wield it."

"You underestimate their powers," said Nighteye petulantly.

"They know nothing of the Dark Gods," sneered the Voidal. "But it is their play. Let them do their worst."

"What will happen?" said Elfloq, moved now by growing anxiety.

The Voidal shook his head. "I cannot say. But Death will walk your city. I cannot leave until he has reaped his harvest. He is the fee for my summoning."

"What of the Orgae?" went on Elfloq. "What part do they play?"

The Voidal looked confused. "Who are they?"

"The sea people. In the Weedcoves and lower Tiers. Their restlessness has not gone unobserved. Are they involved?"

"When I possessed the hand, I was plagued with dreams, visions, prophecies, and I often saw in them something of what was to come. Yet the dreams visited upon me by your Masters showed me nothing of the future. Thus my vision is limited, my power truly usurped."

Elfloq frowned. "What if you were to regain your hand, your power? Could you then say what is to come?"

"Only if the Dark Gods wish it known."

"But the Seven will perish?"

"The Dark Gods are mocked by none. Greater beings than your Masters have fallen to them."

"If the Seven fall, the Orgae will rise, storming the city, for they will think the power of the Csarducts broken!" cried Nighteye.

"That would be so, if the Seven fell," agreed Elfloq. "And there would be new gods in Quellermondel. Or should I say, old gods returning?"

"Would that we could know!" exclaimed Nighteye.

"If the Orgae rise and take back this city," added Elfloq, "the Csarducts would come from beyond in force and destroy Moonwater utterly."

The Voidal listened to them in silence.

"Then—we shall all perish," mumbled the unhappy Nighteye.

"Unless we prevent the fall of the Seven."

"We have only this man's word that they may fall—"

"I am not overfond of risks," said Elfloq. "And I prefer to control as much of my own fate as I may. There are too many bleak possibilities in this affair." He turned back to the Voidal. "How may we prevent this catastrophe?"

The dark man shook his head. "We are mere pawns. We control nothing."

"But the prophecy?" said Nighteye. "If you reclaim the hand, you will see what doom shall come to Moonwater—"

"Doom?" echoed Elfloq. "If it is to be that, then I shall make for some more salubrious place, with all speed. And if my Master is to perish, then I shall find another!" He glanced slyly at the dark man, thinking on what might be.

"What's to be done?" said Nighteye glumly. Elfloq had severely dented what little peace of mind he had.

"I will confront your sorcerers," said the Voidal. "The hand is destructive beyond their understanding. I will plead for its return, otherwise the Dark Gods may begin an indiscriminate punishment for the theft. I have no love of that vile member, but it will leave a bloody swathe of chaos until it is returned." He held up his incomplete arm.

"You cannot leave, chained as you are by the spells of Endellys," said Nighteye.

"Then release him!" snapped Elfloq impatiently. "Surely it is obvious we cannot ignore his plight."

"I can weaken the hold of the spells," said Nighteye, "but to free him—I doubt if I am able." But he set to chanting and muttering, making airy passes with his tiny fingers. Elfloq added what weight he could and the Voidal drew in his breath, steeling his wiry frame. There came a crackle of energy: the air was very hot for a moment, heavy with powers, but the Voidal rose stiffly, swinging his legs from the slab and standing shakily. He drew his blade and it began to hum, its metal alive.

"This is the Sword of Dispersal," he said. "Let me test these spells." He flicked it easily to and fro, lively as a serpent's tongue, absorbing the last of the binding spells and converting them to so much empty air.

"Is it done?" breathed Elfloq.

"It is," nodded the dark man. "My thanks to you both."

"My own fate is certainly cast with yours," Nighteye said to Elfloq with a scowl. "Though I am fickle in my disloyalty."

"On the contrary, you are very wise," Elfloq laughed, though nervously. "So, no dallying, lest your master come to examine his erstwhile prisoner. Let's away to the upper city."

"Take me before Quarramagus," said the Voidal, no longer drugged, but purposeful and assured.

They came by devious means to the tower of Quarramagus, for the wily Elfloq knew the most tortuous methods of entry and was careful that his two companions should go undetected. Quarramagus had long since explained to the familiar the intricacies of the passages and corridors to the upper portion of the sorcerous tower, and Elfloq was thus once more able to avoid the numerous blasting spells and malefic demon guards that prowled the place in profusion. Outside the doors of the chamber of the sorcerer, the three halted, Elfloq speaking further runes and spells.

"How do you wish to enter?" he asked the Voidal.

"Is the Mage within?"

Elfloq listened, then nodded. "I sense him—resting, I think."

The Voidal indicated the thick doors. "Open them."

Elfloq obeyed, but hopped aside to allow the dark figure first entry. The Voidal strode into the chamber, sword drawn, and glared ahead of him. A black-draped dais was before him, its cloth soaked and dripping; upon it, picked out in wispy candlelight were the glittering shards of some shattered vessel.

"The Moonglobe!" whispered Elfloq at the Voidal's waist.

"Gods of the Pits! Where is the hand? It was imprisoned within."

The Voidal shook his head. "We are too late. It must have already begun its dreadful work. I smell blood in here." There was a squeak of terror behind him: Nighteye had popped out of being, preferring the astral.

"A fickle ally indeed," commented Elfloq with a sniff.

"Be silent," said the Voidal calmly, ears cocked. Elfloq immediately listened. There were curious giggles coming from an alcove, hidden by purple silks. "What lies there?"

Elfloq shrugged, not anxious to look. The Voidal walked across the bizarre designs and motifs on the floor and reached for the drapes with the tip of his sword. Blood seeped in a thick pool from behind them. More eerie laughter came to his ears. Elfloq kept cautiously at bay, ready to follow Nighteye on to the astral at a hint of danger. The silks parted. There, cowering against a stone wall, tittering like an imbecile, was Quarramagus.

"Your Master?" the Voidal asked Elfloq.

The familiar nodded, shuffling forward in amazement. "He is—insane," he breathed, seeing the mad eyes.

The cowering figure held up an arm and the Voidal understood, for it ended in a black and withered hand, the same that had been stolen. Elfloq squawked as though singed by fire and leapt well back.

"Ambition has done this!" said the Voidal scornfully. "He has cheated his companions and sought to graft the Oblivion Hand on to his arm." He pointed to pools of blood that led to a grisly hand in a corner, the mangled hand of the Mage of Spells. "He sought to wield the power for himself. His perfidy has undone the combined power of the Seven and breached their defences."

Elfloq nodded, grimacing at the two repellent members. "What now?"

But a sound behind them made them both turn to face a new dilemma, for the six remaining sorcerers of the Csarducts stood there, arranged in a half circle, their featureless heads directed at the two intruders.

"What treachery do you work here?" snarled Zomakh.

The Voidal stepped aside so that the sorcerers could look upon the mad thing that had been Quarramagus. The withered hand had now altered in appearance. It had left the Mage and was crawling across the floor towards the six, settling at the heart of a blasphemous design upon the floor and flattening itself. Each of its fingers pointed at one of the six, for there were now six fingers where there had been five.

For a period of several heartbeats the scene froze. Elfloq felt his every fibre shaking with terror, being as he knew, in the presence of some colossal, imperishable evil. Then the six sorcerers broke ranks, and as one, turned and fled from the terrible severed hand. The Voidal alone seemed calm. He walked to the hand and looked down at it with more loathing and disgust than Elfloq had ever seen before upon the face of a man. The dark man bent down, obscuring the hand, but when he turned to face the familiar, he had two black-gloved hands, as though he had never been without them.

"Is it over?" said Elfloq tremulously.

"Over? It is never over. And this has only just begun."

"What are we to do?"

The Voidal considered. "We can only wait. The familiars are your allies, your close fellows?"

"Well, no—they are—well," spluttered Elfloq, but then shrugged. "Oh, yes, I suppose they are my fellows, my kindred."

"Go to them all. Tell them that the sorcerers of Quellermondel are doomed. The familiars must flee. The Dark Gods have no quarrel with them, but they are without pity." Elfloq looked greatly disturbed, but nodded, glad to be able to quit the frightful chamber and the presence of the man who could face this impending catastrophe with such unnerving calmness.

Jundamar, Mage of Prophecy, and the five other sorcerers were gathered in the tower of the former, all listening intently to the trilling voice of Dagwort, Jundamar's familiar. Dagwort had come rushing to Jundamar's side the moment his master had returned from the ominous events in Quarramagus's tower, telling the Mage of the alarming things that portended in the city. Jundamar had called the remaining sorcerers to him at once and ordered Dagwort to repeat his dire warnings.

"Masters," said Dagwort, voice almost failing him in the presence of so many hallowed Mages, "I have been watching events in Quellermondel while you have been engaged in your late workings. While below, in the very Weedcoves, I listened to the whispers and susurrations of the Orgae. It seems they fear your power no more, for they plan to rise up through the city like a tide and reinstate themselves as its masters. They have their own prophets, who have been silent since the coming of the Csarducts, but who are now inciting the Orgae to rebellion, telling them that the time of their Old Gods is at hand. Soon they will rise."

"Who is behind this?" growled Zomakh. "Is this another of Quarramagus's treacheries? We have seen how he cheated us by seeking to use the Oblivion Hand for himself—is this how he worked its power upon us?"

The others pondered this, nodding; it seemed that Zomakh spoke the truth.

Quar Mordo spoke. "Whatever the dreadful schemes of Quarramagus, he is mad in his tower. Should we fear the lowly Orgae? Ridiculous! Let us bring down a curse upon them at once and smother their dreams of conquest. We must assert our power immediately."

This met with unanimous approval.

Lucedrix held up a hand and they turned to him. "Some good may come of Quarramagus's foul treachery yet. Through it we may easily demonstrate to the Csarducts that he was singularly responsible for the invoking of this Voidal and that he tried to use the creature's power to overthrow the Csarduct Dynasty."

"Excellent," nodded Zomakh, and his comment was quickly endorsed by the others.

"I submit," put in Tephlemytho, "that Quar Mordo, as celebrated Mage of Pain, devise the nature of the destruction of the Orgae. And quickly."

Quar Mordo bowed. "A means of chastisement has already come to mind. The Orgae must be severely punished, but not destroyed utterly. When this is done, they will still have their uses."

"Of course," the others agreed.

"I thought, perhaps, if we were to render their fighting arms useless—"

This met with the unanimous approval of the sorcerers.

"Very well," nodded Quar Mordo. "I will undertake the necessary working. The Orgae rising will be stillborn."

Elfloq entered again the apartments of his erstwhile Master, Quarramagus. He was less fearful now of what he would find, though still wary of the dark man he had left here. He came across him sitting in a carved chair, staring out into apparent nothingness. At the tread of Elfloq's gentle feet, the Voidal came alert and greeted him. Elfloq bowed.

"I have spoken with all the familiars, save Dagwort."

"And?"

"They are all undecided, but favour flight on to the astral realm until affairs here on Moonwater begin to balance again."

"They are wise then. But what of this Dagwort?"

"Familiar of Jundamar, Mage of Prophecy. He is most loyal to his Master and will be reluctant to leave his side. They are together at the moment, Dagwort doubtless blathering as much as he knows."

"No matter. I doubt that any course chosen by the sorcerers will affect events to come. This Mage of Prophecy should see this, but it may be that the Dark Gods have drawn a veil over his far-seeing eyes."

Elfloq nodded, looking about him alertly, expecting anything. "May I enquire as to the fate of Quarramagus?"

The Voidal nodded. "He is no more. His heart ceased to function and there is an end of it. Put him from your memory." A shadow crossed his face and Elfloq read enough in it to let the matter lie.

"There is other news," he said.

"Yes?"

Ordinarily Elfloq would have sought to barter his pieces of information, but he thought better of attempting to deal with the dark man. "The Csarducts, rulers of Moonwater and of Phaedrabile, are gathered in the royal palaces of Dan Zar Enzo, where they are conducting an orgy and a great feasting in honour of victories won in the extension of their empire. Many of their great Conquistadors are there. Soon they will visit this very tower, intending to consult the oracle of the Seven so that they may know of their next conquest and of its fruitfulness, though I cannot see why they ask! They sweep all before them."

"The Csarducts? Many of them, and their greatest warriors?"

"Indeed, the very heart of their ruling body. A unique gathering."

"Now I see all things at once. I see why the Dark Gods have sent me."

"Oh?" said Elfloq, unsure how to press for more truths.

"The death of Quarramagus was the first of three dooms sent to Moonwater. Three dooms—the hand, the arm and the body. The second doom will soon fall."

Elfloq grimaced. "What will you do?"

"I?" said the Voidal with a dry laugh. "I can do nothing but wait. I will not help these accursed Dark Gods, though it would amuse them to hear me say it."

Puzzled by the enigmatic reply, Elfloq nodded as though in comprehension. "I will wait also."

Quar Mordo laughed unpleasantly. He had cast the magics. Now the stinking Orgae would feel his venom. Out into the shadowed city the spells had dissipated and soon they would reap their unsavoury harvest. Quar Mordo sat in his tower, crouched over the optic mirror—its surface shimmered like a silken pond and within were the images the Mage sought.

The Weedcoves. Dark, festooned with trailing streamers of seaweed, curling with knotted vines of subterranean root. Here were the mooncoral havens of the lowly Orgae; seeping into them came the cruel spells of the sorcerer, the bane of all, sparing none.

Quar Mordo again laughed sharply as he saw the first of

the amphibian folk stricken, and thereafter the curse spread like a virulent plague, so that the fighting arms of the dwellers in the sea were withered and made useless. Throughout all the dwelling places, all the harvest rooms, and all the far reaches of the Weedcoves the potent magic wrought its fallowing curse. Quar Mordo turned from the mirror, his pineal window, nodding to himself with satisfaction.

"Let the Orgae rise! The Csarduct Dynasty has nothing to fear from cripples!"

Jundamar looked out from his tower. The growing sense of dread that had been no more than a subtle streak in his dreams had now become an awning of doom drawn over the city of Quellermondel. The Seven had obscured the moons with clouds to shadow their evil work, but they had not gone—thick black billows of cloud had come scudding across the ocean, whose sprinkled lights had winked out, leaving the waters dark and oddly lifeless: a strange phenomenon for Moonwater, for without the moons or the sea-glow, the all-pervading darkness weighed down on Quellermondel like a choking mantle. Jundamar knew now that there were greater forces at work than the Seven had estimated, and that to control them would need a tremendous fusion of powers. His early doubts expanded with the darkness that had come and gloom settled even deeper within him than it had outside the tower.

Each of the other sorcerers secretly scowled at the artificial night that had drawn itself over the city. They watched from high windows and from their crystal globes and from their mirrors; they saw the low-born of the Tertiary Tiers bolting and barring the doors and windows of their hovels, all hiding within so that the alleys and backwaters were devoid of life or movement. Even the slinking cats and the scuttling alley rats were gone. On the Secondary Tiers it was likewise; all had gone within as though to be touched by the shadow of night meant instant pain. Only on the highest levels of the city was there any sign of habitation. Nowhere else was there light, sound or movement.

Then, beginning under the sea, in the Weedcoves, came the first of the movement. Wriggling, squirming movement. Like the coming of crabs or spiders it began, shrouded in the darkness. A tide unlike any known before on Moonwater, living, surging slowly upward beyond former levels. The six remaining sorcerers of the Csarducts did what they could to rip aside the weed veils that cloaked this strange surging, but failed. Everything had been obscured save the sure knowledge that there was movement, upward. Out of the sea it moved, and on through the alleys and backstreets of the dingy Tertiary Tiers. Up it went, silent but purposeful. The dark clouds over the city thickened, making pale the lights in the highest spires.

It drifted up on silent legs to the Secondary Tiers, blotting out the lower, still encountering no living thing, ignoring the locks. Jundamar cursed with fear, for he had caught a brief glimpse of the substance of this remorseless flood. Dagwort, near at hand, muffled his own terrors and then withdrew discreetly, fleeing at last, knowing that the sorcerers were indeed doomed. Up into the Primary Tiers the black tide lapped, and those who were foolish enough to stray into the streets died horribly.

Quar Mordo was watching in his optic mirror, and now, as the mass came into the dim light, he gasped. He thought at first it was a natural army of crawling horrors from the depths, some clawing crustacean force, but now he knew otherwise. From the caverns below the city had come an army of living hands. Countless, seething, rolling forward like the sea itself, it came on upward, groping blindly but with certain assurance. One for every hand I withered, Quar Mordo realised. Doors were being splintered aside on the Primary Tiers and the retainers of the Csarducts were dragged forth and grimly pulled to bloody pieces. Nothing could avail against the boiling waves of monsters.

"They have turned our magic back upon us!" cried Quar Mordo.

Now the first of the remorseless hands were swarming up the walls of the sorcerers' towers so that there were six living, wriggling fingers of flesh pointing at the clothed moons, all alive with the rising army. Each of the sorcerers rushed up their spiral stairwells to the uppermost of their turrets and there made their defence, hurling spells and blasting rituals downwards. It was useless. The hands moved on in their thousands, easily climbing the rough mooncoral walls. Some were destroyed and fell away, but the numbers were immeasurable.

As one, they smashed their way into the upper turrets of the six towers, battering down the doors, tearing apart the metal windows set against them, ripping away stone and mortar. Jundamar and the others all began a terrible shrieking. Terror clutched them icily and then turned to panic and ultimately madness as the fingers of the hands pointed. The six set up a maniacal laughing, eyes distending as each saw the carpet of hands closing in on them across their marbled floors. The laughter rose to a pitch that was drowned in pain as the first of the hands began grasping, tearing, rending.

Elfloq listened. The tower had become deathly silent now that all his Master's guardians were gone with him to dust. Yet he had heard a rising wind out in the city; it had sprung up from the ocean and now rose and rose, eddying about the seven towers, strengthening into a cyclone. "The wind," Elfloq breathed, "is unnatural. I hear strange laughter within it—the mad shrieking of demons."

The Voidal shook his head patiently. "The last of the sorcerers shouts out his pain. Madness has claimed them, though it is only the beginning. Soon they will be no more."

Elfloq shuddered as though the wind had beaten a path through the stone of this tower. "Are we to flee, or will we succumb as well?"

"We are safe enough. Come with me." The Voidal then led the familiar up to a small room and out through a wooden door on to a tiny balcony that overlooked Quellermondel. Elfloq saw columns of shadow moving back down into the depths, but could not identify the things that made up the swiftly subsiding tide. He felt that it was better not to know.

"Watch, Elfloq. The last of the dooms comes to Quellermondel. This is to be the end of the Csarduct Dynasty."

Elfloq looked across dizzying distances to where the sea was barely visible. What Gods walked behind the night there? He waited.

"Our revel within your splendid palace flares with brightness and extraordinary inventiveness," smiled Hor Zar Argo, notable Csarduct Conquistador of the First House. He addressed his immediate commander, Dan Zar Enzo, lord of Quellermondel. "Yet it seems the lively fires within cannot match the formidable murmurings of the atmosphere without."

Dan Zar Enzo belched and gave a surly grunt, watching the garish antics of the orgy around him in the huge hall. "You swill words around your mouth as though tasting wine! I am a fighting man, Argo, and prefer simple words."

"Indeed, but it would seem one could build a totally new language about the whimsical nature of the climate of Moonwater. This world fascinates me. I could state, simply, that there is a storm brewing outside, but to do so, with respect, sire, would be to dismiss rudely what must surely be a unique phenomenon."

"Fires of the Bloodworld, Argo! You are more confusing than my wine!" Dan Zar Enzo belched once more, laughing emptily.

"May I venture to suggest, sire, that you look—but briefly—at the storm? I assure you it is of a singularly ominous nature."

"Oh, very well. Cool air will not be unrewarding. Lead on," growled the huge Csarduct. As he walked with Hor Zar Argo out into the lavish balcony of the upper palace, he was followed by a number of the Csarduct revellers; soon a company of them stood together, looking out over the shadow-clung city.

"Storm?" said Dan Zar Enzo. "But there is no sound! An unfamiliar darkness, I grant, but all else is peace."

"I hear the sea," said Hor Zar Argo. "And there were frightful gusts but a while ago."

"The sea is dark," said another of the Csarduct lords. "Where are its shimmering lights?"

"Where are the lights of the city?" said another. "All is pitch."

126

Dan Zar Enzo gazed up at the sorcerers' towers. They were as black and lifeless as blasted trees. The huge warlord scowled. "All is not as it should be," he conceded to Hor Zar Argo. He turned to one of the many ubiquitous guardsmen. "Alert the soldiery at once! Be ready to move at a word." The guardsman bowed and vanished in an instant. Dan Zar Enzo leaned on the balustrade, staring out at the sprawling mooncoral city for a sign of movement. Now he heard the rush of the distant sea. One by one the seven aquamarine moons slipped out from their coy hiding places.

"The work of your sorcerers?" asked one of the lords, though he drew back dubiously.

Dan Zar Enzo pointed. "There. What transpires?"

The sea was alive with movement, as though whipped by a tornado. It began to undulate like the back of a gigantic beast; waves built up and rushed in like wolves on the lowest of the mooncoral structures. Greater waves began to gather and heave forward from out of the ocean deeps. Vibrations shook the very palace as these huge waves thundered down on the city.

"An undersea upheaval," muttered Hor Zar Argo.

"The sorcerers shall answer for this!" roared Dan Zar Enzo and turned. As he did so, the wind roared and gusted out of nothing like the rasping breath of a monstrous god, and all the doors to the festive chamber slammed shut, afterwards proving immovable. The Csarducts dragged out their killing swords and turned their attention to the city once more. The ocean had suddenly come awake and now surged forward and upward, shaking the foundations of the city, crashing inwards and creating huge fissures and splits in the walls of mooncoral. Towers began to splinter and crumble as the water rose. Out at sea the waves lifted themselves like questing beasts, thousands of feet high, as though all the oceans of Moonwater came to the affray, racing down on Quellermondel, hanging over it now like fists. The wind fumed and boiled and clouds closed for the last time over the moons.

Living streamers of water reached up, licking like tongues at the Tiers, dragging them down. Dan Zar Enzo screamed as he saw the hideous faces that leered from out of the immeasurable walls of water. Up and ever up they rose, blotting the stars, as though all the gods of his private hells had come to crush him and his city. Millions of tons of water cascaded into the alleys and houses, towers and palaces. Like ants the populace were swirled out of their holes and sucked down into aquatic oblivion. To the howling Csarducts it seemed that their innards were gripped and squashed by huge fists of water. Moonwater had come to life and its ocean extracted a terrible revenge for the tyranny of the Csarducts. In the deepest of the deeps, secure from the maelstrom, the Orgae listened.

One tower survived the cataclysm, and in it the two figures watched, one placidly, one in terror. The Dark Gods had unleashed their awesome reckoning.

"We are doomed!" wailed Elfloq, gripping the cloak of the dark man, but the latter remained still, watching the thunderous collapse of the city where avalanches of mooncoral plummeted down into the whirling chaos.

"It will soon be done. Flee to the astral, Elfloq. There is time."

"But what of you? Surely you have the power to escape! I cannot desert you."

The Voidal turned a look of surprise on him. "No? But it is through me that this has come about," he said, indicating the destruction that surged about them. "This was your world."

"Aye, but not by choice. I have lost my place in Quellermondel, but I have gained a greater prize! My will!"

The Voidal nodded sadly. "Yes, your fate is yours to do with as you will from now on."

"But—you have smashed the power of the sorcerers! You, too, are free to quit this madness and be your own master."

The Voidal felt the shaking of the tower. Soon it would fall. "Free, Elfloq? Would that I was. But not yet, I think. Now—go! The tower will collapse."

Still Elfloq paused, almost ignoring the booming approach of the mighty wave army as it sought to finish its brutal work.

"I will gladly accompany you and serve you if you wish it!" he shouted above the din.

"Flee!" cried the Voidal as the towering water began to fall,

like the sky dropping. Elfloq blinked out and the Voidal prepared himself for the darkness that he knew would immerse
him. And the fresh nightmares.

"Well met, little familiar," he breathed as the waters came
down. "Perhaps you shall serve me yet. Well met in hell."

ut in the limitless mists of the astral, Elfloq drifted. He
felt the briefest of droplets of water, like the start of rain,
and knew that Quellermondel had been reclaimed by its
rightful heirs. But there was no sign of the Voidal. Not here.
This would never be a sanctuary for one such as him.

"But I will find you," the familiar whispered to the mists.
"And serve you well. Oh, yes."

And he set off at once, gripped by a determination that
those who had known him would have appreciated.

V

URGE AND DEMIURGE

*Just as the omniverse is full of balladeers, informants. gossips, songsters
and other purveyors of information, so it is liberally spiced with havens, sanctuaries and boltholes, and it is more often than not in such places that the tongues
of the former group loosen most readily. In my own travels, especially those un-
dertaken incognito, I have learned more in an hour in such diverse haunts as
Cloudway (of which I shall speak more fully in due course) The Inn at the
Edge, Mindsulk and High Crofels than an entire week in the administrative
courts of any number of deities and their high priests.*

*No matter what one's station, one can always glean something of interest,
of value even, in these sequestered places.*

*Elfloq was a master at extracting information, and I doubt if there were
many others who knew so many diffuse and curious agents and points of con-
tact.*

Not all of them, of course, were reliable.

—Salecco, sometimes named by his enemies, The Indiscreet

Asylis has been variously described by both mortals and
immortals as a squalid city, a den of iniquity, as a sprawling hovel fit only for criminals and as the repository of
freaks, delinquents and indiscretions of nature. This is scarcely
fair. Asylis is certainly of the proportions of a city, though no
one has ever had the time or inclination to attempt to traverse
its entire perimeters. The buildings, to be honest, are not pleasing to look upon, being ramshackle and crumpled together, almost as though the gods had taken the indeterminate whole and
squeezed—this has led to the houses, inns and storeplaces being
very narrow but tall, top-heavy like overhanging trees. As for iniquity—well, there is no more of that here than in any of the
other towns and metropolises of the many dimensions of the
omniverse. Certainly Asylis is not an evil place. Neither is there a

predominance of freaks and hybrids here, although the place was (as the story goes) conceived as a home for those of the gods, demigods and lesser spirits who had at some time failed to maintain the high standards expected of such entities. They may be disgraced, but Asylis is no prison. All are free to come and go as they please, but few leave, preferring to remain in the company of their own kind.

Having been constructed by gods (and admittedly tossed aside somewhat indifferently) Asylis sprawls in no positive dimension. Indeed, those that know how to use its labyrinthine alleys and crumbling gables can enter most of the dimensions from here. Reaching this place, however, is not so easy, and takes peculiar qualities.

There is another realm of Asylis—a bizarre landscape that threads in sooty confusion from roof to roof, garret to garret, spire to spire, for among the tall chimneys and looming towers can be found a vast terrain, quite unlike any other. This remarkable haunt has its own guardian, or rather caretaker, for Loptoc the Gossip would never consider himself capable of even so much as a hint of violence. Verbally, that would be another matter, for it was his tongue that won him the stewardship of this smoke-pulsating domain. That flapping member has become an almost tangible companion to Loptoc, for he is ever to be found going about his endless chores, tending the flues and chimney pots of Asylis, discussing the vicissitudes of life with this invisible apprentice.

It was thus, immersed in just such a dialogue, that Elfloq the familiar discovered the caretaker of the chimneys. Elfloq, popping into being from the astral, grimaced at the clinging stench of soot and smog, and quickly hid behind a tall brick chimney that seemed must surely topple at any moment. He watched Loptoc thrusting a lengthy rod downwards into the throat of another tall chimney, the fat legs of the caretaker waving about in sooty clouds, words tumbling around him as he leaned far over the brick lip to work.

"Ho, Gossip!" called Elfloq. "Have you time to spare to exchange tales of the outside?" To offer such news to Loptoc was the equivalent of offering raw meat hocks to a ravenous carni-vore. The caretaker emerged at once, his whiskered face bris-tling with cinders, though a crooked grin beamed through the grime.

"Ha, the rapscallion has come to visit! He's not been here for an age. Come to talk to me, has he? Talk then, talk. What tales does he bring? Whose private embarrassments has he been a-prying on?"

"Tales enough to make your ears burn," Elfloq laughed. "Terrible things are abroad. Empires are falling."

"Pah! How dull—he brings me nothing new. Empires fall every day. There are multitudes of empires out there, of men and gods. The stars teem with empires! In the end they all fall. And those who were once mighty—"

Elfloq grunted, for Loptoc was evidencing all the familiar symptoms of a pending outburst of nostalgia—of how he had once been a proud and notable demiurge, serving under the mighty god, Hadro-Hadro, builder of a million worlds, and of how he, Loptoc, had sadly fallen victim to his own tongue (his own tongue, that should be his truest friend!) and had bungled so many of his creative chores that he had been severed from service and cast out by Hadro-Hadro to dwell here in Asylis, where there were many other such inept unfortunates. Loptoc was fond of narrating how no one appreciated the stresses and strains placed upon gods and demiurges. Mistakes were inevita-ble.

Yes, mused Elfloq, he looks in the mood to babble it all once more, though my ears still ring from the last time I heard the entire recitation—aye, and of how he tripped over the coils of the same wriggling tongue here in Asylis, showing himself to be incapable of tactful silence and of being too attached to idle (nay, harmful) tittle-tattle, his tongue having bruised too many of Asylis's inhabitants for their comfort. Then it had been up to the chimney world for Loptoc, an outcast among outcasts. It was a world where visitors were few and thus, though Loptoc would never admit such a thing, welcome.

Elfloq had been in two minds whether to come here to Loptoc, but since the fall of Quellermondel and the untimely demise of his former master, he had spent far too long searching in vain for the mysterious dark man who had brought about Moonwater's debacle, the Voidal. Any port in a storm, he mused.

"If my news is so boring," said the familiar, "I'd best be on my way, having much business to attend to—"

Loptoc's grubby fingers pinched at Elfloq's wrist and clamped. The demiurge managed a good-natured smile. "Nay, nay! He was ever impetuous! Let him come over to the heat. Let him warm himself. All news has some merit."

Loptoc wobbled off over the slates, more ape than man. He was no taller than Elfloq, though far stockier. He was in direct contrast to the buildings of Asylis, which had the appearance of being crushed inwards, for he had the build of a man who looked as if he had been squashed from above, as though an angry god had leaned on him a little harder than he had meant.

The two beings squatted like gargoyles around a low-built chimney from which warm air rose in rippling hot currents. Both held out their hands to warm them, though for all its mist, smog and smoke, the rooftop world of Asylis was not cold.

"So he has some news of interest?" said Loptoc, pulling at the strings of a little bag beside the chimney. Elfloq knew there would be victuals within, for Loptoc was expert at monkeying down the chimneys and acquiring things from the kitchens of inns and such like. The familiar was correct, and shortly was given a juicy piece of raw meat. He chewed it with relish and settled himself, peeping at the bag to see if there was wine within.

"Empires may fall," he told Loptoc, "but we like to be the first to know, do we not? I would not bring anyone history."

Loptoc's fingers couldn't decide whether to pick at his teeth or his nose. Half way between them they became distracted and dug instead into his beard. "I would not give him fly-blown meat."

"Then I have word that will interest you."

"He is always a mine of news, this rapscallion," Loptoc sniffed. "He never comes here without bringing a feast. I fear that such small repast as I have shared will be a poor exchange, and certainly insufficient." He passed over a dark green bottle.

"I am not ungrateful," Elfloq grinned, sipping the wine, which was deceptively good. "But, of course, there are things that I must know."

"Does he seek knowledge for his Master, I wonder, or does he seek to add to his own trove of titbits? He would make a good Loptoc, I should say, for his nose is as long as mine, and his head as full of knowledge. But nay! Alas, his tongue is not so loose!"

Elfloq finished chewing. "I will tell you my tale," he said, and at once launched into an involved and complex narrative concerning the fall of the mighty Csarduct Dynasty, which had bridged stars, and of the demise of its ambitious sorcerers. It was not like the familiar to give such an unprompted recitation, but he knew that it were best for him to tell his tale first, without asking for a random one of Loptoc's. This would mean that once he had concluded his tale, he would be entitled to ask a tale of the Gossip. Indeed, protocol dictated that Elfloq could ask for specific information. Elfloq knew that had he asked his questions first, he would certainly have received evasive answers.

Loptoc realised at once that Elfloq was manipulating him, and under normal circumstances would have countered with an immediate interruption and temporary suspension of the tale. The two would then have haggled until a suitable arrangement had been agreed upon. However, Loptoc was intrigued by the momentousness of Elfloq's tale (as the familiar had anticipated) and allowed him to go on.

Elfloq considered it to be in his best interests to leave out certain details of his story, rather than stir up a potential hornet's nest of interrogation by his lone listener, but Loptoc was quick to sniff out some of the omissions, having expected Elfloq to be evasive.

Loptoc grunted, unable to disguise his fascination. "Then if the Seven sorcerers of Quellermondel have gone to their doom, why then, so has his Master, Quarramagus! He is now without a master, which is not well for him."

Elfloq had grudgingly fancied that Loptoc might seize on

this, but still, it would do no harm unless Loptoc happened to gossip to certain beings. "That small matter is in hand. I will have a new master very soon. All I seek from you is word of where I can find a certain person. I am sure that your whispering chimneys would already have divulged it, just as I am sure that your ears miss not a murmur that escapes from the city below, where men and gods alike converse indiscreetly around their hearths."

Loptoc belched loudly, signifying brief contemplation. "Well, his tale was a good one, and one which I can easily barter below for things that I need. News of this person—can that be all he wants? None of my rich sagas? No long ballads—I have a new one fresh from the very lips of Glandrool the Voluptuary, who was cast out by his fellow gods for attempting the seduction of no less than three goddesses—"

"Spare me the bawdy ballads! All I ask is the whereabouts of one person," repeated Elfloq.

Loptoc's eyes narrowed and he dabbed at the soot on his cheeks. "He asks such a small thing. Perhaps I view it from a false position. Perhaps it is not such a small thing he asks. Perhaps, typically, it is a vast thing. Well?"

Elfloq hesitated, but there was no way he could avoid stating what he wanted. "I seek a man garbed in darkness. Some call him—ah, the Voidal, I think it was."

Loptoc squawked as if a hot ember had bitten into him; his last chunk of meat disappeared down the dark chimney orifice. "Is he mad? Better he should summon up the Seething Plague, or demons, or Death! Does he speak that name so lightly? What can he want with such?"

Elfloq swigged at the wine, and it appeared to have an immediate effect. "It was he who brought down the Csarducts and their Mages—and he who freed me from my unsavoury service to Quarramagus. Why, I even had some part in it. Thus I am in his debt and seek to repay him," gabbled the familiar, but at once realised he had volunteered information that he had meant to keep secret. The wine must have weakened his guard—he was not used to it. No doubt it was one of Loptoc's tricks.

Loptoc looked even more aghast. "Repay him—with service? This is lunacy! But—wait. What is this? He has not told me all. His beautifully woven tapestry of the fall of the Csarducts is missing certain threads, and they would seem vital to the perspective of the work. What had the Voidal to do with it?"

"I was coming to that," Elfloq said sheepishly. Reluctantly he retold his tale, including much of the information he had omitted earlier.

Loptoc snorted at the conclusion. "He escaped with his life," he said, referring in his oblique way to Elfloq. "The Dark Gods spared him."

"Oh, doubtless they had reasons," said Elfloq. "But I have much to do. My stay with you cannot be protracted, alas. Will you say where the dark man may be found? Have you word?"

"Does he think the thoughts of the Dark Gods are at my disposal? Does he think such terrible beings would as much as look in the direction of this miserable place? Does he think a single one of Asylis's inhabitants would as much as whisper a word of the dealings of the Dark Gods?"

Elfloq grinned. "Of course! And Loptoc the Gossip would hear."

Loptoc mumbled sourly, not amused. "I suppose it is true that I am found owing to him. He has the right to ask something for his tale."

Elfloq examined his clawed hands, attempting unsuccessfully not to look smug.

A sudden crafty grin spread itself over the sooty features of Loptoc. "Hmm," he sniggered. "Fair swap, eh? Yes, I will deal with him as he has dealt with me. Two tales he told me. The first, concerning the fall of the Csarducts, was pretty but lacking in finery. He sought to obscure the facts—he thought it would be injudicious of him to let Loptoc know that he is in the debt of the dark man."

"It hardly seemed relevant," protested Elfloq feebly.

"But Loptoc found him out. His second tale was closer to the truth. Very well! I shall impart to him two tales also, a fair trade. This is the first:

"I have heard talk lately of a battle. Nay, a war, for I heard that it would embroil the entire fortunes of two great nations, the Poldarrians and the Vobandisheks of fabulously rich Elotrine. What turmoil! What bloodletting! All because the Houses of each nation worship gods that are the antithesis of each other, and minor gods at that! Yet how common this is among that rabble, mankind! Other nations have perished in their entirety because of these two gods. I have heard that the Dark Gods have decided to make an example of them both. By ending them for all time. Poldarrian and Vobandishek were not spoken well of and I assume that they will come to the brink of extinction, possibly topple over it."

Elfloq nodded, enrapt. "I know the world of Elotrine. The dark man will be there, the axis on which the downfall will turn?"

"So went the whisperings from the chimneys."

"Then I must speed away to this war with all haste—but first, Loptoc, your second tale," gasped the familiar eagerly, though he could read a degree of impish triumph in the Gossip's face.

"I am in no hurry to tell it. Later, when he reaches the world of Elotrine, then he shall have my second tale. I'll send a hearth imp with it. He has my word."

This last was a comfort to Elfloq, for Loptoc never gave his word lightly.

"You would not cheat such a valuable source of knowledge as myself?" appealed Elfloq, still dubious.

"No more than he sought to trade me half a tale garbed as a whole."

"The dark man will be at the hub of this war between Poldarrian and Vobandishek?"

"I heard two erstwhile gods discussing how the Dark Gods had decreed war on these Houses. They said that the dark man would bring disaster, and why should they lie?"

Elfloq considered, then nodded his thanks. "I'll come to you again another time," he promised, then was off, winging into the smoke and slipping at once on to the astral.

Loptoc gurgled, enjoying his wine. He had done nothing to invoke wrath or penalties. And he had a very excellent new tale to exchange down in his favourite kitchen.

Elfloq's speedy flight across the regions of the astral brought him to the distant world of Elotrine, home of the two warring nations spoken of by Loptoc. The familiar spent some time winging about the world, darting in and out of the astral, but eventually he found what he sought.

He flew over a battlefield of immense proportions, which seemed to span an entire country. But there was little movement down there. Indeed, there was little life. Only broken things stirred amongst the corpses. There were whole fields of the slain. Countless thousands had died in what must have been a dreadful volcano of violence. Already the scavengers were gathering to the feast.

Anxiously Elfloq flew backwards and forwards over the battleground, nose wrinkling with the awful miasma of blood and death seeping up to him. He did see a few men moving about, but they were human scavengers, pulling at corpses, searching for loot. He had no mind to speak with them.

He heard a buzzing beside him and spun about, half expecting to be attacked by a blood-maddened vulture, but it was a small dark being even more diminutive than himself, a hearth imp of Loptoc's.

"A message," hissed the imp. They were not noted for garrulity. "From Loptoc."

"Ah, yes, his second tale. Well?"

"Loptoc says, the war was yesterday."

Satisfied that it had done its duty, the hearth imp disappeared.

"Yesterday," echoed Elfloq. He cursed Loptoc's cunning. "The dark man is not to be found here. Then I must look elsewhere." He popped back to the astral. "Yesterday," he muttered again.

VI

THE OCEAN OF SOULS

As the alert reader of my saga will have perceived by this point in the narrative, there are a number of strands to the work; just as the accomplished weaver must needs leave certain strands dangling for a time while working on various parts of his tapestry, so must I, too, occasionally desert my characters. Rest assured, however, that Elfloq's part in the warp and weft of my saga is a crucial one—I have not abandoned him, as you shall learn in due course.

Meanwhile I must turn my attention to the threads I left hanging loosely earlier in my working, for at this point they are needed again in order to bring the wider picture into focus.

—Salecco, Shadow Loom Virtuoso

There are dimensions and dimensions, but as I have already been at pains to point out, there are also places neither in between nor beyond them and that seem to bear no tangible relationship to them. Thus it is with the Ocean of Souls, a limitless, timeless zone created by certain Gods who enjoy the creative diversity of reincarnation. It is a unique universe, to which none may come and from which none may go forth, save at the whim of the Gods who created it. It is a dream region, briefly glimpsed by the souls as they enter and depart on their short voyage back to the reality of a new incarnation in one of the dimensions that interweave the omniverse. The Gods who designed and constructed it alone know its secrets, its paradoxical workings; they draw into the Ocean of Souls those whom they will, and they release from it whosoever it pleases them to release.

It is an utterly dark place, for there are no suns or stars to light it, and no worlds coursing it. There is only the fathomless Ocean, rich with the dormant souls that dream, of former lives perhaps. It is a domain of sleep, of death between lives.

To watch over the Ocean of Souls and to attend to the duties necessitated by it, its Gods have placed within it a Keep, and have set within this Keep a master, a lord of the dead. He has many names. He it is who dispenses the whims of the Gods and sets the souls upon their way, scattering them about the omniverse as he is commanded.

In his Keep, the demi-god is called Necral—his sprawling domain is known simply as Skull Keep, and none save Necral and his few minions know of it. It has the vast skull head of a man and the body of a naked giant, reclining lifelessly in the emptiness that surrounds it as though drowned: it is the body of an old, deceased god, though it is preserved in its state for eternity, sorcerously embalmed, perhaps, and set to drifting in the Ocean of Souls. Within its immeasurable proportions, riddled with halls and cells, are the secret places of Necral, Keeper of the Ocean, where the chosen dead await their rebirth.

Ceaseless movement surrounds the corpse Keep, as though a plague of feasting worms have made the place their haven, but these are no scavengers, merely the shadowed minions of Necral. From out of the black ocean the Dead Fishers pole in their narrow barges, bringing to Skull Keep the chosen. Into the mouth of the forgotten god they take their burdens, to be received within by the Revivers. From the cavernous eyes of the skull fly the Sowers, carrying on their winged backs the reborn souls, taking them to whichever place they are to be incarnated.

Over all this presides Necral, watching everything from his sequestered chambers high in the skull of his Keep; he is as ageless and deathless as the Gods who have set him there. His emotions are a blank book, his thoughts secret, his place in the scheme of things fixed, unchanging. For only the Gods may bring change to this place of brooding doom.

Necral sent his probing intelligence up into the highest levels of the huge dead skull, wherein had been set the Chamber of the Omnivorous Eye. Here the bone room was dominated by a massive, glittering orb, constantly sparkling with sentient inner light, spreading its bright rays from a thousand facets. It was the Omnivorous Eye of Horabis, who had

140

once been a great demon, but who had elected to serve the greater Gods of the omniverse by rendering his fealty to them—he had given up his one great Cyclopean Eye, which looked out at all parts of the omniverse. Necral was forever gazing into this miraculous Eye, for therein he could see all things. Mostly he took note of all those who were dying and nearing death out in the many dimensions, so that he could prepare a place for their souls in the great Ocean outside the Keep.

Scintillating light flashed as Necral's mind probed down into the countless mirrors of the Eye, mirrors which turned their images inward to the room of bone. In each facet, men were dying, but one window on the dimensions attracted Necral's fullest attention and he focused upon the events in it avidly.

It was a world called Elotrine.

There had been a battle.

It had been no skirmish, but a great, surging tide of chaos. Thousands of armoured warriors had died, bloodying acres. Perhaps kings had fallen—even Gods. Smoke eddied in gusts over the battlefield, while gaunt scavenger birds winged noisily over the slaughtered. Bodies were heaped in mangled piles, heads gathered in grisly mounds. Blood had drenched this field of mortals where the mirthless Reaper, Death, had sated himself avariciously. In the distance a castle burned, streaming out black tatters of smoke, spangled with red embers. A few figures moved like ghouls amongst the many slain. These were the robbers of the dead, who came to every aftermath, stripping from tangled cadavers what riches they could find.

There were five of them, working in a group, and already their arms were ringed with purloined bands of gold, their belts hung with trinkets and jewels taken from the dead. These armies that had clashed and destroyed each other had been of great Houses, men of pride and substance, fighting for powerful monarchs, used to the plunder of priceless kingdoms. Well could they have afforded to go into battle bedecked in riches. But such riches could serve them no longer. They would go to the Skull Keep with nothing.

Those five unsavoury brigands came across a heap of

death-locked corpses and paused, using their bare feet to roll over the slain, noses wrinkling at the stench of death. One of the men smiled at what he saw.

"Here's a pretty sight! What d'you make of this, Gruul?" He pointed at the black-clad warrior he had exposed with his careless foot. The dead man was smeared in blood, his dark clothes clotted with it. The five bent over him hungrily like jackals preparing to feed.

"Mercenary, by his dress. Neither Poldarrian nor Vobandishek wears such black finery. What manner of fabric is this? Hoo! What jewels does he wear beneath his mesh of armour, eh? If he is a mercenary, I'll warrant there's a fat belt of gold!"

They cackled. A sword was drawn and its point hooked under the shirt of the fallen man. As the point thrust beyond the fabric, the man's eyes flickered open; the thieves gasped. "Alive!" cried one.

But his companion spat. "Nay, nay, Thorg, you are mistaken."

A grin spread quickly across the crooked features of the other and his companions chuckled at his meaning. The sword slipped deeper under the shirt of the reviving man, cutting down in a neat, precise incision. At least it would be a clean, painless death. The shirt frayed and fell apart, but there was no expression of pain in the open eyes, and more curious than that—there was no blood.

"Cut deeper, Aug," grinned Gruul. "It is you who are mistaken!"

Baffled, Aug pulled away the whole of the ripped garment. As he did so, he flung up his arm to shield his eyes from what lay beneath. He cried out and staggered back, blundering into his rough fellows, who cursed him obscenely. Gruul avoided the tumbling bodies and the yelping Aug to stare down at the victim. Where his chest should have been was a gaping hole, not a neat, gushing wound, but a black abyss that looked outwards like some cosmic window into the deep reaches of star-pocked space.

"Madness and chaos!" shrieked Gruul, lurching back.

Seeing this incomprehensible vision, the other men howled in confusion, turning and feverishly scrambling over the mounds of the dead in pell-mell flight.

The dazed man in black looked down at himself and saw the void: it seemed that he began to implode into it, collapsing within himself into a dizzy vortex of dreams.

All this Necral observed through the Eye of Horabis, musing in silence. He knew the fallen man: it was the immortal, the one who could not kill and who could not die as men died, for the Dark Gods had decreed it. He was the Voidal, and it was time for him to return once more to Skull Keep.

Necral turned from the Eye apprehensively, not eager to study the dark man further. Let the passage of this frightful harbinger be brief, so brief, he mused.

Out of the left eye socket of the gigantic skull fluttered a host of black shapes, their necks short and thick, their myopic eyes like huge, bulbous orbs, glowing with lambent green fire. Their bodies were squat but strong, their wings thick, flapping silently, ghosting them out over the Ocean of Souls as they carried their comatose burdens to the very portals of life at the edge of the many dimensions. These were the every-moving Sowers, bearers of the reborn, working tirelessly in clouds, replenishing the dying with the living.

On the sturdy back of one slumped a figure, a torpid man, dreaming the dazed sleep of one who is about to know again the mystery of rebirth. As the Sower swooped on into the darkness, guided by blind instinct, the man registered only passing images, dreams that would quickly be forgotten in his new life, for no one alive ever recalled Skull Keep. Death remained a mystery its Gods guarded jealously. Yet as the Sower crossed the Ocean of Souls, there were faint lights down upon its surface: it was there that the black Dead Fishers poled their long barges through the murk towards the mouth of the Keep, their way lit by the blue nimbus controlled by the Keeper, Necral.

In one of the flat barges was stretched out a single body, that of a man dressed entirely in black, a sword strapped at his side in an ebon scabbard. Usually the barges contained several dead each, but this barge contained only the dark man—each barge usually had but one Dead Fisher to pole it, but in this there were several of the hooded figures. And commonly the dead were naked—certainly no weapons ever came here. Perhaps it was these facts that netted the curiosity of the flying Sowers, or perhaps their interest had been seeded some other way. Several of the Sowers did drift down over the solemn scene, vaguely curious. Their minds were puny, geared to the perpetual task set them by Necral, but some flash of insight now made them aware of the uniqueness of the slow-moving barge of death.

The man on the back of the most daring Sower dreamed on, but the Sower came close enough to the barge bearing the dark man that several of the Dead Fishers waved it away with their dripping poles. The creature lurched in mid air and the dreaming man swung precariously from side to side. A sizzling bolt of blue energy zipped by the Sower, warning it off on its voyage and the creature's green orbs bulged even wider with terror. It shot upward; from its back tumbled the sleeping figure, plummeting into the darkness that was the Ocean of Souls.

None of the Dead Fishers had ever shown emotion, for they had no need of it in their grim, mechanical toil; yet now there was a sense of great urgency about them. An ageless pattern had been shattered as the falling body dropped out of sight beyond the blue nimbus of light. At once the Dead Fishers acted—they began to pole the barge urgently from its course, towards the spot where the body had disappeared. This event was unprecedented in the history of the Ocean and must quickly be rectified lest there were dire repercussions. Already such a corruption of the rhythm of Necral's domain would have to be reported.

The barge drifted on, its now anxious crew scouring the depths for the fallen man. Then a pale hand rose up like a gnarled branch. Arms reached out and fastened on to it. In moments the body was tugged up over the low rim of the barge and the man was dropped on the wet boards. Around him huddled the Dead Fishers, thankful for having secured him. Until they realised what had happened.

He was no longer ready for a new life. He lived again in the body that the Dead Fishers had taken to Skull Keep, the body in which he had died, victim of a murderer's knife. This could not be permitted.

The Dead Fishers stared upwards, looking for the Sower, sensing its flapping shape circling them like a desolate bird searching for lost young. It would have to return this man to the Keep.

When the man had hit the surface of the Ocean, he had found his dreams acutely emphasised. Gone was the lethargic vagueness, the lack of continuity. Everything had become clear, a joined sequence, ultimately reality. He was aware. Now, shaking droplets from his eyes, he peered at his bizarre surroundings, etched in pale blue light. He was on a flat boat, moving towards a distant mass that was shaped like a giant, sprawled in the darkness.

Impossible.

Around him the Dead Fishers gathered, highly nervous, realising that he was aware, another fact without precedent here. They sought to bring the Sower down so that it could carry away its burden and restore the order of things. The man looked down at the dark figure reclining in death. Its features were sharp, picked out morbidly by the garish light. They were familiar. Who was this being? Where was this place? What dimension of nightmare had swallowed them? Rough hands made to drag the man away, but he fought them instinctively. Somehow they meant harm, he was certain.

With a sudden twist, he wrenched a long pole from the hands of one of his assailants. Above him a black shape winged down like a huge bird of prey. He swung the pole and punctured a leathery wing: a tortured shriek followed and the thing plunged out of sight into darkness. Now the guardians of the barge were in a panic. They rushed upon the man, who they thought insane, but he attacked them with scything sweeps, battering them desperately aside. Bones crunched and robed bodies

doubled up in unaccustomed pain; the barge rocked danger-
ously. Completely unprepared for such a ferocious onslaught,
the Fishers were quickly beaten back, falling over the sides of
their barge into the waiting blackness. The man saw his advantage and was quick to follow up, crushing the skulls of the last
Fishers to resist him.

As his final victim flopped overboard, he put down the pole
and turned his attention to the corpse in the bottom of the
barge. He leaned over the dark man, whose eyes began to flicker
open. Their green depths made the features even more familiar. "I know you," said the dark man.

The other touched at his ears, as if they had been damaged,
mystified by something. "And—I know you."

"Where is this place?" said the first.

But the other shook his head. He pointed to the nearing
mass of Skull Keep.

The dark man rose on his elbows and looked at the huge,
prone body. He nodded. "I have been here before, though it
may only have been in a dream."

The other frowned in agreement. "This may be a dream,
too, for there is much mystery about this place. Shall we investigate?" he grinned.

"I think we have no choice."

And so the barge drifted on, now poled by the man who
had fallen from the sky. For some reason he kept touching his
ears, as though they would fall away from his head.

As they drew nearer the floating mass, always watching for
signs of an attack either from the Ocean or from above, the dark
man tried to recall where it was that he had met his companion
before. Something about the man's preoccupation with his ears
was the clue, for there was a significance in it that he did not
understand. The other poled on silently, watching the amazing
Keep, the dead husk of a giant, who must have belonged to a
race of superhumans. From its eye sockets the two men could
now see the twin clouds of Sowers, constantly going out into
the ink of the heavens.

"By all the Gods, this is a dismal realm," murmured the
dark man. "What manner of being is that before us? I feel I

know it, but my mind is hazy." As he spoke he could faintly discern other barges—they all plied a path through the impenetrable murk of the waters to the gaping mouth of the dead giant, where broken-toothed portals awaited them. It would not be wise to enter, for they would immediately be discovered and possibly attacked. The dark man pointed way off to the long arms of the dead being. "There," he said. "Let us make for the hand. I see no life there. We need time to plan carefully."

The other nodded, studying the solid forms of the twisted, lifeless fingers beyond. He began to pole away from Skull Keep and drifted along the towering walls that were the body of the dead giant. Across darkness the barge slipped in absolute silence.

Eventually it came under the shadow of those colossal fingers, nestling in the space between them, out of sight, hidden in the chasm from the watchful eyes of anything that might fly overhead, or from the beings in the other black barges drifting over the lake of black glass. The two men moored the barge deep between the massive fingers, waiting to see if they had been pursued, but they had not.

The dark man looked across at his companion, realising that the latter had been studying him closely. "You say you know me?"

Momentarily the other's eyes lit up. He nodded, his lips framing one word, clearly and distinctly. "Voidal."

The dark man echoed the word, frowning. But then a gate in his memory creaked open and in that shadowed place, shards of recollection gleamed. "Voidal!" he exclaimed. "Yes, I recall. The Dark Gods would still keep the truth from me." He was nodding, lost in a sudden deep reverie.

His companion's eyes were fixed on him. "Once you helped me." His words were a little slow and ponderous, as though he was not used to speaking. "I had become the prisoner of a particularly pernicious creature. But I invoked your name and you came to free me and those who were incarcerated. But my freedom had a price." He tapped his ears grimly.

The dark man looked puzzled. "Your ears—"

"My hearing. I was made deaf. And yet here, in this unwholesome realm, I can hear once more! I am glad enough of that, though I wonder what price I must pay for such a miraculous restoration. Is this your doing? You told me we would meet again, but it amuses the Gods to toy with me."

The Voidal nodded. "You are not alone in that."

"It is strange," mused the other thoughtfully. "I seem to recall my life almost as a series of dreams. I am a Songster by profession. I possessed the most beautiful instrument, Layola. She was my love, my inspiration, trapped within that living frame. Priceless to me, and sadly of much value to other, greedy thieves. When I lost the use of my ears, I could no longer hear the loving voice of Layola. I knew despair then, and I sank myself into its pit. I could not sing as I had, I could not make a living. My life became a weary trudge from one tavern to another, each dive more despicable than the last.

"Envious eyes watched me, my Layola. One night, drunk to the point of insensibility, I slumped in an alley. The thieves found me and took my Layola. Something in my sodden brain stirred: I struggled, and for my pains got a knife between my ribs—" He winced as if he could still feel the pain.

The Voidal saw the look of surprise on the Songster's face.

"But—I died! My life leaked out of me as I watched the murderers flee with my Layola—"

"That's why you are here," said the dark man.

The Songster looked down at himself, studied the place where the knife had entered him. "Repaired, though there is a long scar. Then, did I live?"

"These are not dreams," said the Voidal. "I will show you something. Come with me." He gestured for the other to follow, then began clambering up the difficult surface of dried flesh that still clung to the hulk of the dead god. Up the wrinkled ridges of a petrified finger the two men went until they had reached the highest joint. There, clinging to tufts of dried hair, they watched the weird processions to and from the Keep.

The Voidal pointed to the sombre barges, their cargoes of naked dead.

"They are all dead," said the Songster.

The Voidal pointed up at the winged shapes. "Living souls, as you are."

148

"Living! The dead come here to be—restored?"

The Voidal nodded. "I recall the place now. It is the Ocean of Souls, known to us only in dreams."

"Then the murderer's knife did kill me. And I was being borne away to a new life—"

"While I was to be cast out into the omniverse once more by the Dark Gods. Your unwitting intervention has broken their grip on my destiny. Yet for how long? They will snatch it back." He lifted his gloved right hand and stared at it hatefully. "For the moment it is lifeless. But here, in this void of death and rebirth, perhaps I can use it for my own ends."

The Songster drew back in horror.

"It will not harm you," said the Voidal. "Ironically it may yet be the boon of us both."

"But where must we go? How are we to escape? Can that hand shatter the walls of this world and set us adrift on more familiar seas?"

"I think not. If we are to escape this realm, we will need the aid of the Keeper, Necral. Here he is omnipotent. We will have to go to him. Somehow we must wrest from him the secret of the exits. By force, by guile, by trickery. Somehow we must use him!"

Glumly the other studied the lines of the remarkable Keep.

"We must find a way in and reach Necral before he discovers us," said the Voidal.

"Your sword—the Sword of Silence—"

But the dark man shook his head slowly. "No, this is not the weapon that stole your hearing, Grabulic."

"Ah, you recall my name."

The Voidal looked up, suddenly more alert. "Yes! My memory has been so poor, so fractured, and yet there are things I recall. Dreamwarp! The rogue Island—it restored something of me. The Dark Gods have not erased it."

"What about the sword? Will it help us?"

"Its powers are not for use against dead flesh."

"I see," muttered Grabulic, disappointed.

"Grabulic, you were being taken away to a new life, in a new form. You have no quarrel with the powers here. Return to the barges—take the one we stole—and you will yet be placed in the omniverse where you belong. You'll recall nothing of this. I make no demands on you. Once I freed you—now you have helped me. The debt is paid."

Slowly the Songster shook his head. "If I am reborn in some other form, it will be without my Layola. The Gods will keep her from me. I—I need your help to find her. I don't care what it costs me."

The Voidal smiled grimly. "There's much of mine that I'd take back from them. Together, then, though you risk everything."

"So be it."

They began the difficult trek over the titanic corpse. It soon became evident that they had underestimated its sheer size and extent, for they had gone along steadily for what appeared to be several miles, yet had made no real progress. The hide was thick, pale and tufted with coarse hair, matted in places that made progress difficult. On and on it stretched, this repellent landscape, with no sign of variation or ingress. Yet the two men did not complain, keeping up a slow, dogged pace.

Eventually they saw movement ahead and shielded themselves behind a ridge of flesh. From this point of concealment they were able to look down into a steep declivity and see clearly what transpired there. Both were stunned. The landscape of the body had been altered unnaturally. It had been quarried. Below, a strange, pale-skinned group had gathered amongst the workings. They were stunted, man-like beings, remarkably thin and stick-like. Their hands ended in clawed talons, their feet curled in a prehensile fashion. Some of them squatted on their haunches, while the bulk of the party began to attack the flesh of the Keep. They needed no tools.

"What are these?" murmured Grabulic, but that much soon became evident. They were feeding on the rotting flesh of the dead giant; their cruel claws ripping off chunks of it in strips and cramming it into mouths filled with pointed teeth. Already they had excavated a deep hole in the centre of the workings, evidently the work of many, many attacks. The Voidal scowled, searching his mind for a clue to their history. He could find none, but his face evinced a rare smile as he turned to his companion.

"Here may lie our means of entry. Fate favours us. Come, prepare for a dispute, for I doubt that they'll allow us entry without a fight."

Grabulic had retained the long pole from the barge and as the Voidal leapt up from concealment and slipped silently down the slope, he followed him, intent on giving a good account of himself. They were upon the feasting horrors before the latter realised. Steel sang as the Voidal drew from its ebon scabbard his sword, though it seemed no more than an ordinary length of steel in this dismal region. He took up a belligerent stance and at once the creatures cowered back.

"What are you about?" the dark man challenged.

One of them crept forward hesitantly, its mirthless features twisting pathetically as it whined at him. "No harm, master, no harm. We are the grovellers. We do but tend the flesh of the Keep that has been preserved by Necral. It is our lot to keep it in a semblance of health."

"How—by eating it!" laughed the dark man.

"We do but take what sustenance is allowed us, no more."

The Voidal drew nearer to the gaping wound that they had inflicted. "You have cut deep. This can do the Keep no good. The Keeper will not be pleased."

Their bloodshot eyes squinted in terror of the blade and he saw their shaking fear. Grabulic swung his pole so that it whooshed through the air ominously, deterring any potential attack. "What is your name?" the Voidal challenged the leader.

"I am Larg the low-born."

"We are the vassals of Necral," the Voidal told him. "Nothing escapes the Keeper." He motioned for Grabulic to inspect the wound's darkness and depth. The latter nodded and climbed down into the workings.

"What will you do with us?" said Larg nervously. "We are too useful to be destroyed."

"You should be punished," said the Voidal. "It is for Necral to decide."

They began gibbering, hopping about like frightened children. Larg looked sheepishly at the huge wound. "Spare us, masters! We are worthless and harmless. We did but steal a few morsels of flesh."

The Voidal ignored him as Grabulic emerged from the wound. "Is it deep?" he asked him.

Grabulic climbed out. "Deep?" he laughed. "Why, there is an entire system of elaborate honeycombs within! How far it extends I could not even begin to guess."

The grovellers began to mutter in anguish. Evidently this was an unqualified breach of whatever contract they had with the Keeper. The Voidal smiled. "I see—a few morsels. Tell me, where do these tunnels lead?" He made a suggestive movement with the sword.

Larg looked pained. "But a short distance, sirs. They are necessary—to the good of the Keep. They—ventilate the aged skin. They are mere burrows in which we shelter ourselves. The Keeper would not dispute it."

Grabulic shook his head and the dark man again made a pass with his sword. "I think not, Larg. I think perhaps these tunnels go much further. Like worms in a tree, you have burrowed far and wide—no doubt throughout the entire Keep! Is it not so?"

None of the creatures answered and the Voidal knew that he had struck the mark with his guess. Larg shuffled closer to him, eyes fixed upon the cold sword. There was a gleam of distinct cunning in his eyes. "A word with you, warrior," he whispered.

"Speak."

"Our secret is out, but it is nothing, a mere item of no import. I have other knowledge that would be more useful to you. It would give you more power than you have."

The Voidal's face remained grave. "Yes?"

"I will not yield it freely."

"I see. You wish to barter this knowledge for my silence in the matter of the labyrinths?"

"You are a reader of minds!" nodded Larg with the gruesome semblance of a smile.

"Your mind would be open to the wind. Well?"

"Do we have a bargain?"

"Perhaps. But you will have to provide me with more than a promise if I am to dismiss what I have discovered."

"Very well," grunted Larg. "I will show you." With that he stepped to the mouth of the wound. "Follow if you will."

The Voidal obeyed, dropping down to the floor of the tunnel, Grabulic behind him, grinning in spite of the gruesome surroundings. The smell of corruption here was thick. Larg began the journey down the cramped tunnel, while behind the two men the rest of the grovellers followed. Down into the rotting flesh of the Keep they went, the tunnels twisting and turning like dried up artificial veins, intersecting and crossing at steep angles. The entire body must have been riddled, as if by maggots. The flesh was desiccated, flaking and crumbling. One by one the grovellers dispersed, taking different tunnels until only Larg remained to lead the way.

They had been travelling endlessly, through what must have been the excavation of centuries, when Larg came to an abrupt halt in the stifling darkness. Only his eyes lit the pitch air.

"We near the place. Even the Keeper has no knowledge of our passage so close to his sanctuaries in the Keep."

"Necral sees all," ventured the Voidal.

Larg snorted derisively. "All, warrior? You have seen the inside of this place, rotting and decomposing. The Keeper is just as raddled, or has he kept that from you?"

The Voidal said nothing, though he mused on the information.

"The place I will show you is most hallowed. Only the Keeper knows of it, save Larg and his grovellers. We have not shared our knowledge, knowing that one day it would be a useful weapon."

"I see," nodded the Voidal. "And that day has come?"

"Look beyond," said Larg, pointing to a narrow slit in the wall through which a shaft of light arrowed.

The Voidal stooped to press his eye to the vent. He drew in his breath at what he saw, motioning Grabulic to look, which he did. He, too, gasped involuntarily.

There was a large chamber there, hollowed out of the body of the giant as if some huge internal organ had been removed; the walls were slick, tinted red as though the flesh still pulsed with life. Veins stood out like blue pillars. But it was not the structure of the chamber that had caused the Voidal and Grabulic to gasp—it was the things within it. For here in choked abundance there were frightful creatures that had the appearance of hybrids, as though men and non-men had been crossbred and mutated to produce the most outlandish of beings. Their outer characteristics were hideously exaggerated, and as the two men looked in at them, they saw that they were all female. Some were lovely of body, but had sub-human faces, others' bodies were wildly grotesque but had beautiful faces; still more were unspeakably horrific. All were chained, some linked to the walls of the chamber by membranous filaments, flowing through which was a familiar crimson fluid. Sizes varied—there were dwarfish, squat-faced beings and tall, gangling spiderish things. Some there were that crawled in dark corners, away from the pulsing mass of bodies near the light.

"What anteroom of hell is this!" cried Grabulic.

Larg sniggered unpleasantly. "Hell, master? There is no hell here. This is the Keep that rules over the Ocean of Souls. There may be other Gods with their places of paradise and their hells, but not here."

The Voidal scowled down at the scrawny figure. "This is the work of Necral?"

"It is. I told you—his mind is as debased as his rotting Keep. This is a place he puts aside for his private, uninterrupted amusement."

"Then he has indeed created a hell for those unfortunates. Who are they?"

"Hybrids. Bred from souls that he has secretly culled from the Ocean. He tortures them and moulds them for pleasure, then discards them when they displease or bore him."

"Discards them?" echoed the Voidal. "He returns them to the Ocean of Souls?"

"Nay. There is a place, deep down in the frozen entrails of the Keep. There, among mouldering bones, the discarded ones are tossed, too crippled to complain. They soon reach their own oblivion."

Grabulic grunted in horror and the Voidal's thoughts clouded as he turned away from what he had seen.

"If you wait long enough," said Larg, "Necral himself will materialise beyond in one of his many forms. Then you shall see him sport with his countless toys."

"We have seen enough," growled the Voidal. "Lead us to a place where we can enter the halls of the Keep."

Larg hesitated. "And our bargain, master? Will you say nothing of our tunnels?"

The Voidal nodded. "Aye, nothing. Go back to your gluttony."

Larg snickered in satisfaction and began leading the two men out of the tunnels. He came to a long flap of loose skin—a broken valve—and lifted an edge of it. The mouth of a disused organ, it led into the inner chambers of the Keep. "Here we must part," said the groveller.

"Come on," said the Voidal to Grabulic, and they slipped out of the dark and to the edge of a huge chamber that had a ribbed ceiling far overhead. Its arches were made of bone, yards thick, and from them hung vats of ignited blubber drained from the very walls. There were no columns here, only more ribbed bones ten times thicker than a man supporting the place, a gigantic stomach. They had gone but a few steps when they saw that they were standing on a ridge which was an extended artery, a black pipe leading into one of the walls. Below them, working in the glow of the blubber lights, were scores of beings, diligently buzzing around line upon line of naked cadavers that stretched out into the far reaches of the great hall. These workers were Necral's Revivers, who prepared the dead souls for rebirth. Countless numbers of the naked bodies were being partially reanimated and led away gently to openings in the sides of the chamber, other dried veins that led away like drains. The reborn ones slid down these to other halls, ultimately to be removed from the Keep by the Sowers.

"Do you have a plan?" said Grabulic.

"Necral has committed a grave error in creating that foul place we saw. He has compromised himself. We must find him and confront him."

"But surely he will submit us to a similar, dreadful fate if we reveal what we know!"

"I think not. Come." The Voidal led the way along the great artery and on through a tunnel that led off from the immense chamber of the dead. They found yet another open vein that served as an upward tunnel, moving along the internal passageways of the Keep. "We must be in the skull itself. Perhaps Necral already knows we are here." Grabulic did not share his calmness.

Suddenly there was movement around them, which came from all sides. From up out of the floor burst shadows, and from out of the walls came others, rupturing the flesh heedlessly in their desire to ring the two men. Both stood still, weapons poised. They saw now what it was that confronted them. They were rotting dead men, flesh peeling from them, eyes white, hands no more than clawed bone. A festering stench wafted from them as though they had been vomited up from some remote charnel pit. Their vile bodies closed in, arms reaching out, but they did not press home their attack.

"They have not come to destroy us," said the Voidal. "These are Necral's creatures and will save us a further search. They will take us to him."

"Then he knows of our intrusion."

"Yes, but I wonder how long he has watched us."

Goaded on by the shambling zombies, the two men moved ahead as directed in silence, again travelling the dim passageways of the Keep. Ever upward they were herded, until at last they passed through a constricted tunnel that led like a throat into halls of pure bone. Here they debouched into a vast room, where a few blubber cressets sputtered like haunted eyes. before them was a pit that seemed to drop down into an infinity beyond reality. Around its far edges they could see line upon line of the zombie creatures, all motionless, awaiting their commands.

Presently total darkness descended as every one of the

winking lights snuffed out. The two men were walled in a black chasm that pressed in on them menacingly. A deep voice came across at them from somewhere beyond.

"Behold, the two men who seek to cheat the Gods and avoid the eternal chain of life and death!" it mocked.

As the echoes died away, the Voidal spoke, his voice ringing out over the unfathomable pit. "Keeper! Show yourself! We do not fear you, nor your reprisals."

A brief silence greeted this, but at last came a bubble of laughter, rising and swelling. Light seeped back into the chamber. Beyond, across the chasm, was a massive head, cloaked in a black hood, all features hidden. But neither the size nor covering of that head caught the eye, as did the mass of writhing evil about it. Congesting the darkness were innumerable demon-like beings, fawning and squirming about the robed figure, depraved, lunatic acolytes of the master of the dead.

"The Gods are not mocked, nor is your arrogance more than a passing breeze to us!" laughed the hooded being.

"Then listen well, Keeper of the dead!"

More laughter rocked the cavern. "Very well. If I am to hear you, I shall. Then I will place you once more in your cycle."

"You know me, Keeper."

"Yes. *Voidal*, sometimes called Fatecaster. Long have the Dark Gods used you. Did you think to outwit them by escaping your cycle of lives?"

The Voidal was impassive, but Grabulic could sense him thinking.

"You have stepped off the path of your predetermined destiny," said Necral, "but the track you follow will only lead you back to your preordained path."

"Not if you set me upon some other course."

"I? Do you think I would go against the decrees of the Dark Gods? In my own right, I am also a god, yet there are limits to what I would take upon myself!"

"Within this realm you are omnipotent," said the Voidal.

"Indeed."

"In this realm, you create the laws."

"Within the bounds set me, that is so. But the boundaries, the properties of the Ocean of Souls, they are my limits."

"And Skull Keep?"

There was a momentary silence. The hooded head moved in the darkness. "Skull Keep serves an eternal function, one which I perpetuate. It also has its rigid laws."

"Yet you are able to introduce new laws, set new precedents here."

This remark seemed to disturb Necral. "As a god, I have some powers!"

"You mould the destinies of all who pass through Skull Keep."

At this the Keeper laughed. "Do I? No, Fatecaster, not all. Even I must obey the word of others: why, my own fate is not my own. You will ask again that I re-shape your fate—destroy what has been woven for you by the Dark Gods and design you a new one. But I cannot. What I do, they will undo if it displeases them. And if I should disobey them, what would be the price of my folly? I would not ponder such a fate!"

"Will you not at least show me my destiny?"

Again the Keeper laughed, mockingly. "Show you! Even if I knew it, why should I reveal it to you?"

"I think you do know it. You know a great deal about me. And before I leave this place, I mean to share in that knowledge."

Necral laughed convulsively, while the things that squirmed about him chittered and hissed along with him. "Are you threatening me? You are nothing!"

"No threat, Keeper, no. But I will strike up a bargain."

Necral's laughter continued, but was not now so mocking. "Bargain? But you have nothing that I desire. Not unless you can trade the secret of your destiny for my own!" Again the terrible laugh.

"Perhaps I hold a key to that," said the Voidal calmly.

Silence smothered him at once, and beside him Grabulic shook visibly with panic. Within Necral's black hood, twin orbs blazed briefly, red stars ablaze in some hellish outer dimension. "Don't toy with me, Fatecaster! Speak openly. What do you mean?"

"I have said that you are able to create your own laws in this realm. Further—I have witnessed the application of these powers."

"Where? What have you seen? There is nothing in Skull Keep but the endless rituals of the dead."

"Rituals which a god such as yourself must find intolerably tedious and monotonous, Necral," nodded the Voidal.

"What do you mean?"

"Surely you must have sought ways to alleviate such boredom? Surely you have created pastimes, games, unique circumstances with which to stimulate yourself in your endless sojourn in this dismal place?"

Necral's fire-eyes gleamed wickedly. "What have you seen?"

"I have seen your private hell, Necral. Its images are burned upon my mind. When I pass from this place to my next life, those images will go with me, just as I must carry—this." He drew from his cloak his right hand and held it aloft, balled into a leather-gloved fist.

Necral emitted a strange sound that may have been a gasp or a groan. "Cover that abomination!" he cried.

"You know it?"

"Of course! Cover it I say! You have no power over it!"

"You fear that it may point to your own heart?"

"Cover it!" snarled the Keeper and the things about him surged forward like hounds on taut leashes.

The Voidal did as asked. "Very well. As you say, I cannot control its whims. It is not my own hand—"

"What have you seen in this Keep?" persisted Necral.

"Your chamber of horrors filled with creatures that were once women, now condemned to a vile fate to satiate your macabre appetite."

The hood nodded slowly, resignedly. "As I feared. But— how did you come upon that place? By chance, or were you guided by some force?" There was a cold fear in the Keeper's tone now.

"It seemed to be chance," replied the Voidal enigmatically. "But remember that the images of what I saw will remain with me. Although my memory is blighted, you shall not wipe that away."

Necral considered this, fearing the intervention of powers greater than those of the Voidal, or of himself. "What do you want of me? Be warned—do not ask for control of your destiny. It was never mine to give you."

It was the Voidal's turn to weigh his thoughts and for a while he was silent. At length he spoke. "I am no more than a means to an end, a vessel. This hand that curses and despatches doom is not mine to control. Tell me, Keeper, who am I? What have I done? How am I to reclaim my soul, my destiny?"

"You ask much. I cannot answer it all."

"Satisfy me or I shall betray you to those who control us both!" said the dark man, anger rising in him.

"You understand nothing! Power is relative, you fool! Even gods have their limitations."

"Then answer those questions that you can."

Necral sighed heavily. "I cannot divulge the nature of your crime. Only the Dark Gods can tell you that. But there are laws that govern your punishment. Your identity is bound up with your crime. The Dark Gods have decreed that you must atone for your sins by wandering the omniverse, bringing doom to those who displease them, for they have many enemies, including certain Gods. The hand you carry, the Oblivion Hand, has greater powers than either of us could comprehend. You are able to carry it secretly between the dimensions, where the Dark Gods cannot go without detection. You seem to be mortal, so Gods do not fear you, but you are everlasting. You think your wandering is erratic, but each step is part of a vast plan. One day you will have done enough to atone for your crime. Only then will you be released. Perhaps then you will learn what it was you did."

The Voidal listened in silence, as did the fascinated Grabulic.

"You also carry a sword of a peculiar nature. It is cursed with strange properties."

The Voidal indicated the shivering Songster. "It was because of the sword that my companion lost his hearing. It was a cruel fate, the more so if in all his future lives he is destined to be deaf."

"The Sword of Silence rendered him deaf as a punishment."

"Why?"

"Who aids the Voidal, hinders the Dark Gods. This man summoned you, invoking your aid to free himself and others from a world of nightmare, where he had been set as punishment for his scorn of certain Gods. Grabulic, in fact, mocked all gods through his songs. His gift was his voice, for he sang as few men have ever sung. But he chose to use it indiscreetly."

"How long is his punishment to last?"

"What is time?"

"I will not have his pain on my conscience."

"Hah! It was not your doing. The Dark Gods decreed it."

"Nevertheless, I want him freed of their curse. Send him back to life with his hearing restored. Let him always be Grabulic, and let him sing as he once did."

"So you demand even more of me?" growled the Keeper.

"Since you cannot answer all my questions, grant these other things."

"Very well."

The Voidal ignored Grabulic's indrawn breath of shock. "You were speaking of the sword, Keeper. Well?"

"It is one of thirteen, one for each of the Dark Gods. Each sword has an individual property. You always bear one of them. They are as much a key to the power of the Dark Gods as that accursed hand. Find the being that forged them. He will tell you more than I can."

"Find him? Where? Where is his lair?"

"I know only his name, which is Thunderhammer. He it is who has also forged a prison for your soul."

The Voidal spoke the name softly, several times. "I will not forget it."

"There is one other thing I can give you. I see that some of your memory has repaired itself. I can strengthen that, in exchange for the memory of what you have seen in Skull Keep. I will also open the gates of your memory on other times and events. And you shall see Grabulic restored. He shall hear again and he will ever be Grabulic. Perhaps this will help him to be more diplomatic in future?"

Grabulic's mouth was too dry for him to answer, but the Voidal spoke for him. "I accept your terms."

"I would rather you left without the images of what you have seen here."

"So would I. Seal the bargain."

"You may not like what you learn, Voidal."

"Even so, I would look back at my recent past."

"Then go to a chamber of rest. You will dream for a while. After that you will be returned to the many dimensions, to follow the path laid for you by the Dark Gods."

Dreams.

Fashioned by the Keeper. Some were fragments of memory, some the tortured convulsions of the dark man's own mind. The distinctions were not always obvious: Necral was secretive, devious. But the Voidal saw the interwoven threads of fate, time and the many dimensions, spun in an apparently chaotic pattern, though whatever messages were written in the fabric of creation were understood by the eyes of the Dark Gods alone. To share their cosmic workings, to have it all mapped out clearly, would have brought madness rushing in.

Flashing through this tapestry of time and space, the dreaming mind of the Voidal fastened on images brought into focus before it by the manipulations of the Keeper. Past lives, future ones, worlds, some to be born, others long dead, heaved and span. Cascading showers of molten stars burst across his inner eye. Single embers curled across space and he saw down to their depths, to the races and cities that infested them like bacteria.

Conflict dominated the shards of dream and memory. Sometimes single conflict, as men fought bitterly with bare fists, sometimes swords. Armies marched; towers fell in roaring flames, swept over by human tides that quenched the infernos of blazing worlds. Gods roared defiance at each other across immeasurable gulfs, while down in the rotting cores of worlds, others crawled, hiding from even the light of dead stars.

Death, deterioration and regeneration. The cycle went on infinitely. Life pulsed in waves throughout the omniverse, drawing in and thrusting out, ebbing and flowing, the Gods its titanic moon, directing the tides. Whatever mighty purpose they intended for it all was hidden by the vastness of the canvas upon which they worked. The Voidal caught only glimpses of colour and movement, his own place in the scheme of eternity masked.He saw himself stumbling along a broken path of destiny, drawn from one dimension to another by the beings that invoked him. Always he had to obey their summons, always to discharge the debt of the summoners. Death walked behind him, and only when they met could he move on. But would it end, or was it a circle?

Always he saw himself in darkness, so many facets of himself hidden from him. So much had been stolen.

Another dream focused on the face of a woman. Gaunt, eyes ringed with shadow, face drawn, pale, so pale. Briefly it flickered across his vision, lit by a dim moon. Then gone again. But the seed of memory was planted. She was part of him, but what?

A final image. Revealed as if by the rays cast by a dying candle. It was a mountain—black, colossal and sombre, guarded by demons that were amassed like flies over its rubble. From near its peak came the glow of a huge fire. Sounds echoed downwards—the sounds of a mighty smithy, forging some glinting blade for the gods themselves. Thunderhammer. The Voidal would remember him, and his mountain. When his journey brought him to it, he would know it.

"Wake, Voidal!"

Through heavy lids the dark man looked up into what he thought must be another dream. But he knew at once that it was not.

Grabulic the Songster was looking down at him. "It's over," he said.

The Voidal shook himself and rose from his cold bed of stone. They were in a small chamber of bone. "The dreams—"

"They are over."

"And you?"

"Oh, I have had my share, too. It seems the Keeper has kept the whole of his bargain with you. I remain as I was, though I still bear the scar of the murderer's knife. But my hearing! I hear every sound, every breath that is taken in this place of death. Every breath! The power alarms me—I hear the coming of something dark and damned. I am to be winged away very soon, and I am glad of it."

"You have atoned for your sins, Grabulic. And I have discharged my debt to you."

"Indeed you have. And done more. You recall the beautiful musical instrument—"

"Layola. Aye, and what she was before."

Grabulic's eyes lit up. "I shall begin the quest to recover her. I will find her, I swear it."

The Voidal smiled, for the man appeared to be fully restored, his audacity, his cunning, his wit, they all shone from those revitalised eyes. And the sadness, the sense of deep loss.

"You will find her," the Voidal said. "And perhaps restore her."

"I will never despair of that, not now," Grabulic smiled.

There was a sound near the doorway and he turned. "Ah, this must be my very escort. Well, I must away. Once you chose to call me friend, Voidal, and for that we have both suffered." He looked down at the dark man's right hand. Suddenly his voice was fused with anxiety. "No matter what the darkness decrees, I hope we shall remain friends."

"Our paths will cross again," said the Voidal. "At least, it is my will."

"Until then," smiled the Songster.

"Find your beautiful Layola," the Voidal told him and with no more ado, the Songster exited with the shades that had come for him.

For a time the Voidal was alone in the near dark. He reflected on what he had dreamed. Uppermost in his mind was the woman. Who could she be? His wife, his mistress, his kin? He knew that his destiny had set him apart, yet he must find her. In her would be strength. And the mountain, where Thunderhammer laboured for the Gods at his forge. Yes, the Voidal would know that place.

Sorrow taunted him now, for the woman's face haunted

him. Now that he had seen her, there would be pain until he found her. His burden, his enforced fate, had been wearying, frustrating, but the price for his repaired memory was a fresh misery.

Somewhere the Dark Gods were laughing.

A flutter of wings brought him from a deep reverie that had verged on another dream. Something lurched beneath him, sharpening his awareness. Around him was darkness. From below him came the whispering sound of a sea, and he stared down to see the Ocean of Souls skimming by like black glass. On its surface the barges drifted by occasionally, still-life figures. The dark man rode upon the back of a Sower: it took him away to rebirth somewhere ahead in oblivion. He felt sleep of a sort drizzling over him, but the sound of the fluttering wings was broken by a laugh near at hand. Gazing across the void, he saw another winged creature flap from out of the dark. Upon its back sat a hooded figure, its face hidden.

"I trust your dreams were wrapped in revived memories, Voidal," came Necral's voice from the hood. "Our bargain is done. I thought it would be prudent to accompany you out of my realm myself."

"What of the Songster?"

"It is as you wished. He is already awake somewhere in Phaedrabile. He will be content—for a while. As long as he is mindful of his tongue, he will not be troubled by the gods."

"And where am I to be cast?"

"I have not been told. You must obey the laws of the weird cast for you. There may have been hints in your dreams."

"Perhaps."

"So, what of me?"

The Voidal looked cold, pitiless, almost as if another creature looked through his eyes. Slowly he drew from his cloak his right hand, a mechanical motion, drugged.

The scarlet eyes in the hood of the Keeper blazed in terror. "What! You have deceived me!"

"No," answered the Voidal in a strange voice. "You have deceived yourself." He turned and pointed back at the gigantic body of Skull Keep.

Necral watched that dreadful pointing finger, but it did not turn to him. In a moment the hand was again drawn out of sight.

"I had many dreams," the dark man told him. "In one of them I saw a cycle of demi-gods as it revolved endlessly. Some of the demi-gods perished and were replaced, each one serving a time at a task allotted by other, greater Gods. Yonder, in the form of Skull Keep, lies the dead husk of the demi-god, Chandrehozer, who was once the Keeper of the halls of the quick and the dead, as you are now. In his ageless sojourn as Keeper, he sinned many times, using the dormant souls for his amusement. For this he was punished; he was made sterile, caused to decompose slowly; there he lies, eaten away by the things that burrow secretly inside him. He has reached the end of his cycle, for corruption and decay have raddled him utterly. See!"

Necral looked at Skull Keep in horror. The hands of the dead giant twitched, and as they did so, their flesh began to crumble into dust. Other parts of the huge body were turning to flakes and sloughing away. Huge cracks appeared over the pale mountain of chest and in the bleached skull.

"But—the Keep!" cried Necral. "The halls of the quick and the dead! They are indispensable—what is to become of them?"

"Others greater than I have decided their fate," said the Voidal. "They will be rehoused."

Necral, stunned, fell silent, but then let out a cry of sheer terror. "What are you saying?" But as he spoke, his shape began its own transformation, his body bloating like a gigantic maggot, squirming as its folds of fat bulged, shredding its flimsy garments. The hood fell away to reveal a blotched, bulbous head that must have been conceived in the wildest nightmare of a lunatic. Pocked and scarred with weeping sores, the product of Necral's disgusting excesses in his anteroom of hell, it began to run with hissing slime.

"You are the new Keep," said the Voidal dispassionately.

"Treachery!" came the scream from lips that were already melting and slithering down the rotting chin. "Your memory—I cleaned away what you saw in my dungeons in exchange for your past! Yet you have retained everything and cheated me! I demand justice! The Gods will not cheat me!"

The Voidal shook his head. "I recall only those things you showed me in dreams. I remember nothing about your dungeons."

Necral's head had become an amorphous mass, its dripping filth beginning to dissipate in wispy clouds. The Voidal emitted a hollow laugh that seemed to fill the realm of night with stentorian contempt.

"Then why am I punished—just as Chandrehozer before me was punished?" shrieked the fading voice of Necral.

"Those who aid the Voidal hinder the Dark Gods, just as you, yourself, told me! I am the Voidal, their pawn. Neither man nor god may succour me! To do so is to invoke their wrath. I am used. You should know this, Necral. Your slide into a pit of self-centred madness has rotted away your own caution. You have forfeited your right to be lord of the dead."

As Necral screamed out his final anguish, the last of the old Skull Keep began to collapse into dust clouds. Countless figures drifted away from the debris like fleas leaving the dead. Necral, now grown monstrous, blotting out the darkness, began to drift into the cloud of dust that was all that remained of Chandrehozer. The head of the Keeper had become a hideous mask of bone, a white skull, devoid of flesh or corruption. Necral's leprous body, thick with layers of fat, was finally hidden from view in the ensuing storm as the former Keep disintegrated.

The Voidal was carried on inexorably over the Ocean of Souls. When he at last looked back, it was to see a remote corpse floating in darkness. Necral had become Skull Keep, and if there was a new Keeper there, he neither spoke nor made himself manifest to the dark man. As the Voidal watched, the countless shapes that were the grovellers began to wing in to the new, fleshy body, eager to satiate their renewed hunger.

Sleep now began to exert an iron influence and the eyes of the Voidal became heavy with new dreams.

The Dark Gods had tricked him once more, for none of what had transpired in Necral's realm had been his own doing: he had been used to instigate Necral's downfall. Now he must go back into the omniverse and tread his weary path anew, at their whim. And yet, they had permitted him to take something back from them. New memories, new clues: the woman, the smith. And Grabulic had been made whole again.

Perhaps, the dark man mused, he had partially atoned for his crime. One day he would learn all of it. Then it would be time to think of revenge. But not yet, not when the Dark Gods could add it to his list of sins and use it against him, prolonging his restless wandering.

VII

ASTRAL STRAY

Coincidence is a state of mind. It is the Gods' way of obscuring destiny.
If, as some would have it, fate is woven by servants of the Gods,
Cloudway must be one of the many looms on which they work.
And Cloudway could be mistaken for the very crossroads of coincidence.

—Salecco—Philosopher, Sage, Exile

Threaded through the many dimensions of the omniverse like a wisp of silk runs the astral real; its own dimensions are as nebulous as mist, often no more substantial than dreams, though the Gods know its swirls and eddies well enough. Here in a shadow region dart flickers of light, swift as thought, entities that linger only briefly as they utilise the astral, moving between dimensions or across them. Most astral dwellers have masters and are linked to them by unseen strands of power, although there are some that move rudderless and blind in a sluggish drift, afloat on a seemingly mindless destiny. Imps carry the spells of sorcerers, ghosts bear the messages of the dead, while elementals are at the beck and call of those earthly beings powerful enough to control their turbulent natures. Familiars often pass through the astral realm, those creatures of witches, warlocks and other wielders of dark power who ever seek to gain more. It is said of these familiars that without a master they are as a man without a soul, or a warrior with no sword, or a dragon without fire. Of those familiars whose masters have perished in some calamity or twist of fate, there are a few, and for them the astral provides a haven, albeit a temporary one, for without a master their lives ooze from them as wine from a cracked pitcher.

lfloq spread his delicate wings, preparing for a last upward sweep before drifting down to rest on the interminable vastness of the astral that loomed out of the drizzling mist below. He had been scanning for an age, looking for somewhere to lie up before moving on in his determined quest. To go back to an earthly dimension was always done at great risk, as his kind were the prey of numerous denizens there, human or otherwise. No: he had decided since the untimely (though wholly welcome) death of his erstwhile Master, Quarramagus, that he would seek a respite from the trials of earthly life here in the astral gloom. Since he had had no success with Loptoc the Gossip, nor with a number of other usually reliable sources, he felt as secure here as he was likely to feel anywhere. It would do until he could again pick up the threads of his new quest.

What was that? Somewhere below, etched against an auroral backdrop, rose a hill crested by thick growths that had formed themselves into a curious whole. A wood? Here on the astral? And yet, Elfloq mused, screwing up his batrachian features in puzzlement, there must be many things here that he knew nothing of. In that wood he may well find a place to rest, and he did admit to himself that the place had a peculiar atmosphere about it, as though conducive to rest and refreshment, rather than unease and unpleasant dreams. He would at least make a cursory inspection.

Over the shrouded landscape he flitted, hovering above the impenetrable canopy of the strange wood, the trunks of which were hidden by trailing festoons of dark verdure. Cloud drifted veil-like over the silent foliage. There did not appear to be a way in: Elfloq muttered petulantly as his third circle overhead appeared to consolidate this fear. However, at that moment arrows of remarkable light angled out from the hitherto closed entrance high up, and a black shape flapped up into the starless astral skies. Cautiously Elfloq approached the place where the light had speared forth, pulling aside thin branches. Below him on a knotted branch sat a bent manikin, squinting through glassy eyes.

elcome to Cloudway," grunted the being, whose limbs were as tough and gnarled as the wood about him.

"Cloudway?" echoed Elfloq. "I have heard of this place." He considered: if he were to admit to being without a master, it might exclude him entrance to Cloudway, though he knew it by rumour to be a haven, shared by beings of all kinds. There were said to be no rulers here, man nor god.

"If you came by chance, then enter," said the manikin.

"Indeed I did," affirmed Elfloq, nodding vigorously.

The manikin touched something and branches swished aside like skirts to allow the streams of light to escape once more. Elfloq muttered brief thanks and passed within. He alighted on a thick beam hewn out of living wood. Below him, at a deceptive distance, was the floor of Cloudway, not like the ferned carpet of a wood at all, but in the nature of the floor of a great hall. There, masked by the smoke that drifted hazily up from scattered tapers, were those who had broken their astral journeys for a time at Cloudway. Elfloq's bulbous eyes smarted in the smoke, as he looked hard to see if there were any he knew below, particularly any that might be hostile, for in his short life he had incurred the wrath of many beings. However, all were strangers.

He drifted down, away from the astral travellers, who had spread themselves through the great hall, either singly or in small groups. All quaffed whatever brew they had been served, or inhaled the fumes from the red bowls that had been placed before them on scarred wooden tables. In one corner, near a fireplace, a huge shadow loomed, now and then emitting a stream of curses, boomed in a voice that would have cracked stone. Elfloq shuddered, making a mental note to keep well away from the lone figure.

Against one of the walls was a counter, and Elfloq walked over to it, he hoped inconspicuously. He was wondering if he would find any clues to the whereabouts of the dark man.

Someone unseen coughed discreetly, moving out of shadow like a cat and looked over the counter and down at Elfloq. He had a scarlet patch over one eye and a mouth that had moulded itself into a perpetual, enigmatic smile. "Greetings, little familiar. I am your host, Eye Patch of the Smile. What magician's task brings you to Cloudway's haven?"

Elfloq recovered his jerking wits and cleared his throat. "Uh—chance brought me here. I have heard, though, that Cloudway offers rest to the needy."

"Certainly! Yet I would have thought that a familiar such as you would have had no time to dally here. Your master must be lax indeed to allow you such temporal latitude."

Elfloq followed the rhetorical words with a scowl. "If you must know, I find myself—temporarily—without a master."

"I see! Perhaps you are en route to a new one?"

Elfloq's scowl deepened, emphasising his ugliness. "That is so."

"Then you shall have whatever refreshment you require. Food? A drink? Something more potent? We always have a goodly supply of dream powders. Why, but a short time since we were visited by the noted apothecary, Tygo of Ptolemidyne, whose potent herbs are famed throughout the many dimensions of Phaedrabile—and doubtless others soon. Tygo left us many of his powders in appreciation of his brief stay."

Elfloq mumbled disapproval. "Food will suffice, and a place to sleep."

"For as long as it pleases you—or your new master." Eye Patch winked roguishly as he left to prepare the promised repast, which only served to underline the familiar's nervousness. Even here, at this sanctuary, it was better not to be known as a creature with no master.

While Elfloq waited, a door somewhere banged open, and a keening wind whipped into the hall, stirring the spirals of smoke and roaring angrily before being choked off by the closing of the unseen portal once more. From the darkness at the rim of the hall there now came a hunched figure, cloaked in dismal, smeared raiment, his eyes haunted, his face haggard. He balled his fists and knuckled them together in a perpetual motion of anxiety, constantly looking back over his shoulder as though an army of imps were about to leap upon him. Slumping at the counter beside Elfloq, he began banging upon the wood for attention. There was no response. No one in the hall spoke or rose to question the frightened man's rash behaviour.

"Our host will be but a moment," ventured Elfloq, hazarding that there could be little to fear from a man so bemused by terror himself.

The man's wild eyes fixed on the little being half his height beside him. "I cannot stay here long," he groaned, the sweat on his brow gleaming in the torchlight, adding harsh angles to his aggrieved expression.

"Cloudway is a haven to all," said Elfloq. "All are safe here, so I am told. What is it that ails you, if I might ask?" he added, unable to quell his curiosity (which had ever prompted him to probe into corners where others would have been less anxious to explore).

The man shuddered, corpse-white hands gripping the counter as he looked back again. "The Gods have deserted me! They torture me!"

"But even you are safe here," Elfloq said consolingly.

The man would have replied, but Eye Patch arrived. Surprisingly he had brought food and drink for both the familiar and the stranger, as though he had known the latter would be here. "With us again, Delirion? Have you not yet outdistanced them?" he said with one of his knowing, infuriating smiles.

"You know I cannot! Do not taunt me!"

"My apologies. Sit in Cloudway awhile. Why not share your troubles with our small friend here? Perhaps he knows of a way to ease your burden."

The frightened man frowned at Elfloq, who took his repast and went to one of the tables, muttering curses. Delirion shuffled after him and set his own food down. "Why should an underling like you be able to help me?"

Elfloq picked at his nose indifferently. "I am not without sorcerous knowledge," he said pompously. "My master was—that is, is—"

"Hah! Sorcerers, wizards, warlocks! Useless against the foulness that reaches out for me. There is no spell to disperse it." He snatched at and chewed upon his meat, staring wide-eyed at the walls as though they would split to reveal something wholly unspeakable.

Elfloq drank some of the heady ale. It was delicious. He belched, enjoying the unique equality of Cloudway, his confidence mounting with each breath he took, or rudely expelled. "Will you not at least speak of this horror? I will pass on nothing of what you divulge."

Delirion spat a sliver of bone to the floor. "Why not? Listen to this, then, and tell me, little familiar, if you know of a worse fate that ever befell a man. Once I was of high blood—never mind of what House. I had great power, and I spread the glory of the Gods in many places, far and wide throughout worlds where they had never before been worshipped or even acknowledged. I had great riches, and my mansions overflowed with treasures, both mineral and fleshy, for many were the beauties that sought to woo one as favoured by the Gods as I. In my self-indulgence I became bored by it all, so that at last none of my treasure would satisfy me and none of my women could slake my thirst for pleasure.

"It was then, on a distant world that I have since cursed a thousand times in my nightmares, that I came across the mausoleums of Vandi-Nuessa, legendary Lamia of Lamias, empress of the infamous wantons who rule the night on all the worlds of Nyctath the All-Night, the forgotten dimension. There, at the heart of the mausoleum citadel, I came upon three dreaming lamias, all incomparable in beauty, all desirable beyond words. In silent trine they slept, awaiting the dispersal of the false dusk before rising to go about their gruesome nocturnal business.

"Overcome by their eerie beauty and my uncontrollable lust, I broke the seals of their rest and one by one I ravished them before they awoke. It was like a rape of the dead, but I was as one possessed! All of them I ravaged, then fled cackling like a madman. Before night had come, I was gone, drunkenly boasting of my foul sins to my followers, who returned my laughter with sycophantic mirth of their own.

"But the Gods—they spat upon me for what I had done. Vandi-Nuessa swore that she would find and destroy me, even if it meant pursuing me to the death of the very omniverse. She invoked the Gods and they applauded her lust for revenge."

Elfloq was nodding, spellbound. Delirion pointed with trembling finger to the invisible portal through which he had entered Cloudway. "Out there! Somewhere, drawing ever nearer! They seek me yet and always will. I cannot rest, for they pursue me inexorably. My sins! My sins pursue me! Vandi-Nuessa's three lamias that I ravaged—wherever I go they follow. Nothing deters them, for being dead they cannot perish, not by my hand. Know that Vandi-Nuessa's lust is like a madness, and once crossed she never forgets and never, never forgives. They will tear out my organs, one by one and suck every drop from me!"

Elfloq grimaced and hurriedly sipped at more ale, though somehow its taste had soured. "But—you are safe here in Cloudway."

"I cannot stay here forever! I have been before. They will wait for me out there, no matter how long it takes. They cannot enter, unless bidden by any but the host, it is true, but they wait. I must flee again soon."

"Are they close?"

"Always," sobbed Delirion.

"Is there no way to forestall them?"

"They are as remorseless as time. They may be held in abeyance, but for a short while only."

"Could one such as I delay them somehow?"

Delirion looked surprised. "You? Why should you aid me?"

Elfloq smirked. "Of course, it would not be merely as a favour. There would be a small price."

"If you can truly forestall these monsters, you may ask of me what you will, though I own no more than what you see. My riches are long since lost," replied Delirion wretchedly.

"All I desire is knowledge."

"You may gladly share all of mine."

"Good," nodded Elfloq, picking at his food. "Tell me, have you heard anything of a man known simply as the Voidal, or sometimes as Fatecaster?"

Delirion frowned. "No. Nothing. Who is he?"

Elfloq looked disappointed. "You speak of your cruel fate, but his is indeed worse. He bears the grim destiny forced on him by the Dark Gods, though he does not know the reasons. He committed some vile crime against them—"

"At least he has life—death is ever at my elbow—"

"The Voidal cannot die, being immortal. His punishment is for all time."

Delirion snorted. "Then why do you seek him?"

"It was he who brought about the death of my former Master, whom I confess I loathed. I have no master now, which is not desirable. The Voidal is cursed, but he has power—such as I have never known the like of!"

"So you seek to attach yourself to him? Well, perhaps there is one here who can help you find him. Though not everyone is as loquacious as we are."

Elfloq's eyes, already bulging with inner visions of power, bulged further. "Here? In Cloudway?"

"Yes," nodded Delirion, but there was craftiness in his expression. "I will gladly point him out. But first—you promised to aid me. Will you still forestall the three that pursue me?"

"If possible—"

"It is, it is, just for a while. Long enough to allow me to escape them and find another dimension to hide in. I have said they cannot enter here without being asked. So—invite them in. They must then stay here until you leave, for by Cloudway's laws, they are then bound to you as under-host. Wait as long as you can. I will travel far!"

Elfloq fidgeted, tugging at his ears as he considered, but at last he gave a nod. "Agreed. But—you swear they will not harm me?"

"I do. It is only me they want. Besides, no harm will befall you in Cloudway. Now, the one you want is in the far corner, there by that dying fire."

Elfloq almost fell out of his seat, for Delirion had singled out the monstrous figure of the being that had let out such dire curses earlier. At least he now appeared to have subsided.

"No one speaks to him, being afraid of him. He is the one they call the Broken God. Beware of his temper, small one. His powers have been crushed, but as you will see, he is somewhat larger than thee!" Delirion laughed for once, but the sound was cold and empty.

Elfloq grimaced but got up. "I will speak to him."

"I will wait until the lamias knock upon the door. When I see you open it and invite them in, I shall be gone."

"So be it." Elfloq sauntered across the darkness of the great hall. It seemed far across its deceptive dimensions to the place where the Broken God sat in shadow. By the time Elfloq drew near, he realised that the man was a giant, thrice the height of any normal man. He was sleeping, snoring noisily, his bristling upper lip trembling as the giant breathed. Elfloq flew up on to the high table and stood before him. The familiar was non-plussed, for he could not decide upon a way to awaken the sleeper, nor could he be sure that to do so would not invoke the giant's wrath. He knew that no harm was allowed to befall anyone while within Cloudway, but the sheer bulk of the being before him made him hesitate. However, one lid fluttered and a watery eye stared down at Elfloq like a glittering moon.

"Think not to pilfer my victuals—there are ample at the counter," said the giant, preparing to flick Elfloq aside as he would a gnat.

Elfloq held up a tiny hand and spoke, somewhat tremu-lously. "Sire, I have not come to steal, only to speak with you."

The Broken God blinked, surprised. He leaned forward, the lines on his face like deep channels of pain. "Speak with me? All creatures shun Murtegg and have done so for an age. What would you speak to me about?"

Elfloq detected sorrow not ire, so spoke again. "I wish con-versation, that is all. Being a visitor to Cloudway, like yourself, I thought perhaps I would exchange tales."

Murtegg leaned back in his great seat and chuckled. "You and I? What could you possibly tell me of interest?"

Elfloq pursed his lips and for some moments was silent. "Perhaps you are right, giant. You think me insolent and despi-cable. I'll not disturb you—"

"Stay, stay! Excuse my rudeness, for you are the first to speak to me for an eternity, save our host, who pities me and al-lows me to remain here for as long as I wish—a unique privi-lege. The travellers that come shun me, for I am a god." His eyes misted over as he spoke and he shook his head in misery. "I was a god. No more. I am now only Murtegg, the Broken God."

"I have but simple stories of my own humble existence to exchange for your stories, which must surely be epic in girth—" began Elfloq, seeing that he had not underestimated the giant's need to talk to someone.

"Well," breathed Murtegg, "I am infinitely lonely and must remain so. You are the first to break my monotonous existence here. You see, I cannot leave, though sometimes I wish that I could."

"Perhaps I can weaken some of your chains," suggested Elfloq, his mind piecing together the possibilities of a plan. "But will you not tell me your unfortunate tale?"

"Very well," Murtegg sighed. "It is the tale of the Falling Gods. Few men have ever heard of it, so doubtless a familiar such as you are can have no inkling. It was long, long ago, for even we gods measure time. When it began, there was a harmony about the omniverse, for the gods that thrive in darkness and those that create in light went about their tasks without bitterness to each other. Yet among the gods there is often jealousy and the lust for power. Thus certain gods of the darker places sought to elevate themselves and to overthrow the might of the greater divinities. To do this they had to destroy power to enhance their own. And light was the power they sought to destroy."

Elfloq listened avidly while Murtegg looked away into an infinite distance, across whole universes as he re-created his history.

"And in those days there was one particular great place of power, known as the Burning Beach. Upon this cosmic stretch a million broken shards of light had been crystallised in particles and heaped up like diamonds upon a forbidden shore. Nothing and no one could attain this Burning Beach for the celestial sea that washed it was alive with reflected powers, scintillating with refracted rays that could destroy. The air above the Burning Beach was smouldering with heat and energy discharged by the potent glow of the Beach—nothing could fly over or through it. The ground beneath the Beach was saturated with the energy too, while the land beyond the Beach opened on to places where only the greater gods could move. From the Burning Beach emanated myriad bolts of stellar energy, sparkling into the omniverse, feeding the many gods that dwell within and around it.

"From time to time, a god might walk upon the Burning Beach and take to himself one of its glittering gems, for they were as many as the grains of sand on all the worlds of the omniverse. Yet those who walked in darkness could not attain the Beach and thus coveted its brilliant power, sworn to destroy it. Thus they poisoned the minds of those who guarded the Beach, telling them that if they betrayed its safety they could harness its powers for themselves. Alas, for the watchers agreed to do this! They allowed the sea to spill over the Burning Beach, and while the unique tide clothed it, permitted the countless spawn of darkness to stream in from their nether hells and steal away the glittering gems, until, as the tide receded, nothing of the Burning Beach remained.

"But darkness had not reckoned with the might of the gods of light, for their anger was colossal. Bitterly enraged by the enormous crime, they set about destroying utterly the fiends that had betrayed them and so began the War of the Falling Gods. Into this great sundering came many, many gods and demigods, many of whom had not been involved in the original crime. Thousands fell, losing all powers. The great vaults of the omniverse rang to the exploding energies and the destruction of universes as the forces clashed. From one end of the omniverse to the other, all was pandemonium. Bitterly the gods drove out darkness and sought to punish every being remotely connected or tainted by it. For a thousand thousand millennia the terrible persecutions went on. The gods became awesome, infinitely suspicious and utterly merciless. Only the most powerful survived, the remainder stripped of all puissance, maimed.

"Eventually the extreme retribution began to ease and once more the gods became merciful. They even became, in time, tolerant, so that they allowed other powers to exist without crushing them. Justice spread. The reign of persecution had ended and a new era of peace had begun. Darkness had not been destroyed, nor can it ever be utterly so. Slowly its powers grew again, until now, I see beyond this place into the many dimensions, it has stretched out evil wings almost as fully as before. Darkness and light are in equilibrium once more, for the gods of light are too merciful."

"And you?" prompted Elfloq. "What part did you play?"

"My part was infinitely small. By chance I came upon one of the stolen grains from the Burning Beach. I coveted it, thinking it would make me something greater than I was. But the thing was cursed—as are all those lost fragments. For my greed I was struck down and crushed like an insect. Now I am no more than that, an insect. The fragment was thrown from me and I was told to find it again and watch it until one day, perhaps, it will be taken back to the gods. Perhaps. If I did not watch it, I was told, and left it, I would be dissipated. So here I sit and watch, and wait."

"You mean—it is here?"

Murtegg pointed to a black box beside the fire hearth. "There. I dare not leave it, for I have not the courage to quit Cloudway and be dissipated. I fear that it will never be taken from here, for the gods have cursed it."

Elfloq was trying to picture the vast scenes described by Murtegg. Had the Voidal been a part of that chaos? He must find out. "Your story is so enormous, I could not hope to equal it. My own life is exceptionally dull by comparison," he said.

"Oh, but I would be glad to hear it—"

"I think, unhappy Murtegg, I may otherwise please you."

The giant lifted his huge goblet and guzzled noisily, putting it down and looking with interest at the familiar. "If that is so, speak out!"

"Once, no doubt, you had goddesses on your arm. Once they must have swooned to your touch, vied for your caresses. Long ago, how you must have loved them!"

Murtegg banged his fist down on the table and swore vehemently so that Elfloq had to take to the air to save himself a bruising. "Of course, damn you!" growled the giant. "I had a dozen such goddesses! Why torture me by speaking of them? I have not had one share my bed for a hundred lifetimes, nor any woman!"

"Then I can indeed offer you something," went on Elfloq. "You shall again be a god, or at least you shall feel like one."

"Do not mock me, little familiar—"

"No, I do not. I have what you desire. They shall be yours,

to keep and to sport with for as long as you wish. Not far from here."

Murtegg was nodding thoughtfully. "You would exchange them for a simple story, one which any of the Fallen would tell you? Or is there more that you desire?"

Elfloq tried to appear nonchalant. "Well—there was something else. Just a smattering of knowledge."

Murtegg laughed so that the hidden rafters rang. "You have done me some good already! Your impudence tickles my ribs. What do you wish of me, cunning one?"

"I seek a new master. Once I was owned by a great sorcerer, whom I took to be the greatest of all, a man who sought to usurp colossal powers and become a veritable god himself. But he was destroyed—him and his world, together with a great dynasty of conquerors. I watched as all this went down to damnation at the hands of one man, a man said to be the pawn of certain gods. It is this man that I would serve, for he has access to undreamed of power."

"Who is he?"

"He has no identity, no name, save that of—Voidal. Who is he, giant? Where may I find him? How can I bind myself to him?" said Elfloq breathlessly.

Murtegg grunted. "Stars, so you are not without ambition, too! But I do not know the name. What gods does he serve?"

"I know them only as the Dark Gods. Once he did them a grievous wrong, and so they—"

Murtegg held up a hand for silence, his face pale. "Him. Yes, I know of him."

"What can you tell me?"

"You foolish, misbegotten cur! Do you think the Dark Gods would permit you such forbidden knowledge? No man may aid the one you speak of. No creature may call him friend and escape the wrath of the Dark Gods. Greater by far than any other was his crime! I will tell you nothing. It shames me to say so, but I fear the reprisals."

"But our bargain—"

"Bargain! To take what you offer in exchange for eternal agony!"

"But, can you not even tell me how I may please this Voidal?"

Murtegg stiffened, thinking. "I will say this. Give me what you promised and I will give you something in return. A fragment, no more."

"I accept," said Elfloq eagerly.

"There are many things the man you speak of desires. You must give him one of them. Hah! but you know that, which is why you interrogate me, cunning one. Well, you shall not have the information from me. I will tell you to whom you must go. But first I will tell you what to seek of them, if you dare. Ask them where the woman may be found: his woman. He would gladly give up the search for his purloined soul to find her again. Find out where she is and tell this Voidal. If the Dark Gods permit it, you will be his ally ever after."

"Whom must I seek?"

"Where are your gifts?"

As though in answer to that, there came a loud rapping at another unseen door. Elfloq tried to grin as he flitted from the table and across the hall, calling to Murtegg to follow. Grumpily the Broken God rose and did so, cursing as he stood at the walls. "Well?"

"They are without."

"Who?" sniffed Murtegg, listening to the shrill sounds beyond the rattling door that were not made by the wind.

"Open it."

Murtegg threw the door open and in the night stood three black-cloaked women, their white faces framed in their hoods, their blood-red eyes blazing like angry fires. "By the powers, what beauties are these!" cried the giant.

"They are yours," said Elfloq, who had flown up to alight on Murtegg's shoulder. "Are you not going to invite them in? If you do so, they are bound to remain with you for as long as you stay in Cloudway. You need not be alone."

Murtegg looked again at the strange women, who were keenly scanning the tables and dark corners of Cloudway. Elfloq had already seen Delirion dart for a hidden alcove by another door, out of sight of his nemesis. Murtegg grinned hugely. "Welcome, beautiful travellers!" he cried, bowing and stepping aside. "Please come this way. Step in from the chill night and let Murtegg fill you with warmth!"

The three lamias of Vandi-Nuessa smiled evilly and walked haughtily into Cloudway. Somewhere a door banged shut as Delirion fled once more. Elfloq was well pleased that Murtegg had done the inviting, for he was more than a little glad not to have to deal with the lamias himself, nor need he do so again. He breathed into Murtegg's ear. "Well? Are you pleased? To whom must I go?"

"Go to the Divine Askers. They serve the Dark Gods as their questioners and they are the ones who extract all knowledge that the Dark Gods seek. Nothing is hidden from them. But be warned, little familiar. I doubt that they will grant anything you ask. Likely they will torture you—indefinitely."

"How do I find them?"

"Go to Eye Patch of the Smile. Below this hall there are many cellars, with stairs that lead to places most travellers would never guess at. Walk with care, small one, if you find the path to cruel Hedrazee, lair of the Askers. Remember, the Dark Gods hear even the dust that falls at the far end of the omniverse."

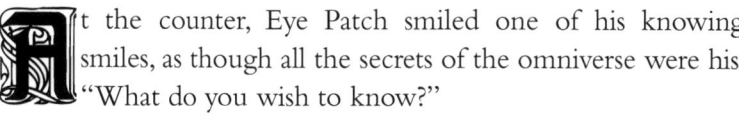 t the counter, Eye Patch smiled one of his knowing smiles, as though all the secrets of the omniverse were his. "What do you wish to know?"

"A way to—the Divine Askers."

Eye Patch chuckled. "The Askers? Strange that you should seek them, for they are usually the ones who seek out their, if you'll excuse me, victims. However, that is none of my business. I am your host and am here to assist as I can. Follow." Saying this, he took up a firebrand and beckoned Elfloq to him as he passed through a door.

Elfloq hopped behind, surprised to find beyond a stairway of wood that led not down but up. "Is this the correct way, host?" he said dubiously. "I was told that your exits to other realms are below in your cellars."

Eye Patch grinned back at him. "Indeed they are, and they certainly open on to many dimensions. However, as you perhaps know, Cloudway has magical qualities—for example, the fingers of coincidence are rarely idle here and weave the most contingent of fates for its visitors, regardless of status."

Elfloq digested these words as he climbed the creaking stairs in the wake of the sputtering brand. The tiny embers seemed curiously not to affect the wood. Eye Patch stood in a narrow corridor before a low door. "Here you may find what you seek."

"A gateway to the Askers?"

"To their clandestine retreat, Hedrazee? No. But herein are two of them, travelling like yourself and resting here in Cloudway for a while."

Elfloq grimaced, but he was resolute about his course. He must find the Voidal. He dare not exist without a master much longer. "Very well."

As he made to knock, Eye Patch bowed and set the brand in the wall, retreating into the darkness without another word. Elfloq knocked and it seemed that there was a distant echo. After a moment the door opened inward. Strange incense drifted to Elfloq's nostrils as he walked into the low room. There were bizarre hangings and black candles dripping tallow. Two figures stood beside a divan, dressed in resplendent scarlet robes. Their jet-black hair tumbled down over their shoulders to their waists, their swarthy faces caught by the glow of the candles.

"Who dares to disturb us?" said one, drawing in a deep breath as though drugged.

"A fellow traveller," said Elfloq. "Our host told me you might help."

"Do you know who we are?" said the other man tersely, his lips pressed into a thin, hard line.

"Yes," said Elfloq, but the first man indicated his companion.

"This is Zobbarkh, lately First Oligarch of the Torturers' Guild of Azadris, the Bloodworld. He is being elevated from his already esteemed position to that of Divine Asker. I am Darquementi of the Askers, Questioners of the Dark Gods and I am taking Zobbarkh to my colleagues. Cloudway's laws demand that we share such facts with fellow guests, but now that you know who we are, rude familiar, perhaps you will quit us in fa-vour of more amicable company."

Elfloq flinched as the eyes of the two men looked balefully down at him. "I know who you are, great masters. Indeed, it is why I sought you."

Darquementi was taken aback. "Do you not understand! We are Divine Askers! We do the exclusive work of the Dark Gods. Before us are brought all those who must answer to them. It is given to us to draw from them their knowledge and their confessions. It is also given to us to punish and to scourge."

"I wish only to honour and serve the Dark Gods," insisted Elfloq as obsequiously as he could.

"That is well. They have many enemies. Have you come to confess some crime? Or do you possess knowledge we should share?"

"I would gladly confess freely to you everything that I know, omnipotent masters, but such facts as are in my head would surely serve only to bore you."

"Then why in all the hells are you here!" growled Zobbarkh.

"I am on a mission, a personal mission it is true. My last master, Quarramagus of Moonwater, was destroyed, along with the Csarducts. The Dark Gods quite rightly brought them to their doom."

"And you escaped the cataclysm?" said Darquementi.

"The Dark Gods were merciful, lords. I aided in my mas-ter's downfall—actually I was instrumental in it."

"Indeed?" The Askers seemed amused by the bravado of the diminutive figure.

"Your masters sent the Fatecaster to wreak havoc—I aided him when the Seven sorcerers chained him with spells. I freed him!"

Darquementi snorted with scepticism. "Hah! You? You aided the Voidal? Do you think he would have been powerless? I think you exaggerate your own powers somewhat. However, come to the point."

"I had disowned Quarramagus, who worked evil, and now I have sworn fealty to the Dark Gods. As I have avowed, I wish to serve only them."

"Ah—and you wish to do so in a particular fashion. You wish us to intercede for you? Your words are garbled but your thoughts are clearer. Remember who we are."

"I will be honest, lords. I wish to serve the—Voidal. I need a new master, lest I perish." Elfloq felt a stab of freezing panic, for he knew that his words cast his fate into the very teeth of these grim lords of pain. If they were displeased, he would suffer exceptional torture to appease the Dark Gods.

Darquementi nodded. "You are honest, but impertinent beyond words! Do you not understand that the Voidal has been marked by our masters? None may befriend him and he must undertake his punishment alone. That is our masters' decree. We cannot intercede for you without bringing our masters' wrath down upon our own heads."

Elfloq was nodding, his blood still icy in his veins. Yet his ambition burned on brightly. "I have—one small gift to offer your masters, to demonstrate my faith."

The Askers exchanged a brief glance, then stared at the familiar. "I trust that you do not seek to bargain with us?" said Darquementi, his voice suddenly cold.

Elfloq looked horrified. "Never, lords! I bring you a gift, and ask nothing for it—"

"What is this gift?" said Zobbarkh, intrigued.

"Once," said Elfloq, swallowing hard, "there was a great sundering of gods, after the piecemeal theft of the Burning Beach. Many of the gems from that Beach have never been recovered. Doubtless the Dark Gods would be well pleased to recover such fragments—"

"And you have one?" said Darquementi, incredulous.

"Below, in the hall, the giant watches over one, waiting until it is claimed. He would be glad if you relieved him of his duty."

Darquementi studied the familiar, then nodded. "I see. You are clever, little one. It is indeed a worthy gift. One that may, after all, warrant a reward." He turned to Zobbarkh. "What do you say?"

"Noble Darquementi," replied the latter sleepily, "I have been idly sifting through some of the twisted thoughts in our visitor's head, and coupling them with certain other knowledge that I have, may have a solution (quite plausibly divinely inspired). The familiar seeks knowledge, though is far too terrified to ask it of us. He seeks to be a servant of the Voidal, but knows that for the Voidal to accept him, he would have to impart to him something the Voidal badly wants—something, for instance, denied to him by our masters. For example, the knowledge that the Voidal's great love has not been destroyed, but lives. The familiar would doubtless wish to impart to the Voidal news of the actual movements of the woman, her troubled course. To do so, he reasons, would surely bind him to the Voidal."

"Sir, I would never have asked such a thing!" protested Elfloq. "It was merely a vague, half-formed thought, rootless and idle!"

Zobbarkh waved the words aside. "Darquementi has told me of the Voidal and his circumstances at length. It is one of the great secrets of our circle. However, there is a certain irony in what you seek to learn. Why not allow the familiar his fragment of knowledge, Darquementi? Let him take news of this woman to the Voidal. After all, such knowledge would likely evoke various emotions in the dark man's breast."

Darquementi was thoughtful, but a slow smile crossed his features. "It may not please him, but torture him more. It could be done, but I would make one binding stipulation. This familiar must choose his own path. Once given the knowledge, he may bestow it or retain it as he sees fit. Well, familiar, does that suit your cause? The knowledge you want may not be what it seems. We are ever devious, but there may be little we can teach you about that particular art."

Elfloq could scarcely withhold his glee. "I am content."

"Of course, the Dark Gods may not wish you to impart the knowledge, in which case they will quickly destroy you," Darquementi added.

"Without a master, I will die anyway," murmured Elfloq. "I must take my chances." He could not back down now, for he may never again find himself so close to his goal.

"Very well. It will be done. Come closer and look into my eyes. You will see what you must."

Elfloq obeyed and as he did so, Darquementi's eyes appeared as two huge pools which merged into one; Elfloq found himself dropping down into that lake, but then, abruptly, he was looking out over a remarkable landscape. A twilight sky with grim mountains below it and a land that seemed never to have been blessed with true daylight. Elfloq recognised the weird constellations that faintly glowed like dead embers in the heavens. This was the dimension of Nyctath, the All-Night, where light had only a faint grip. Dark things were spawned here, with cold blood and colder hearts. Now he saw a crumbling ruin of a city and therein mausoleums, from which lethargic figures stumbled or crawled. Some stretched diaphanous wings and rose upward into the bleak night. The scene was familiar, at least in memory, for this was the very palace of Vandi-Nuessa, whom Delirion so dreaded. Here were the lamias of the empress, ruler of the night worlds.

Elfloq seemed to float into a central chamber where all was dark and obscured. He saw a lamia rise from her black velvet couch and watched her. Her skin was milk white, her eyes filled with incalculable sorrow. Slowly, hesitantly, she bent down to bite into the flesh of something beside her, as if reluctant to feed. Her fingers touched the strings of an instrument beside her, a thing of beauty, an anachronism in this dreadful realm. It seemed to Elfloq to offer a hint of comfort to the lamia, who must be little better than a prisoner.

Beside her, another lamia stirred from sleep, but before the familiar could study her better the blackness of the light shut down abruptly. Elfloq felt a spinning nausea threaten him but shook his head. Before him stood the two Askers.

"You have seen? Like the Voidal, the lamias are cursed with immortality."

"A cruel fate."

"The Dark Gods are stern masters. Even so, familiar, you have what you came for. And in exchange we will have the giant's charge before we leave."

Elfloq nodded. "You are kind. Now I must somehow find the Fatecaster."

"You have only to summon him by name," said Darque-menti.

"And pay some dire penalty for doing so?" gasped Elfloq, knowing the laws that surrounded the Voidal.

"You are in Cloudway. No harm will befall you here. Summon him and there will be no reckoning."

Elfloq did not look convinced. Since stepping in here, he had begun to feel progressively more like a pawn.

"Well, you must leave us. Our own journey begins anew soon."

Greatly relieved, Elfloq bowed and departed, closing the door with a thump and scurrying down the wooden stairs. Below, Eye Patch awaited him with a leer. "Perhaps you would enjoy a further drink after your conversation?"

"Aye, a large flagon," Elfloq replied with bravado, sitting at a table. He looked around him, but saw no one he knew. Murtegg and the three lamias had gone to find some private part of the establishment. Elfloq sighed, deliberating. To summon the Voidal—to tell him what he knew, that his lover was the eternal slave of the Lamia of Lamias, herself a lamia and chained to her frightful realm, never again to be what she once had been? But how would the Voidal react to such melancholy news? Surely he would curse the one to bring him such knowledge. And if the dark man did thank Elfloq and make him his servant, what then? The Voidal would doubtless seek out his lover in Nyctath, the forgotten dimension. Elfloq would then be bound to go—to face, for certain, the ire of Vandi-Nuessa, whom Delirion had said never forgot a slight.

To summon the Voidal—whichever way the coin fell would presage unpleasantness. The Dark Gods were unkind, after all. Yet—they let the knowledge pass to Elfloq, and they left nothing to chance.

He turned to Eye Patch of the Smile, who brought him the promised ale. "Bring food, too. Plenty of it."

"You have regained your appetite?" smiled the host.

"It's for another guest."

omewhere above them, the two Divine Askers were making ready to quit the haven and return to their secret place of Hedrazee. Darquementi gave a thought to the squat familiar. "He had courage as well as impudence and ambition. He faced me in spite of his freezing terror. I hope that he will not be too discouraged when he discovers how he has been manipulated."

Zobbarkh smiled lazily. "I will fetch the charge of the giant."

Darquementi nodded as his companion quit the chamber. "Yes, I hope they spare you, familiar. There are no chance meetings in Cloudway."

ater it would seem to Elfloq that he had partaken of a little too much of Cloudway's exceptional ale, and that the meeting at the table in the shadowed corner had been a product of his intoxicated imagination.

Not one, but two figures stepped out of the darkness, and Elfloq sat back with a jerk. The dark man he recognised at once, both by his clothes and by his confusion. The other, a gangling fellow in clothes that had once been colourful but which had barely survived any number of repairs, also looked more than a little confused.

The Voidal glanced at him. "I had not expected to meet you so suddenly after quitting Necral's Keep, Grabulic. It seems we are yet tied to one another."

The Songster, for it was indeed he, nodded, looking about at the smoky hall. His eyes dropped to the diminutive figure at the table. "Yes, and we appear to have fallen in with very strange company. Is this the work of your mysterious masters?"

The Voidal grunted, apparently amused by something. "I think not, for once. Greetings, Elfloq," he said, coming to the table and seating himself. "As there are two dishes here, I presume one is for me?"

Elfloq focused on the Voidal, burped, and nodded.

The dark man indicated the food. "Here, Grabulic. Eat your fill if you've stomach for it."

Grabulic grinned, pulling up another chair and beginning at once.

"Did you summon me?" the Voidal asked Elfloq. "You may have avoided the attendant penalty, but for what purpose?"

"The same as before," grinned Elfloq, nervously peering around him. "I am resolute."

"Your interference in my destiny has dragged this Songster into its web. But it pleases me to have him with me for a little longer. However, the Dark Gods will not tolerate this for long, if at all. And you, Elfloq, are in danger. No man may be my friend—"

Elfloq hiccoughed and pushed away his ale, from which he had drained enough courage. "Riddles! I am not a man. And I have not said I would be your friend. Only your servant. The Dark Gods may allow me that."

The Voidal smiled. "To work for your own benefit! No, you tempt consequences you could not dream of. The Dark Gods are cruel, devious beyond knowing. I would not have you punished on my account. Too many have suffered through me."

"Without a master, I am doomed to perish."

"A familiar with such talents—and with such cunning—as yourself could have his pick of any wizard, sorcerer, mage—"

"I have made my choice," affirmed Elfloq. "Listen, Voidal! I offered you my service once before and you declined. But now I have the means to barter with you. I have fresh knowledge. Is this not your goal?"

The Voidal's smile faded abruptly and his green eyes narrowed. "About myself? You have learned something of me?"

"That which will both please and displease you. It may earn me your wrath, even hatred, but I will risk even that."

Elfloq felt the green eyes drilling into him as though they would see his very thoughts. The dark man's voice had become a hiss. "Tell me what you know."

"It will be a revelation, I promise, and I will gladly tell you, but will you be my master?"

The words hung in silence; the very dust seemed still. Grabulic's fork was poised in mid-air, loaded with food. He had stopped chewing, eyes fixed on the bizarre couple who faced one another.

"You understand that you are courting catastrophe?" said the Voidal.

"Yes."

The Voidal stared at the familiar, carefully balancing out needs and repercussions in silence. He emitted a great sigh. "I must share this knowledge. Very well."

Grabulic chewed slowly, realising that something of great weight was taking place.

"It concerns the woman. The Askers said you would know her," said Elfloq, watching the Voidal stiffen. The familiar described the lamia he had been shown by Darquementi, her dread seat in Nyctath the All-Night.

Afterwards the Voidal remained immobile for a long time, eyes closed as if picturing for himself Vandi-Nuessa's dreary domain and the terrible things in it. Then he shuddered, his fists contracting with violent but controlled emotion.

Elfloq flinched, dreading the awakening of the Dark Gods' hand.

"Necral did not lie. She is alive. Yet she is cursed even as I am. Her fate is worse than my own."

"Will you seek her?"

The Voidal seemed to tremble with anguish. "Dare I? Dare I heap more misery upon her? Even if I were allowed to go there—"

"I was afraid to tell you of this," said Elfloq. "I see that it has riven you."

The Voidal shook his head. "My anger is not for you. I will direct it all elsewhere, when I am ready."

A surge of relief douched the familiar. But there was another anxiety to be faced. He had no desire whatsoever to visit Nyctath, in view of his dealings with the lamias, but if he were to serve the Voidal truly, he must obey his master's needs and wishes.

"Then you will make me your servant?" he prompted.

The Voidal's pained gaze returned to him from great distances. "You are adamant? Since that was the bargain, you may serve me as it suits you, familiar. But you are a fool."

"Then how may I serve you now?" replied Elfloq at once. "What do you desire? Information? News? I have a treasure trove, I have contacts everywhere, I—"

"Peace, peace!" the dark man smiled grimly. He turned to Grabulic. "There is one cause I would gladly champion. Grabulic searches for his own lost love."

"Layola," breathed the Songster. "If I could find her, imprisoned in my instrument though she is, I would be content."

"Perhaps Elfloq knows something of her whereabouts, or could pursue news of her on your behalf."

Grabulic at once described Layola to the familiar, and as he did so, the diminutive figure seemed to shrivel up, almost sliding under the table.

"Has the ale soured your brain?" the Voidal asked him.

Elfloq shook his head. "I—I—" he burbled.

"Speak out," said the Voidal. "Come, if you are to serve me, you must have no secrets from me!"

"Layola," breathed Elfloq. "I saw her."

Grabulic leaned across the table, eyes filled with anguish. "Where?"

"She was beside the lamia. Just as you describe her. The lamia's fingers touched her strings."

Grabulic gasped and the Voidal scowled in fury. "You see how they work! The Dark Gods laugh in our faces. Nyctath holds them both!"

"I must go there," said Grabulic. "I must try to regain her, whatever lurks there."

The Voidal stood up, mouth hardening. "I swore to aid you, Songster. So be it. I, too, will visit Nyctath. Somehow it is their will."

Elfloq tried to smother his terror. It was unavoidable—the Dark Gods had known it all along. This must be their fee for allowing Elfloq such liberties. He must go to Nyctath and face the Lamia of Lamias.

"If I might suggest," he said, "I could visit Nyctath easily enough."

The Voidal nodded. "You could. But do not invoke me again, once you are there. It would be your end."

Elfloq pretended to be amused by the preposterous state-ment. "There will be other ways of bringing you out of the void. You'll not find my brain empty."

The Voidal laughed. "No, nor idle. And in the end, what will you gain, for all your dire risks?"

"I am a familiar," chuckled Elfloq, feeling a little better. "I feed on the power of my master."

"Well, you have a sufficiently large appetite."

Elfloq reached again for the ale. "That is so—master."

VIII

EVER THE HUNGRY NIGHT

If there is one thing we can all be certain of about the Dark Gods, it is that they are masters of retribution. And as they seem to know everything, cosmic or microcosmic, we are all subjected to the consequences of our acts, whether we appreciate the fact or not.

To break free of this control, this Nemesis, would set us apart from, possibly above, the Dark Gods.

But still we strive, oh how we strive!

—Salecco, the Determined

In a chamber hung with funereal black, the melancholy figure slumped in his chair of sculpted stone. A few candles burned in alcoves, casting the faintest luminescence about the room, weaving a pattern of shadows, cloaking the figure in a writhing darkness. His shoulders sagged, his eyes probing a remote vista. The walls of his chamber were thick and no sound from without penetrated. Alone in this remotest of places he brooded, as he had done for time immeasurable.

He recalled many things—events that were not garbed in grim shadow, but in bright, effervescent light, which once he had loved. Deeds, events, loves. Though these memories twisted the knife of remorse within his heart, he could not put them from him as he had the daylight. Though he chose to hide here, he could never escape the memories.

It was true that he had loved light, for he had been almost a god—a demigod of unsurpassed beauty, renowned also for his humour. All had loved him, and how he had loved! The sirens, the sylphs, the mermaids, the lamias, the witches, many more—even goddesses. His beauty had been known throughout the omniverse, by both light and dark powers, and he, sadly, chose to squander it for petty amusement, rather than in the service of those who knew best the affairs of the many dimensions. So great was his charm and so great his skill in winning the hearts of all whom he chose to woo, that his pride grew until at last it had superseded even his beauty. And the gods, already tired of his petty affairs, would no longer tolerate his pompous boasts and his impudent claim to be the most beautiful of all.

Thus they punished him for his arrogance. They destroyed his looks and scattered his face like shards of a broken mirror throughout the omniverse, so that none could recall it. In its place they gave him a broken visage, cracked and lined, crumbling slowly like mouldering rock. Never again would he be called beautiful, nor would anyone find him desirable. Appalled by his disfigurement, he fled to this far away world on the edge of its dark dimension, walling himself up in his dismal tower. He was known ever after as Shatterface.

Now, watching the shadows play, he saw them move in a strange way, thinking that his tortured mind must once more be teasing his senses. Yet the stuff of the night was coalescing: something was seeping into the chamber, its form burgeoning forth into several parts which separated and grew. There were thirteen such shapes. Shatterface pressed back deep into the cold recesses of the stone chair, for this visitation could only mean further pain. These were the Thirteen seneschals of the Dark Gods, who had struck him down for his haughtiness.

An arm pointed at him, an accusing tendril. "You have languished for an age in your tower, Shatterface. Will you never again venture out into the many dimensions?"

Shatterface hissed an answer. "To be jeered at by all living things? No. I remain here, unless you have come to eject me. Have your masters no pity?"

"We are not here to force anything upon you. The Dark Gods have not forgotten you. They know how you have suffered. They would offer you a respite from this dreary existence, if you will earn it."

"Respite? If this is true, there will be a price. I know your cruel masters too well," sighed Shatterface.

The darkness pulsed, the disembodied voice indifferent. "We are here to pass on what we have been told, no more. If you wish surcease, you must earn it."

Shatterface considered, but he could not turn down a chance to end this numbing exile. "How?" he snapped.

"There is a man you must find. He, like you, has been punished by the Dark Gods. He is their pawn, drifting at their whim, used against their enemies so that one day, perhaps, he may have atoned for his own sins."

"There must be many of us whom your masters have crippled."

"The Dark Gods do not tolerate evil against them. This man, the Voidal, sometimes called Fatecaster, has learned from treacherous creatures met on his wandering something of his circumstances and his past. He grows bold in his forbidden knowledge. His memory must once again be washed clean."

"By me? But what powers do I have?"

"You will be given the means to wipe away the things the Voidal must not know. You shall have the Sword of Oblivion. Know that neither you, nor any other can kill the Voidal, but plunge the sword into him and you will have pleased the Dark Gods."

Shatterface leaned forward. "And if I do this?"

"Half your face will be restored."

Shatterface cried out. "Half! And the remainder?"

"Be satisfied! We pass on only what we have been told."

"And if I fail? Has this Voidal the means to destroy me?"

"Not destroy, no. You have not earned such rest. But the Dark Gods are just. If the Voidal thwarts you, he will be allowed to retain the things he has learned. You will be as you are, to do as you wish. Return here, perhaps. You will not be punished for failure."

"Failure! No, not after so long a wait. I will pursue this Voidal remorselessly," avowed Shatterface. "Wherever he walks, I will follow."

"That is permitted. Thrice you may try for him, but after that you must forget him. Thrice—abuse that command and you will be punished, *in the extreme*."

Shatterface nodded. "Then give me the Sword of Oblivion! I will do all that is asked of me. Nothing shall deter me—I would ravage eternity for my face!"

The Thirteen began to depart, and in the place where they had been gleamed a sword, stretched out on the stone, its powers dormant but potent.

In the dimension of Nyctath there is barely a seepage of light, as though darkness has welled up, tide-like, to engulf the very suns and stars of that unhappy realm. There are dim embers of decomposing worlds, fading as the great cold snuffs them like candles without wicks. Even the gods have given up this dreary place, which once they populated as freely as any other. Nyctath, once a proud place, is now a region of decay, where night beings lurk in abundance: it is spoken of as Nyctath the All-Night, the forgotten dimension.

Yet there was a solitary god who dwelt in Nyctath, loath to leave, being convinced in his dotage that one day the gods of light would come again to his shunned realm. This lonely god, whose years equalled in number the very stars of the omniverse, burned and tended the last light in Nyctath, and by its ever-dimming radiance set the false dawn and dusk of the scattered worlds. This ancient god, Ozbaak Uderaak, dwelt in the mountainous retreat of Nacramonte on a clinker world that had lost its own name; here he sought to restore light, dreaming that one day he would make incandescent the heavens and spread a celestial glow throughout the entire dimension of Nyctath. Once he had sought to do this without recourse to dubious powers, but as the swarms of night creatures and acolytes of gloom multiplied around him like germs, he turned to whatever powers and mysteries he could find to aid him. Hope and a blind faith were his twin weapons, for slowly his sacred beacons were dimming, the shadows drawing tighter around him. Night was always waiting to pounce and make whole its conquest.

lipping from one dimension to another and between them on the astral was second nature to a familiar. Elfloq, as lively as any of his peculiar kind, popped into exisence in the dismal surroundings that he guessed at once must be Nyctath, the dimension known omniversally as the All-Night. His unfortunate features screwed themselves up distastefully and became even more ugly; however, he had never depended on his good looks to win him any of his numerous ambitions.

He found himself on a slagheap, knee-deep in ashes: a cloud of black dust rose up around him. Stretched out beyond him in monotonous continuity were hummocks that suggested infinite heaps of detritus. The place was dead—extinct. Elfloq doubted if anything could live here. He had miscalculated, though not by much, for peering upward through the smog, he saw a world suspended high in the pitch heavens, a single glow about it like a red halo. That must be the world of the old god, Ozbaak Uderaak, the last wielder of light in this miserable dimension.

Having no reason, nor wish, to remain on this cold lump of rock, the familiar slipped back on to the astral and a few moments later quitted it, this time on the nameless world of the old god. It did not present a much more inspiring terrain than that of the shell he had just left, but at least it was the correct world. Around him Elfloq could discern the sheer cliffs and daunting crags of Nacramonte, its precipitous stone walls and buttresses lifted ever upwards in mockery of the heavens. From somewhere on the rim of the dizzy heights came a red glow—the fortress of the old god must be there, its beacons shedding what little light they could.

Nodding to himself, Elfloq spread his membranous wings and launched upward in a graceful, easy movement, blending with the shadows and flitting high up over the rim. Turrets and towers spread below him, hewn incredibly from the black obsidian and porphyry, some broken and spilling into little quadrangles of the fortress: there were scored marks across many, like the trails of gargantuan claws. In others were faint glows, which suggested witch-fires, while in the central tower, a thick finger that rose up accusingly at the night, there blazed a crimson glow from which billowed waves of heat. The hot air currents buffeted Elfloq as he enjoyed their warmth, and he had to struggle to maintain his arc of flight.

Presently he alighted on a tower near the central one, and having set down deftly among its garish crenallations, scanned the place and its few windows for signs of guardians. He detected none, and so moved around the tower to which he clung. Its figures and statues were meticulously carved, representing warriors with serene faces that seemed much out of keeping with this night-smothered world. Certainly no living beings such as these had walked here for eons. Satisfied that none of them would revitalise and attack him, Elfloq flew from the tower and began searching others. He must find the old god.

At last he came across him, working in a bright chamber, bent over a huge glass dome inside of which there wriggled a mass of creatures so entangled that their individual shapes were indistinct. Yet light shone from them, magnified by the substance of the glass dome. It lanced upwards on to a mirror, directed outwards through the window. Ozbaak Uderaak clapped his hands and stood up, though his warped spine prevented him from straightening. He was chuckling, as though he had made some marvellous discovery.

Elfloq, balanced easily on an external window ledge, felt himself partially picked out by the glow from the amazing creatures. Ozbaak turned, ostensibly to make some adjustment to further reflective apparatus, and his rheumy eyes widened. He flung up his gnarled fingers and a bolt of something white-hot zipped by Elfloq's exposed tuft of ear.

"Avaunt, horror!" cried the angered god.

The familiar fell from the ledge but spread his wings to keep from plummeting. "Wait!" he protested. "I am no night gaunt, but an ally. One who has come to aid you."

"All things that dwell in Nyctath are my sworn enemies!" growled Ozbaak, peering over the windowsill into the night. Clearly his eyesight was no better for the light.

"I do not fear the light," called Elfloq. "Let me show you. Gladly will I bask in it."

This evidently impressed the god, but his expression was one of intense suspicion. "What cunning deviltry do your mas-

200

ters practice now? They cannot have learned immunity!" he muttered.

"I am not from this dimension," said Elfloq. "I am a familiar."

Ozbaak looked far from happy, but waved Elfloq into his tower. The latter hopped down from the sill and spread his arms to show that he bore no weapons.

"Ah," nodded Ozbaak, fingers lost within the entanglement of his red beard. "Ah. Just as you say. Not spawned in the All-Night. I know your genera. Used to have a trio like you. Well, what brings you to this desolate realm? What news do you bring me, eh? What gods have you seen? What do they say of me? Have they decided not to turn away from Nyctath?"

Elfloq finally managed to squeeze his words between the bubbling questions of the old god. "It is all rather complex, sire, but I will explain it fully." Distracted, he wandered over to the glowing creatures. "But—what are these?"

"Beauties, are they not? I had them from a mire on Zitterbab. It wasn't easy. I had to transform myself and slither away from this place. I don't enjoy inter-dimensional travel any more. My old bones are too brittle for metamorphosis. But it was worth it for those beauties—they are glitterworms. Breed profusely and perpetually. Just one of the many ways in which I shall extend the boundaries of light around me. I have taken great sea-stars from the coral depths of the Waterworlds in the Lydex Cluster, and I have nurtured fireweed from Xenidorm's hot satellites—and there, in that shimmering bowl, is a sunpearl from tropical Violovi."

Elfloq savoured the heat and light, turning to the old god. "Well, your fortress is the only source of light I have seen here."

"Indeed. Dawn and dusk, aurora, moonlight, starlight—all come from here, direct or reflected. Without my light, Nyctath would be wholly darkness. But I persist. I sow the seeds that will blossom into clean light again."

"You spread light, year on year?"

Ozbaak looked pained. "Sadly, no. I barely maintain a balance. I fact I sense, though I hardly like to admit it, that it is the darkness that creeps forward, not light. There are so many enemies: darkness has all the allies. Down below us, in the city of the necropoli, the followers of evil muster like maggots. My war with them goes on and on, and when I seek to gain an advantage, they tear it back from me. But as I said, I persist. I shall find a way!" He punctuated this promise with a fit of hoarse coughing. To Elfloq he did not seem a very credible champion, but the familiar admired his mad determination.

"About that dead city," prompted the familiar.

"Ludang? A cesspool, overrun with horrors and controlled by that filthy she-wolf, Vandi-Nuessa. What of it?"

Elfloq was nodding uncomfortably, having good reason to be wary of the mythical Lamia of Lamias. "Ludang? Is that its name? My master has business there."

"Business?" said the old god, puzzled. "No one but an idiot would venture there. Unless they were an ally of those fiends—"

"I assure you, my master is no ally—"

"Who is he?"

"Uh—I do not know his name. He was responsible for the demise of my former master, Quarramagus, who was himself ambitious in all the wrong ways. I had need of a new master, and having aided in the downfall of my old one, was fortunate enough to meet with the approval of my present one, who took me into service."

"Yes, yes, yes. And he has no name? Hrrmph, if he has no name, what else can you tell me of him?"

"Oh, very little, sire. He is greatly secretive, though in such dark times, that is, you'll agree, wise of him—"

"Cease your prattling and tell me of him!" growled Ozbaak.

"Well, to be honest, I think he may have, in some small way, displeased the—uh, certain of the gods—and now seems compelled to wander in what appears to be an aimless way, though in fact, to be sure, he does the work of, well, the gods," went on Elfloq dilatorily, hoping that this vague portrait of his master would shed no light on Ozbaak's memory of him. But the latter had again become interested in his glitterworms and merely grunted.

"I know only," said Elfloq, "that my master is here on a mission of compassion."

Ozbaak regarded him with renewed interest. "Compassion? A unique emotion for this place. Very laudable. Can you explain—without too many verbal peregrinations?"

"Of course. Mt master wishes to terminate the unfortunate existence of one of the denizens of Ludang."

Ozbaak sniffed. "Only one of them? I have striven for centuries to wipe out the entire nest!"

"Yes, I realise that, sire, but my master does not wish to, uh, eradicate this particular creature."

"Oh—enslavement then? Torture and pain, is that it?"

"Well, not quite."

Ozbaak's suspicions mounted. "Do not tell me he wants one for a servant! That is intolerable!"

Elfloq shook his head patiently. "No, no. There is a woman there—a lamia—who is bound to the perpetual service of Vandi-Nuessa, empress of the entire brood. This woman, herself now a lamia, was once the lover of my master, before the gods chained her to her present plight. My master seeks to free her, and make her what she once was."

Ozbaak considered. "I see. Chivalry as well. And bravery, or lunacy, I am not sure which. So, where is your illustrious master now? Hiding outside?"

"No, he is not in this dimension."

Ozbaak scowled. "Not? But how does a mere mortal hope to free—oh, I see! Either he is a demigod or a seraph, or he seeks my divine aid."

Elfloq looked diplomatic. "Well, yes. He is no mere mortal, as I have intimated, and he does need your help. But he will, of course, recompense you for any assistance."

"How?" said the wily god.

"He gave me the authority to discuss that with you," said Elfloq, lying and praying that his master would not hear him, which was extremely unlikely. "What would you want? May I suggest terms that would, I feel sure, be certain to please you, sire?"

Ozbaak nodded. "I am listening, though sceptically."

"Shall we say, the extermination of Vandi-Nuessa? Her complete abrogation? The removal of that menace to your plans, so that she will never again infest Nyctath the All-Night?" said the familiar, with mounting enthusiasm.

"For such a thing—if your master could truly engineer it—I would give all the aid that it is in my power to give!"

"Excellent! Then you have only to do one thing, sire. Summon my master and it will bring him to this dimension. He is in a void and it is his peculiar fate that should anyone summon him, he must come."

Ozbaak's wrinkled face became more so as he smiled and chuckled. "You are more devious than a pack of lava-demons! Undoubtedly you think me an old fool, palsied and eccentric. But I am not so short of sight that I cannot see a kink in your smooth suggestions."

"Sire, I speak openly—" began Elfloq.

"There are more knots in your tongue than are contained in my beard! You have told me that you do not know your master's name. Very well, then how am I to summon him?"

Elfloq sniffed, face contorting with puzzlement. Ozbaak was no fool and he did have a point: Elfloq would have to reveal who his master was. If Ozbaak knew of the curse, he would certainly refuse to complete the bargain. "I said my master has no name. But he does have an appellation."

"Appellation? Is that not the same thing?" muttered Ozbaak, confused.

"He is known," said Elfloq, fidgeting, "as the—uh, the Voidal." He winced mentally as he expected an outburst of vituperative anger from the old god. However, Ozbaak had evidently been wrapped up in his lonely crusade in Nyctath for so long that he had either not heard of the Voidal or had forgotten him and his enigmatic fate.

"A strange name—I mean, appellation," grunted the god. "Does it have a meaning?"

"Certain scribes tend to favour a translation equating to 'he who comes from the void'," said Elfloq.

"How very vague. Perhaps I should know more of this Voidal before ushering him here. However, if your master needs my help to cross dimensions, I certainly have nothing to fear from him. You say I have only to summon him and in return he will give me peace from Vandi-Nuessa?"

"That is the bargain."

"How can he possibly achieve this?"

"Sire, he has powers. Make the bargain and he will honour it."

Ozbaak nodded thoughtfully. His plight was a desperate one. He had tried so many avenues. "Very well. As the gods witness us, I will do it. What must I say?"

"I invoke—" began Elfloq, then realised he was about to say that which he would rather not say. "Uh, simply that you invoke the Voidal."

"Then I do," nodded Ozbaak.

"No, no, you must *say* it. State it. The words—the name."

"I see. The name is a key? Very well. I invoke the Voidal. Is that all? Surely you could have said as much yourself."

Elfloq looked about him at the bright chamber. "No, sire, the invocation would not work for a lowly familiar."

"Well, there seems to be some flaw in the invocation anyway. Unless your master is the size of an insect, for I cannot see him. Or does he cloak himself in invisibility?"

"He will come," said Elfloq with a little shiver. "He will come."

The dark man had been dreaming again. All the old confusions and horrors had taunted him, but he clung to the images of the familiar and of the meeting in Cloudway.

Something tugged at his mind, a remote voice. The dream winked out like a receding star and he found himself awake, standing in near-darkness, surrounded by cold stone walls that formed a tunnel upward to a vague, glimmering light. Slumped down in this corridor was a human form, stirring as he looked at it.

Memories hovered about it like dust motes. "Grabulic?" said the dark man.

The other rose up slowly, trying to clear his head as if to free it from the effects of a protracted drinking bout. "Is this the inn?"

"No, I suspect my familiar has—"

The Voidal did not finish. A flutter of wings nearby confirmed his thoughts. Elfloq solidified from out of the dark man's dreams.

"So you have brought us to Nyctath, as you promised," the Voidal said wryly. "What trickery did you employ?"

Elfloq hopped forward. "None! I merely bargained with the old god, Ozbaak Uderaak, in your name."

"Then he summoned me—by name?"

"Indeed, master. He seems not to know of you, or your fate. I did not enlighten him too much."

"Then what of the reckoning? Does he know that my summoner always pays? Did you tell him that?"

Elfloq examined his small claws and made an effort to clear his throat. "Not exactly, master. But I told him that if he summoned you, you would aid him."

The dark man scowled. "And what did you promise him, again in my name?"

"Well—as the old god is beset on all sides by the forces of darkness and evil and as they constantly seek to wipe out his light and also as the principal enemy that he has is Vandi-Nuessa, Lamia of Lamias, I thought it pertinent to offer Ozbaak the eradication of that very same Vandi-Nuessa. It seemed the best bait, and as you can see, it worked, for here you are!"

The mouth of the dark man curved in a brief, rare smile. "I see. And I assume the fact that you recently crossed the very same Lamia of Lamias and sent three of her servants on a hunt for shadows, coupled with the fact that the same Vandi-Nuessa is notorious for her never forgiving the merest slight had nothing to do with influencing your choice of bargaining matter?"

"Master!" protested Elfloq indignantly.

The dark man nodded. "Well, as you say, I am here in the All-Night. It is what I wish, whatever the price. If what you have learned is true, she is here also, she whom I once loved."

"Then—you are not displeased?"

Again the dark man smiled. "You seem to hold the reins of your destiny, while I have lost mine. There are things that I envy of you, little familiar. But we have work to do, and swiftly. If we

206

have for once slipped the watches of the Dark Gods, it will be for no more than a moment. Take me to the old god."

Elfloq bowed and sprang lightly up the tunnel. The three of them shortly came to a chamber in which Ozbaak was fussing over more bowls and vials, adding chemicals to a bubbling cauldron from which heat and light spread outwards. "One precious cup of starlustre," he muttered, turning to behold the Voidal. He saw in the green eyes that met his a melancholy beyond speech.

"You are this Voidal?" said Ozbaak. "You are the one who will free me of the hated Lamia of Lamias? If she is destroyed, light will establish itself here again."

"I am the Voidal. Do you not know of me?"

"I am trying to recall. In time I will. But for now I will teach you what I can of this evil realm. I will show you where to find the nest of lamias, and I will give you Equumyrion, who will carry you to your goal." Ozbaak looked at the ebon haft of the Voidal's sword protruding from its dark scabbard. "You come prepared, I see. What weapon is that you carry?"

"The Sword of—" the dark man began, but then had to pause. Somehow, however, he knew the name of the sword. "It is the Sword of Light."

"Then it is a worthy blade. And entirely appropriate."

The dark man nodded, though there was no cheer in his face. Had the Dark Gods sanctioned his coming here, after all? Did it suit their purpose?

"Come," said Ozbaak. "Time is short. I will take you and your companions to my steed of light, the miraculous Equumyrion."

They stood upon a high balcony cut from dead rock, overlooking the distantly remote piles and broken ruins of once proud Ludang. The Voidal stared at the sprawling city, hardly visible in the dim lights that flickered here among the crags. On the dark man's face was an expression of some pain, for he knew that his woman was below, just as Grabulic's Layola would be, somewhere in the terrible mausoleums of that husk of a city. As they watched, they heard the din of their invisible tenants.

"I will do all that I can to shed light on that foul place," said Ozbaak. "From here I often ride out upon Equumyrion, so that I may replenish all my pyres and places of light. They stretch away from here in radiating lines, projecting their heat and strength over evil, but they must be re-lit and started anew constantly. When Equumyrion has taken you below, I will ride him myself, circling Ludang with what light I can bring. The lamias fear it, and all those other foul pestilences that pass for living things dwelling below shun it. Hold high your Sword of Light and they may keep it from you, but beware the cunning of Vandi-Nuessa. Time presses—here comes the steed."

Equumyrion swooped from behind a stone balustrade and curved his great wings upward and behind him as he landed. He shone like beaten gold, seemingly moulded from metal rather than flesh. Elfloq hopped back in alarm, preferring to trust to his own fragile wings. The charger snorted like some huge engine as its hooves sent up a shower of sparks.

Grabulic gasped, a mixture of awe and pleasure. "Such beauty!"

Ozbaak put a loving hand upon the steed's brow. "Take them to the city and return for me," he whispered. He motioned the two men on to its back. Both mounted.

The Voidal waved Elfloq down into the night.

Ozbaak looked at him sadly. "What will you do with your woman?"

The Voidal's face clouded. "I cannot take her from this place. But I will free her."

"Light is our strength," called Ozbaak as the great winged charger rushed away, the familiar following in its slipstream.

As the two winged shapes were swallowed up by the night below, another figure moved in the crannies of the black mountains, peering intently from a crag to watch the graceful descent. It saw Ozbaak go back inside his tower, but paid him no further heed. The one he had come to undo had flown below. Glad of the thickening shadows, Shatterface picked his way down the sheer cliff wall, patient in his descent, knowing that he would eventually come upon the Voidal in Vandi-Nuessa's mausoleums.

He touched the haft of the Sword of Oblivion as if in reassurance and the night hid his terrible smile.

Aquumyrion dropped into a wide plaza flanked on all sides by heaps of debris and shattered walls. The Voidal and Grabulic dismounted, the Songster patting the long nose of the golden beast, which neighed softly and then took to the skies once more, as quiet as any shadow. Elfloq appeared from the night, and the three figures studied the mouldering necropoli of Ludang.

"Will you recognise the place you saw in your vision, where the lamias nest?" the Voidal asked Elfloq, who gave a nervous nod.

A pale wash of false dawn from over the distant crags of Nacramonte barely outlined the dread buildings as they crossed the pitted plaza. Perhaps the architecture had once been splendid, but now there was only dust and the droppings of beasts, the walls cracked and beslimed. There was the stench of death and decay in the air, while in the unseen places there were rustlings and slitherings as though a deep pit of evil had released creatures best left in their dark lairs: an evil that throbbed like the incessant beat of a drum.

Elfloq indicated a narrow thoroughfare leading away from the open plaza and as they came near to its black mouth a terrible hissing sound escaped from it. It seemed that a tide of reptiles had come spewing forth: Elfloq took to the air at once, but the Voidal swept from its scabbard the Sword of Light. It blazed like a torch, revealing in the glare a multitude of horrors, not serpents at all, but revolting things that writhed, bloated bodies alive with feelers and clutching feet. Eyes like pins gleamed by the hundred as the searing light that haloed the Voidal and Grabulic drove the horror back, for they saw now that it was a *single* beast.

From the fallen towers and broken buildings there came grunts and croaks as other parodies of life gathered. Elfloq was glad to drop into the ring of light. The dark man motioned for him to lead on, and with a shudder the diminutive being did so. Down the straight road they went, the light throwing alleys and windows into a white glare, and always something screamed or shrieked as it fled back to darkness. They passed charnel houses and ruined places, and from within came whispers and murmurs of madness. The sounds were hellish, the stink of death and ordure worse; swarming flies buzzed about the light in thick clouds. Behind the group, things stalked, wary of the light. Eyes stared hatefully from every nook, while overhead could be heard the unmistakable flap of wings and the hiss of avian life eager to drop for the feast.

"There," breathed Elfloq, pointing to a cluster of mausoleums. "The central one is where I saw—"

The Voidal nodded, jaw tightening. He flexed his right hand, but the movement was for once his own. The Dark God to whom it belonged remained dormant. To enter that place, then, would not be its doing. "We'll wait until Ozbaak can aid us with more light. There must be countless thousands of these blasphemies around us. Sooner or later, some of them will be goaded into attacking us in spite of the sword."

Grabulic was constantly looking over his shoulder. On a tumbled building at the edge of the circle of light, he now saw a figure, standing stiffly and watching them. The Songster pointed.

"Lamia?" said the Voidal, hardly able to see more than the flowing black silks and a white blur of face.

"Yes," nodded Elfloq. "They cover themselves, master, but that is one of them."

"They know we have come. We must put our trust in the light. Look!" The Voidal indicated the heavens, where a new glow suffused them. High overhead, Equumyrion flew, and behind him glowed a comet trail as Ozbaak spread what light he could. To and fro over the dead city the old god passed, pausing only to light up his beacons on the crags that ringed the city like teeth. The light was still poor, but it sharpened the features of the city. Dreadful wailings and murmurs of fear rose up in response to it: the Voidal and Grabulic sensed the slow drawing back of the dark beings that had been closing in.

"To the mausoleum," the dark man said. "We must find the women."

The first of these grim buildings stood before them, its pillars leaning, its roof partly fallen in. Beyond it were others, all built to surround the central pile, wherein Elfloq had seen the lamias of Vandi-Nuessa.

The dark man held high the Sword of Light. "Horror awaits, little familiar. I will not curse you if you choose to hide on the astral while I act."

Elfloq would gladly have so fled, for he had never before experienced such terror, but if the Voidal were to be his master, he must honour him. "I will go with you."

"And I," murmured Grabulic, though he bore his own terror like a banner.

The Voidal smiled dourly. "Then come."

Vandi-Nuessa's great central mausoleum was built on a foundation of bones culled from a thousand centuries, cemented with blood and piled upwards with stone cut from fallen meteors, all carved an age before by slave armies. Uppermost of the tortured piles was a blood red finger in which the Lamia of Lamias reclined on a divan of stretched human skin, its pillows stuffed with human hair. On the outer wall of this tower the carved face of a giant demon watched over the city, its eyes windows that housed two lenses. In these lenses the empress could study her dead city and see all things that moved within it, even those that crawled with the worms in the lowest of the catacombs.

She saw the approach of the Voidal and his two companions. As her crimson eyes focused on the diminutive figure of Elfloq, they blazed with feral anger.

"So that sub-human filth dares to come here after making fools of my servants! No one cheats me of my spoils and laughs over their fortune for long! Well, familiar, I will tear every scale from your body and fill you to the brim with the burning poison of my personal bite! Come to me. I luxuriate in your arrival!"

She turned her attention to the dark man and sneered at the vision in the lens. "Voidal!" she scoffed. "I am not moved by your coming. You are not here at the behest of your masters, but for your own ends. It is the woman you seek! To free her. Well, I may give her to you without a struggle, for she can never bring joy to you as she is, nor can any man comfort her. And you can never hope to take her with you on your aimless travels, so what foolish plan have you conceived? Go into the heart of my mausoleums and find her. We are more than ready for you!"

The three figures moved on, oblivious of the watcher and her words.

Through high portals cut from single slivers of basalt the three figures passed, crossing the very threshold of the central mausoleum. They were cautious, for they had not been attacked in spite of the unseen multitude. As they went inside, darkness closed in like a fist, but the Voidal held high his sword, banishing the shadows for a little distance. Elfloq watched the tombs and altars warily, expecting to see a host of lamias rise up to join battle, but none appeared.

"Where are they?" he asked nervously.

"The light pains them."

"And she whom you seek?"

The Voidal ignored the implication. "We must open the tombs. She may be within," he said bitterly, his resolve set.

A movement ahead made them all start, but still nothing attacked. They passed on through festoons of web, rotting candlesticks. Their footsteps echoed high up in the vaults where bats rustled, hating the light. Something crunched under the Voidal's boots and he looked down to see the remains of human bones. Elfloq drew back, for a carpet of the grisly relics stretched ahead of them.

From the darkness beyond came sounds suggestive of a beast feeding. The Voidal stepped forward slowly, holding the sword ahead of him like a brand. Something moved among the frightful remains. It was a lamia, cringing back from the light. Its long gossamer gown was smeared with blood and its pale, tapered hands held raw meat. Elfloq mumbled a curse deep in his throat as the Voidal walked on alone. Grabulic, nauseated, held back.

The dark man stood over the lamia, which cowered on its haunches, face hidden by clawed hands, thin body sheathed in

212

the darkness of the gown. It presented no menace, but merely whispered as the Voidal bent down and pulled the hands away from the face. The mouth and cheeks were crimson, the eyes squeezed shut against the detested light: the face had been human, but bestial depravity had distorted its features, making it all animal now, while the hair was lank and matted with filth, the teeth razor sharp and unnatural. Blood ran from the lips in a trickle.

But he knew her.

A single cry of despair escaped his lips as he looked at she who had been his lover. *He remembered.* Memories that had been hidden from him came back urgently. "What have they done to you?" he said hoarsely, holding the Sword of Light away from her so that she would not suffer, but she whimpered like a dog, devoid of any understanding.

From around the mighty hall there now came the shuffling of feet and the sibilant hissing of other beings crowding in. Elfloq looked about him to see a host of slender shapes gathering, their faces shielded from the light by thick, black veils. Vandi-Nuessa's servants had surrounded them. Grabulic backed up against a broken pillar, as if he could blend with the stone. He felt his insides melting with terror.

One of the night creatures stepped forward. Only its scarlet mouth was outlined by the light, lips pursed in mocking contempt. "Have you found what you came for?" she challenged in a piercing, icy voice. It was the Lamia of Lamias herself, her wraith-like figure seeming to coalesce from the very darkness.

The Voidal turned his withering gaze upon her. "Is this your work?" he snarled, indicating the lamia at his feet.

"She was deposited here by beings more powerful than I. Even I must bow to those masters who rule beyond Nyctath."

"The Dark Gods," the Voidal breathed.

"Yes! I do not serve them, but I do their work if it pleases me. They sent her here to be secreted among my slaves. That is how she was when she came. She serves me readily enough. I am simply her keeper."

The Voidal shuddered as he looked upon the wretched creature, once a woman, at his feet. "The same Dark Gods who cursed me with immortality have cursed her with a parody of the same."

"And what will you have of her now?" challenged Vandi-Nuessa as her servants thronged, rising from the crypts below the mausoleum. "You dare not take her from this dimension. Perhaps you will stay with her and make her your mate once more!" The red mouth opened in appalling laughter, revealing twin rows of gleaming fangs.

"I may be the pawn of the Dark Gods, but I am not without some power. I will free her from your repugnant clutches! And I will destroy all those who stand in my way."

"I am sure you will," laughed the empress mockingly. "Take her where you will. Nyctath is peppered with barren worlds where even I do not walk. I will not hinder you. She belongs to the Dark Gods before me."

Elfloq hovered near to the Voidal's side. "Do not trust her!" he hissed.

"You would let me pass without dispute?" the dark man said to the empress.

"If you agree to my terms."

"Which are?"

Vandi-Nuessa pointed venomously at the familiar. "Give me that worm! Forsake him and deny him further service to you—give him to *me*! Cast him at my feet and you can have whatever you wish."

Elfloq gasped, body shuddering with renewed terror. He had not foreseen this unthinkable possibility.

But the Voidal shook his head. "I owe you nothing. Stand aside or I will let the light eat out whatever passes for your soul. I will give you death everlasting!"

Vandi-Nuessa's mouth spat her contempt. "I think not, man from the empty places. You are immortal, so think yourself invulnerable. We will teach you the fallacy of that! My servants will suck the sweet red juice from you. We could never drink you dry, but each day could draw from you the renewed wine of life. You will suffer a thousand times more than she has! Let us see how you fare against my thirsty sisters!" So saying, she waved her minions forward and as one they swept to the attack. At once the Voidal swung the Sword of Light above his head in blinding circles.

"Hold the woman!" he cried to Elfloq, who was himself cringing at the dark man's feet, but the familiar had the presence of mind to do as bidden and gripped the lamia so that she could not flee. Thankfully she had no appetite for the battle. The lamias tried to claw at the Voidal as they sprang in, but his weapon tore into their gowns, scorching their flesh, charring them with every impact. He seared their arms, shrivelling them so that as one they were forced to fall back. Screams and frightful shrieks rent the air, but the Voidal ignored the agony he had unleashed. His own bitter anger and hate spurred him on and he tore into them furiously. Three times the ring of lamias closed on him, but against the terrible Sword of Light they were helpless. They fell back, moaning.

The Voidal faced the empress, his own stare fuelled by the very fires of hell. "Shall I burn every last one of them from your nest? If you force my hand, I will destroy every last thing in this charnel house!"

Vandi-Nuessa shook with silent anger and frustration. "Take the cursed woman with you, if you can find a place of shelter. And that stunted halfling you call servant. *I will find him*. My wings are long. The omniverse itself cannot shield him fro me!"

The Voidal had been looking to see where Grabulic was, but the Songster had somehow made himself invisible. The dark man turned to Elfloq. "I must carry her. You must raise the sword for me."

Elfloq looked astounded, but took the bright weapon from his master.

"Lead us," the Voidal told him as he swept his lover up into his arms. She seemed to be in a dream, faint and silent, her body wrapped in her gown as though it were a shroud.

Elfloq stepped warily forward, holding the Sword of Light away from him as though it would explode in his face.

"We are leaving," the Voidal told Vandi-Nuessa. "If you try to stay us, I will finish what I began."

The red mouth twisted spitefully. "Go where you will, Voidal, but this entire world will follow you. You will fall foul of us in the end. Then we will bring you back to these chambers and lavish our constant attention on you. Your lover will be the first to feed upon you." As she spoke, the empress drifted to one side, fearful of the Sword of Light that Elfloq brandished so effectively. Around the hall the broken lamias moaned, nursing their burns.

Elfloq neared the portal to the plaza. As he did so, the woman shifted in the Voidal's arms, groaning. Her gown fell open to reveal her body from the waist down. The Voidal gasped in horror, for it was not the body of a woman, but of a beast with hooves.

Elfloq spun round to see what was amiss and missed his footing, stumbling. At once Vandi-Nuessa leapt forward, her fangs barred and gleaming like tiny knives, ready to tear and shred. Over the tripped form of the familiar she spread herself like a great bat. The Voidal stood as though turned to stone.

Cursing, Elfloq twisted and thrust upward awkwardly with the Sword of Light. He felt it slide easily into the belly of the descending Lamia of Lamias as though made of smoke. Her awful cry split his ears as she took the full length of blazing sword. The black-clad body crashed down over Elfloq, smothering him, and the two of them tumbled down the stairs to the plaza beyond. They landed with the lamia uppermost, and from its back protruded the end of the sword, still burning, sizzling with her life fluid.

The screams were frightful. A uniform sigh went up from the lamia host, which pressed forward. Vandi-Nuessa's body stirred, flopping to one side. Elfloq emerged breathlessly, staggering to his feet. The great sword had gone home to the haft. "Master—I cannot withdraw it!" he shouted, tugging at the hilt.

"Then leave it!" replied the dark man. "If you pull it free, she will rise again. Come, let us flee before these abominations attack." He turned to see another figure emerging from the darkness of the mausoleum. It was Grabulic: the Songster clutched something to his chest, half concealed inside his shirt.

Together the three of them raced down on to the plaza, the

chorus of near-hysterical screams behind them swelling as the maddened lamias stood around their fallen empress, whose agonies were fading.

Elfloq pulled up in the centre of the plaza. In front of him stood yet another figure, wielding a heavy sword of its own. The Voidal stopped and stared across at the man who confronted them. He was dressed in linked chain, the head encased in a helm that allowed only the eyes to be exposed. These were hellish, as though they belonged to a demon from the Abyss itself.

"Stand back, Elfloq," the dark man told the familiar. "There is greater evil here than the things we have just quitted."

Elfloq obeyed as the Voidal swung the woman down. Neither the familiar nor the dark man now carried a weapon.

"Do you know me, Voidal?" said Shatterface, lifting the Sword of Oblivion.

"Show me your face."

Shatterface laughed coldly. "No one has seen this face, nor shall they. It is not mine!"

"Why are you here?"

"The Dark Gods sent me to take away all the things you have remembered."

The Voidal drew back slowly. "They resent my discoveries."

Shatterface moved forward confidently. He had said all he need say. One stroke now would be enough. As he moved, the skies began to brighten and a wash of false dawn flooded above them. Elfloq looked around him anxiously for some means to stay this grim avenger. The air abruptly whistled to the falling of a great body. Shatterface glanced around, confronting whatever interfered in his business.

It was Equumyrion, ridden by the old god, who seemed greatly agitated. The bright light that bathed them all served to send the oncoming lamias into renewed panic and soon they had scattered, disappearing into vaults and temples where they continued to shriek their outrage.

"Ozbaak!" shouted Elfloq happily. "You have come at an opportune moment."

The Voidal watched the old god approach. "Vandi-Nuessa

is destroyed as I promised. Listen and you will hear her anguish as the Sword of Light drains the last of her power."

Ozbaak came close to him, seemingly heedless of what had transpired. Shatterface was nonplussed, though his weapon was still poised.

"You are the *Voidal*," Ozbaak said to the dark man, staring down at the unconscious woman in the man's arms. "I have recalled everything. I was a fool to have forgotten you—you, whom the Dark Gods have marked!"

"You know who I am? What sins I have committed?"

Ozbaak nodded his head in a mixture of sadness and scorn. "Everything."

"I see that it does not please you," said the Voidal. "But will you tell it to me?"

Ozbaak nodded slowly. "I may be wrong, but for the good you have done here, yes, I will tell you. All gods have deserted me, so why should I respect the rules they have forged? I shall tell you *everything*!"

Shatterface pushed forward, a step from Ozbaak. "Out of my way, old fool! You prate about revelations, but I am here to wipe away all that he has learned."

Ozbaak glared up at him. "What is your part in this?"

"Unlike you, *I* serve the Dark Gods. Here is my assurance of that." As he said this, Shatterface drove home the Sword of Oblivion into the vitals of the old god, who sucked in a huge breath in surprise. His eyes widened, then began to dull. He slumped to his knees, gasping.

Elfloq sprang forward, appalled. "You have murdered him!"

"No," said the Voidal, again loosing the woman. "Ozbaak is a god. The swords of the seneschals cannot destroy him, aged though he is."

"I have merely washed away his memory," snorted Shatterface. "He will tell you nothing." He pulled the Sword of Oblivion from the old god, who collapsed on to the cold stones. "I have but one stroke left to deliver, Voidal."

The dark man drew back, but Shatterface followed, supreme in the knowledge that nothing could foil his cause. He laughed mirthlessly as the Voidal lifted his right hand. "You would match your hand with my sword? Oblivion cancelling oblivion?"

But the Voidal knew that the hand was dormant, its power temporarily absent. No, not absent, he realised, *but in the sword*. And there would be no escaping the bite of that power now.

As Shatterface stepped inexorably nearer his victim, the air was suddenly filled with music, a swelling, dizzying wave of chords. And the music, so compelling, so utterly haunting, froze all of the figures in the plaza, as if the gods had woven a spell of a different kind. With it came a voice, a voice so pure, so perfect, that it reached inside each one of them.

Grabulic, who had taken his instrument, Layola, from the mausoleum, played it now, and it was her voice which so enriched the air. Shatterface's resolve wavered: in that song he heard the voices of his own past, the powerful echoes of all that he had lost. The Sword of Oblivion sank floorward, its tip resting on the stone.

Another sound intruded as hooves rattled on the same stone; a snort of anger billowed from the flared nostrils of the great golden steed, Equumyrion. The beast rushed forward, leaping into the air, wings extended. With a crash it came down before the bemused Shatterface, who barely turned aside to escape a crushing. He lifted the sword, striking at the charger's neck, but the blade rang on metal, useless against it. Shatterface regained his senses, but Equumyrion, eyes blazing, rose up and defied the puny man. It was over quickly as the horse trampled him, spread-eagling him on the plaza floor. The Sword of Oblivion rang as it skidded across the stones and was still. Equumyrion stood back in triumph with a last derisive neigh.

The Voidal bent down to look into the eyes of the old god. Ozbaak was alive, but his breath came in rasps as though he was, after all, expiring. The music, too, gently subsided.

"Ozbaak!" cried the dark man anxiously, holding the aged head gently. But the old god merely coughed and managed a weak smile.

"I have paid for summoning you," he murmured, closing his eyes. "You bring death, Fatecaster, but see, light returns!"

A movement beside him made the Voidal look up. Shatterface, his body a bloody ruin, crawled like a smashed serpent towards him. "Voidal," he said through his pain. "Voidal—this is not the end. I, too, am cursed with immortality, and this—body—is but a shell. This is not my end, though I wish it were. I shall find you again—"

"But why?" asked the dark man softly.

"Take off my helm."

The Voidal did so, seeing for the first time the face of the twisted form before him. It was hideous, a mass of flaking skin and crumbling flesh.

"I will find you—and win back—my true face," gasped Shatterface. His eyes closed and his head pressed to the stone. In a moment the body began to disintegrate.

Elfloq meanwhile had sauntered over to the Sword of Oblivion and picked it up. The danger passed, the familiar had regained all of his old swagger. He swung the sword carelessly. "Here, master. Since the Sword of Light remains lodged in the carcass of Vandi-Nuessa, take this in its stead."

The Voidal rose and stared at the weapon. Then slowly he took it and sheathed it.

Equumyrion lowered his neck and nuzzled his master's head. The Voidal went to the old god and lifted up his ailing form, placing it carefully on the broad back of the steed, which seemed to please it. In a moment it had spread its wings and had risen up into the skies.

"But—but—" began Elfloq, "how will you climb up to Nacramonte?"

"It is no matter. Our work here is over. Look!"

Overhead, Equumyrion climbed higher and higher as though about to quit the world altogether and soar out into space. As he did so, the body of Ozbaak began to glow, expanding and becoming a searing ball of light that encompassed rider and horse. Up and up they swept, the light spreading wider and wider, washing the landscape in bright hues, driving back the night dwellers below ground.

"What is happening?" gasped Elfloq.

"It is the old god. He is becoming a *sun!*" replied the

Voidal. "See how he soars outward into Nyctath. The gods have *not* deserted this place. They have heard him—his punishment for summoning me is no punishment at all. Ozbaak has gone to rest at last, after eons of struggling alone. Perhaps he, too, had some terrible sin to wash away."

"Daylight comes! The worlds of Nyctath will be strong again," said Elfloq, skipping round the Voidal like a child. He did not need to mention that the threats of Vandi-Nuessa no longer hung over him.

"It will take time." The Voidal looked down. "There are more transformations to come." He pointed to the body of the woman. She was changing, altering as the rays of new sunlight daubed her in beauty. The bestial features of the lamia were melting like snow. New hues came to her cheeks; her hair rid itself of its tangles. The beast legs re-shaped and became human once more. The Voidal bent down and covered them with her gown. Her eyes opened, glittering with natural fire.

The Voidal felt strange, forgotten emotions stirring within himself, for she was again a woman, and to him, above all others. "She is as she was," he whispered.

Elfloq looked pityingly at him. "But, master, how will you quit this place? You are bound here until summoned again. And she cannot travel with us."

Suddenly the woman stared at her surroundings. Her eyes widened in fear as she looked at the Voidal. "You!"

The dark man reacted as if she had struck him. "You remember?"

Her hands went to her head as though it ached terribly. "Gods, but what has happened? What has happened to me?" She began to sob, holding her head in her hands, shaking wildly and crying.

"What is it?" said the Voidal.

"Leave me, leave me! The memories! They scream at me. Gods, but they crowd in on me like an army—so many."

"But—it is over," whispered the Voidal.

"Over! But I *see* things—I have been the vilest of the vile for an age! I dare not recount the things I have suffered, the

things I have *done*—here. No, I cannot believe such things!"
Again she sobbed.

Elfloq touched his master's arm. "Perhaps by waking her, master, you have opened a door on her worst fears."

Someone cackled horribly and they looked across the plaza. Vandi-Nuessa tottered there, the Sword of Light embedded in her chest. Power ebbed from her visibly, but she pointed at the woman. "See how the Dark Gods mock you yet! You have freed her, but at what cost! She recalls it all, Voidal! But such foul memories will make her life miserable forever. Ask her and she will tell you all of it. Who you are, what you did, why you both were punished. But once the floodgates are open, she will never be able to face you again! She will live on the rack for eternity! Hah, but the Dark Gods are cunning!" With a last choking rattle of laughter, the lamia fell forward, the final energy spent.

The woman was still sobbing, as if to compound all that had been said.

The Voidal's face clouded. He understood the depth of the deceit of his tormentors. "To live with such things could only lead to madness," he murmured. "You deserve peace, even though I am to have none."

He drew out the Sword of Oblivion. "Forgive me. I cannot carry you from here. But your evil memories will not remain with you, nor will those that might have comforted you. Forgive me." And he eased the Sword of Oblivion into her heart.

Elfloq cried out in consternation. "Master! What have you done? She will remember nothing. Not even you—"

"She will be free, Elfloq. Whatever pain she has suffered was through me. Memory of me would only be painful to her. She may even have hated me. I would rather not know. It is enough that she rests."

"Is she asleep?" said the familiar, for the woman had sunk to the stones.

"Yes. She will recall nothing when she wakes. Let us find somewhere to set her down in comfort. There will be a new world waiting for her when she rises."

"And what of us?"

"You are not chained to me, though I am glad of your service."

Elfloq helped the Voidal to lift the girl. "I have no love of these Dark Gods, who seem so cruel."

"Speak softly. They miss nothing, little familiar."

A shadow fell over them both. It was Grabulic. "They may not be cruel in everything," he said. As if to demonstrate his odd statement, he turned. Behind him stood another woman, her face wearing a look of uncertainty, her fingers interwoven nervously.

"Layola?" said the Voidal, rising.

"The light has freed her," smiled Grabulic, holding up his instrument. "She is restored." He reached out for the woman's hand and she took his eagerly. He pulled her to him and gave her a look of such utter devotion that Elfloq turned away, embarrassed.

Layola let herself be pulled into the Songster's arms.

"You sing like the goddess you are," the Voidal told her. "And you are both blessed. You have served out your sentences, I am certain."

"Then the Dark Gods are capable of mercy," said Grabulic, fingers tenderly caressing Layola's face. "Perhaps they will show it to you in time."

The Voidal's features hardened. "One day I will be free of their curse. And then, perhaps, I will find her again."

Elfloq looked at the dark man's unconscious woman. A single tear fell from the ugly features of the familiar and splashed upon her skin. But there was no time for sentiment. There was work to be done. Plans to be made.

And so ended the beginning of the dark man's quest. He had recovered something of what he had lost, but at a cost. And he was yet the pawn of the Dark Gods. My various sources, some of which are, I confess, more than a little dubious, agree on one thing: light finds a way into the darkest of crevices. After all, darkness cannot be defined without reference to light.

I recall a fascinating conversation I had once in Effelgung's preposterous Library...but perhaps it will keep until I begin again this charting of the Voidal's dark and tormented genesis.

—Salecco, the Repressed

5992030R00132

Printed in Great Britain
by Amazon.co.uk, Ltd.,
Marston Gate.